MORE...

"A fantastic addition to the world of The Others... grab a copy as soon as possible. Christine Warren does a wonderful job of writing a book that meshes perfectly with the storylines of the others in the series, yet stands alone perfectly."

—*Romance Reviews Today*

"Warren weaves a paranormal world of werewolves, shifters, witches, humans, demons, and a whole lot more with a unique hand for combining all the paranormal classes." —*Night Owl Romance*

"*Howl at the Moon* will tug at a wide range of emotions from beginning to end...Engaging banter, a strong emotional connection, and steamy love scenes. This talented author delivers real emotion which results in delightful interactions...and the realistic dialogue is stimulating. Christine Warren knows how to write a winner!" —*Romance Junkies*

THE DEMON YOU KNOW
"Explodes with sexy, devilish fun, exploring the further adventures of The Others. With a number of the gang from previous books back, there's an immediate familiarity about this world that makes it easy to dive right into. Warren's storytelling style makes these books remarkably entertaining."

—*Romantic Times BOOKreviews* (4½ stars)

SHE'S NO FAERIE PRINCESS
"Warren has fast become one of the premier authors of rich paranormal thrillers elaborately laced with

scorching passion. When you want your adventure hot, Warren is the one for you!"

—*Romantic Times BOOKreviews*

"The dialogue is outrageous, funny, and clever. The characters are so engaging and well scripted...and the plot...is as scary as it is delicious!"

—*Romance Reader at Heart*

"Christine Warren has penned a story rich in fantastic characters and spellbinding plots."

—*Fallen Angel Reviews*

WOLF AT THE DOOR

"A great start to a unique paranormal series."

—*Fresh Fiction*

"This book is a fire-starter...a fast-paced, adrenaline- and hormonally-charged tale. The writing is fluid and fun, and makes the characters all take on life-like characteristics." —*Romance Reader at Heart*

"Intrigue, adventure, and red-hot sexual tension."

—*USA Today* bestselling author Julie Kenner

ST. MARTIN'S PAPERBACKS TITLES
BY CHRISTINE WARREN

You're So Vein

One Bite with a Stranger

Walk on the Wild Side

Howl at the Moon

The Demon You Know

She's No Faerie Princess

Wolf at the Door

You're So Vein

CHRISTINE WARREN

St. Martin's Paperbacks

This is a work of fiction. All of the characters, organizations and events portrayed in this novel are either products of the author's imagination or are used fictitiously.

YOU'RE SO VEIN

Copyright © 2009 by Christine Warren.

For information address St. Martin's Press, 175 Fifth Avenue, New York, NY 10010.

ISBN: 0-312-94792-5
EAN: 978-0-312-94792-7

Printed in the United States of America

St. Martin's Paperbacks edition / April 2009

St. Martin's Paperbacks are published by St. Martin's Press, 175 Fifth Avenue, New York, NY 10010.

10 9 8 7 6 5 4 3 2 1

For my mother, who told me I was a writer before I ever thought it was possible. I love you, Mom.

Chapter 1

In the humming chill of the Manhattan night, a nearly silent buzz made the hunkered shadow twitch in its rooftop perch.

"What?" the shadow hissed into a sleek black mobile phone, but eyes the color of hard frost never shifted their attention from the street below.

"Est-ce que vous à New York?"

The shadow grunted and shifted until the form of a man could almost be seen. Provided the observer was especially perceptive, specially trained, and happened to be on an adjacent rooftop on the Upper East Side with a good pair of binoculars at an inhuman hour of the night. It would also help if the observer himself wasn't human. Dima certainly wasn't.

Vladimir Rurikovich had visited nearly every major city in the world, and this one ranked near the bottom of his list of favorites. New York City simply smelled wrong. It stank of cement and glass and pollution, as well as the millions of human bodies that lived stacked atop each other like cords of firewood. At least Kiev and Moscow could be trusted to smell of snow or vodka or centuries of history. Those things he could trust. Those things reminded him of home, a place he intended to return to just as soon as he finished his current assignment.

"I called in my arrival three days ago," he rumbled back in English, his voice low and rough and impatient. He had never been able to make his handlers on the European Council understand that he could do his job much more efficiently if they stayed out of his way and didn't waste his time demanding reports on his progress.

"We expected a report by now."

The voice on the phone sounded crisp and French and ineffably aristocratic. Dima vaguely recalled a rumor about the Revolution, the Guillotine, and an unlikely escape. He had never cared enough to pursue the tale, but it did go a little way toward explaining why this particular councilman ranked among his least favorite.

"I report when I have information worth reporting."

"Three days and you've learned nothing?"

Grimly, Dima pushed aside the impulse to take his impatience out on the Frenchman and focused on the task at hand. A successful mission provided the only way Dima could honorably return to Russia and his estate near the banks of the Shelon. Even if his employers could be satisfied with anything less, he could not.

"I have eliminated several possibilities," he said grudgingly.

"That is progress of the sort we would wish to hear reported."

"That is not how I work."

For more than three hundred years, Vladimir of Novgorod had stood as the finest—and most feared—member of the European Council of Vampires' elite army of enforcers of the Laws. His skill, relentless determination, and brute strength had brought to justice many of Europe's most notorious vampire offenders, those beings who disregarded the customs and boundaries that had kept the secret of their kind from humanity since the dawn of time.

"Perhaps you will need to make a concession or two." Before Dima could express his disdain of that idea, the Frenchman continued. "The council would like also to hear your impressions of the relations between us and the humans. Of course, we possess much curiosity of the results of the American experiment."

Several years ago, the American Others had managed to force the issue of Unveiling their existence to humans. Reactions had been predictably mixed but perhaps unpredictably—in the eyes of the ECV, at least—peaceable. Still, the ECV and other groups like it maintained a tight rein on the vampire population under its purview in order to bolster the uneasy truce with humankind.

Dima grunted. "The situation appears stable for the most part. Law and order prevails; however, the mortals remain wary of us, especially of vampires."

"We have always focused much of their fear." The Frenchman's philosophical shrug sounded clear in his tone.

To Dima, this made no sense. Were he still a mortal

man, he would have more fear of the shape-shifting
predators like the Lupines and the Feline races than
of vampires. After all, a vampire might feed on human blood, but a werewolf could feed on human flesh.
The mortals, though, didn't seem to feel the same
way. Something about the shifters fascinated them,
curbing their fear with a sort of grudging affection.
The way Dima figured it, it had to be the fur. Cover
a beast in a soft, shiny pelt and humans just couldn't
resist petting it, no matter what the risk to their out-
stretched limbs. But make a beast an enemy of the
sun and the humans shivered at the mere mention of
its name.

"Fools."

"Not so foolish," the Frenchman corrected. "After all, who better than you understands how some
vampires can prove very dangerous to humans indeed? If they choose to disregard the Laws."

Dima grunted, shifting his weight while main-
taining his clear view of the empty street below him.
He couldn't argue with the Frenchman's contention.
The truth of it was, after all, the reason Dima was
here.

The first of the Laws of the Vampire Race stated
that humans must not be drained to the point of death,
because only a stupid predator killed off its food
source. Dead, humans became useless, but alive they
could continue to provide nourishment for vampires
for years or decades to come. The second Law de-
creed with equal adamance that humans should be
turned only under the most extreme circumstances,

or after permission had been granted by the prince of a territory or by the ECV itself.

"I hardly need to remind you of the laws Yelizaveta has broken," the Frenchman said.

He didn't.

The vampire Dima currently hunted had broken both the primary Laws many times, for which she'd been sentenced to spend the remainder of her existence in a palatial but well-guarded prison outside of Moscow. It hadn't helped her cause that Yelizaveta Chernigov had broken a third—unwritten but equally important—Law among their kind: If you plan to kill a prince and seize his territory, make certain he has no living relations to bring the crime to the attention of the ECV; and if you plan to kill more than one prince, be certain to kill them all, because the survivors left on the council will make it their only ambition to remove you as a threat to their own sovereignty.

"Yelizaveta never was very good with rules," Dima acknowledged. "Nor with strategy."

When Yelizaveta took her third territory by force, she made the ECV nervous enough for her to earn their harshest sentence—eternal imprisonment. More feared than death, because death was quick, eternal imprisonment had been known to drive a vampire mad. Even a human with a life sentence had an end to look forward to—the escape of death. A vampire had no such light at the end of her tunnel.

Yelizaveta had served a little over three centuries

of her sentence before the boredom became too much for her and she broke out of her jail, quickly disappearing from the council's sight. The rumors suggested that she'd flown to America, and if she'd stayed there and stayed out of trouble, the ECV might very well have let her go, but Yelizaveta was equally bad at behaving herself. Newer rumors suggested that she was using the United States not as a hiding place but as a base camp from which she could plan her return to Europe with fresh forces at her command.

Clearly, the ECV wanted her stopped, so they sent an enforcer to recapture her. Dima, however, had his own reasons for taking this assignment himself rather than offering it to another member of his team. Any member of the Chernigov clan—though few enough of them remained—got his immediate attention. They had a long history in common with his own family, dating back to the time when his father, Rurik of Novgorod, had led his sons in battle to defend their lucrative trading empire against the scheming of their unwelcome neighbor.

His last confrontation with a Chernigov might have been over 750 years ago, Dima admitted, but some memories stayed with a man, especially when he lived forever.

A sharp memory could prove a valuable tool in his line of work. It helped with the many details he needed to learn in order to track his quarry as efficiently as he expected. Knowing the details of a person's life helped to predict that person's behavior, where he might go or with whom he might associate.

Given what he knew of Yelizaveta, Dima figured it was a safe bet that she had settled on Manhattan for her nest.

Liza had grown up as an acknowledged diamond in the courts of Kiev and Smolensk, the eldest daughter of Kazimir of Chernigov. The position had always inclined her toward a desire for material possessions and crowds of fawning inferiors. What better place to shop and be admired than the heart of the most cosmopolitan city in the United States?

Unfortunately, knowing Liza was in Manhattan didn't mean Dima knew exactly where to find her. If he did, he'd already have her back at Kolomenskoye and be walking through his lands, inspecting his orchards and his flax fields. His position at that moment on a rooftop above East 88th Street indicated he should get to work.

"We need for you to find her quickly," the Frenchman said. "Every day when she remains free makes greater trouble for us."

"Then you should stop calling me for reports and let me do my job."

"Quietly. The council prefers to handle this matter on our own, without interference from the local authorities."

That was another point that Dima hardly needed to be reminded of. The American Council of Others had a reputation for handling matters in a manner their European counterparts found . . . unconventional. Not to say lenient. But Dima had his own reason for avoiding contact with the local council, a reason called Vidâme.

"It is easier to keep quiet when not forced to speak."

"Be very quiet, because any explanations made to the American Council will have to come from your own lips. We mean to see the criminal returned to us for her punishment. We will not allow sentencing by committee, nor tolerate outside interference."

"Fine. Neither will I." Dima hung up the phone.

Reluctantly, he rose from his crouched position, ignoring the leg muscles that protested the abrupt change of position after three hours of stillness. Earlier research had indicated to Dima that a sort of nightclub for the city's Others was located within a few blocks of his perch, and though he knew Liza would not be dumb enough to show her famous face in such company, he had hoped one of her new minions might. Luck, however, had not favored him tonight.

He checked the horizon as he sheathed the long, deadly knife he carried in a scabbard at his thigh. A gray pre-dawn pallor had begun to lighten the sky. The sun would rise in another hour or two and bring an end to the night's work. Until then, he would make a check of the surrounding streets and perhaps make a new acquaintance to refresh his stock of information. For certain, he'd be keeping his eyes and ears open. You never knew when something interesting might stroll right into your path.

Chapter 2

The heels of her black Gina boots clicked on the pavement with the sharp rap of gunfire, which suited Ava's mood just fine. Frankly, she felt as if she'd just fought the Battle of Bunker Hill single-handedly. And without ever letting the enemy know they'd been engaged. She had just come from the house of Vidâme, the well-known former head of the New York's Council of Others and a very public vampire. And she had been more than happy to escape.

Why she continued to attend these events Ava could hardly fathom. Certainly it had nothing to do with enjoyment. She'd stopped looking forward to the girls' nights years ago, and she knew perfectly well that she made all the rest of the attendees as uncomfortable as they made her, but Ava wasn't the kind of woman who gave in. To anything. So every other Friday evening, as regular as the army, she gathered up a bottle or three of good wine, stopped at the cheese shop down the block from her office, then carried herself, her provisions, and her very forced smile to a party that offered her approximately as much pleasure as an IRS audit.

Of course, she'd be a fool if she didn't acknowledge that periodontal surgery likely held more appeal for the other guests than her awkward presence. Everyone always welcomed her with open arms, but she could see that behind their smiles, her friends clenched their teeth whenever she made an appearance. That could very well have been one of the reasons that she continued to appear. Ava Maria Theresa de Castille Markham appreciated nothing so much as the sheer perversity of her own character. Knowing herself to be unwanted was the surest way on earth to ensure that she planted herself in the middle of the action.

You should have let me call you a cab.

The errant thought, coming out of thin air as it did, made the hairs on the back of Ava's neck stand at stiff attention. Damn it, this counted as one of the many reasons she had snuck out of the party after talking to no one other than her hostess. And she'd only done that because the woman had cornered her in front of the coat closet.

Immediately and reflexively, Ava tensed and forced her mind to go blank. She had rules about things like this, and she made very sure that everyone around her knew about them.

As expected, her cell phone rang less than a minute later.

"I'm serious. It's too late for you to be walking home alone."

Ava pressed the slim silver phone to her ear and kept walking. "No, actually it's merely too late for unexpected visitors to barge in without so much as knocking."

"I'm sorry, but that's what you get for making me worry."

"While I appreciate your concern, Regina, I neither needed nor wanted a taxi. I'm a big girl, more than able to take care of myself."

On the other end of the line, the woman Ava loved—and hated—like a sister sighed. "I don't dispute that, but it's two in the morning, Av, and even in this part of the Upper East Side that is not an hour when women should be walking alone."

"Why not? You've done it. Repeatedly."

"That's not the same thing, and you know it."

Silence.

Regina sighed again. "Look, just tell me where you are and I'll come meet you. If you won't take a cab, at least let me walk you home."

The image of standing around like an idiot, waiting to be escorted home by a woman at least six inches shorter and two inches softer than herself, struck Ava as ridiculous. No matter how fast or strong the other woman might be.

The *Other* woman.

"No, I'll be fine," Ava dismissed, shoving her errant thought back into the abyss where it belonged. "Go back to your guests and tell everyone I said good night."

"They barely got a chance to see you all night. You kept disappearing on us. Everybody will be disappointed that you had to leave without saying good-bye."

"Don't lie, Regina. It can cause wrinkles."

She disconnected before Regina could answer. It

would only have been another lie, and Ava didn't need anyone to pretend with her. She could handle the truth; in fact, she preferred it, and she thought she'd done a pretty damned good job of dealing with it over the last few years. Like she'd told Regina, Ava Markham was a big girl.

Having grown up in Manhattan, Ava knew the city like the rooms of her apartment—well enough to navigate blind, deaf, and wearing three-inch heels. The time of day, or night, wasn't going to give her any trouble. She always kept her eyes and ears open, her pace brisk, and her attitude confident. Attackers would take a look at her and move on to easier prey. But just in case any particularly stupid muggers decided to try for her, she had self-defense training, lungs like a prima donna, and a can of pepper spray. She'd be fine.

Her heels beat a steady tempo on the pavement as she shoved her hands into the pockets of her cardinal red trench coat and attempted to walk off her discomfort. Her oversized black Spade bag bumped her elbow with just enough force to maintain her current level of irritation. Now if only she could decide at whom that irritation should be directed.

Some of it had to rest on her own shoulders, of course. It was her monumental stubbornness that kept her running face-first into the same brick wall over and over while expecting a different result. That was the definition of insanity, wasn't it? Or had the guidelines been revised since the news broke that people who thought they were werewolves hadn't necessarily gone off their meds?

Ava gritted her teeth and glared at the empty sidewalk ahead of her. Displacement, she admitted, but healthier than confronting what she really wanted to glare at. She hadn't worked this hard for this long to retain her friendships—strained though they may be—just to throw that away by punching out one of her friends' husbands. And that was without considering the fact that committing suicide by vampire, werewolf, or demon—oh, my!—had never been a personal goal of hers. In the interests of her health and social life, Ava had perfected the ability to pretend that everything was fine and that the good old days remained brand spanking new.

Too bad the developing ulcer in her stomach put paid to that particular lie.

Times hadn't just changed; they'd undergone a metamorphosis that made Jeff Goldblum's turn in *The Fly* look like something out of a beauty pageant. It almost made Ava consider cutting off her electricity and exploring the requirement for conversion to an Old Order Amish church. If it weren't for the fashion limitations . . .

Her cell phone rang again. After a quick glance at the caller ID, Ava shoved it back into her pocket unanswered. This time, Missy was calling, of course. People always thought that not even Ava could be so hard-hearted as to ignore the pleas of sweet, sensible, loving Missy. Her friends believed that if Missy asked Ava to take a cab so that Missy wouldn't have to worry about her friend's safety, Ava couldn't say no.

Well, they could believe anything they wanted, although in this case, they happened to be 100 percent right. Ava couldn't say no to Missy, which was why she let her voice mail answer the phone. If she picked it up, Missy would convince her to take a cab the rest of the way home and Ava would lose the chance to walk off her mad before she reached her apartment. She'd have to take all of these nasty feelings to bed with her. Already today she'd had a rotten night's sleep, followed by a lousy morning workout, and without some form of release before bedtime she would probably end up taking her frustrations out on her personal assistant, who barely needed one more frown to convince her to quit her job and leave Ava up a certain nasty little body of water.

It was better to walk. She'd be perfectly safe. She certainly *felt* safer than she had in the very swank media room of Regina's town house, surrounded by the women she still called her best friends. There had been a time when Ava would have sworn that nothing could come between her and Regina. And Missy and Danice and Corinne. They'd been inseparable, best friends forever, together to the end, one for all and all for one. But that had been before Dmitri had entered the picture. Then Graham. Then Mac and Luc. Before their circle had expanded to include werewolves and witches and even a twenty-four-carat, straight-out-of-another-dimension, certified Faerie princess. Before Regina had turned.

Before Ava had realized she was alone, completely alone, in a room full of monsters.

Swallowing back the fist that tried to lodge in her throat, Ava stepped up her pace and lifted her chin.

She still felt a wave of guilt and shame every time she reflexively used the *m* word. She didn't want to think about her friends like that. She loved those women like sisters, but she couldn't deny the truth. They had changed, changed in ways that went beyond marriage and starting new families and growing older and wiser. They had become people Ava barely recognized sometimes. Some of them had even changed species, and as far as Ava was concerned, you could never trust someone who wasn't quite human.

It always came back to that, Ava admitted. That fact was really the root of her problem, the thing she couldn't get used to, the obstacle she just couldn't get past. How did you relate to your best girlfriends when you realized that some of those girls were no longer human?

Ava sure as hell didn't know. Which was why she'd left when the party was in full swing to walk home alone like the reject from the kickball team. It was an unfamiliar sensation.

People just didn't reject Ava Markham. All her life, she had been the girl everyone wanted to be or be with, the golden child. Born to wealthy parents, raised in luxury, "discovered" by a modeling agent before she'd even been a teenager, by the time she hit eighteen she had earned more money than most people would see in a lifetime, and she had decided to get out, before her dieting turned into starving and her lack of energy turned into addiction and her success turned into last season's news.

After a couple of chic and boring years in Europe, she had opened M and signed some of the biggest names in the business. And that had been before her twenty-fifth birthday. Now, at thirty-four, she occupied a coveted spot at the top of the Manhattan food chain of wealth, beauty, and success.

Was it any wonder then that she felt angry every time she thought about the way things had turned out? After everything she'd done for her friends, this was how they ended up. How ungrateful could they get? The fantasy fixes they'd dreamed up all those years ago had been intended to set them up with the men of their dreams—the *human* men—so that they could live the kind of fantasies that most women spent their whole lives only dreaming about. They were supposed to have hot sex, lose a few clothes and maybe a few inhibitions, not their damned minds.

How could it be that the others didn't understand how much better off they would have been if they had just done things her way? Especially Regina. Regina she had loved like a sister. She had tried to warn her friend about Dmitri Vidâme, because Ava had known from the beginning that there was something wrong with him. She'd seen it right away. Otherwise how could he have managed to seduce her prudish, uptight, ultra-conservative friend so thoroughly that she blew off her closest friends for him after knowing him for all of twenty minutes?

And Ava had been right, too. There had been something wrong with Vidâme; there still was, only she had been too late to keep him from infecting

Regina with the same disease. He had turned Ava's best friend into a vampire, and she'd be damned before she forgave either one of them for it.

Shit.

"Breathe," Ava muttered to herself. She had to force her jaw to unclench before she could get the sound out, and then it took another effort of will to draw the crisp night air deep into her lungs without letting it back out in a frustrated scream. If this weren't a quiet residential neighborhood, she might not have bothered to fight.

Every time she went over this ground, the anger bubbled up inside her like water in a hot spring, fast and sulfurous. She had trusted Regina and Missy and Danice and Corinne, and Ava Markham made it a point not to trust anyone but herself. She'd learned early on that people could only ever be counted on to take care of themselves. They might talk about love and sacrifice, but when it came down to matters of survival, everyone turned into Darwins. The fittest survived because they didn't waste time trying to drag anyone else along with them.

Ava had always taken pride in how well she'd learned that lesson. The cutthroat world of top-tier modeling had taught it to her. She took care of herself and never expected anyone to lend a hand when they could give her the boot instead. Unfortunately, she still hadn't managed to stop trying to take care of other people. She'd been banging her head against that wall for so long, she should have the imprint of the bricks permanently embedded in her forehead.

Cursing herself under her breath, Ava crossed the street and hopped up onto the opposite curb. Anger had lengthened her stride until she was practically jogging, the slim knee-length skirt of her dress stretching against her thighs with each step. With her eyes fixed on the shadowed sidewalk in front of her, she saw she still had quite a distance to go before she reached her elegant little row house in Yorkville. Maybe by the time she got there, she'd have walked off some of this resentment.

Or maybe not.

Few things (short of a targeted bioweapon and a very public acknowledgment of her efforts on behalf of the friends who had stabbed her in the back) could likely dent Ava's resentment. After all, she'd had years now to let it build. It wrapped around her as securely as her trench coat, keeping the world out and her focus in. She didn't realize she'd approached the entrance to an alley until the tone of her footsteps echoed in a slightly lower pitch.

Unfazed, she pressed on, attacking the sidewalk with misdirected force. Even when her peripheral vision caught a blur of dark movement off to her side, Ava didn't think anything of it. Manhattan was home, to her and about 8 million other inhabitants, so people rarely made her look twice.

Unless they leapt at her from the shadows and grabbed her by the throat, dragging her struggling form into the alley with the casual ease of inhuman strength.

I knew it! her mind crowed even as her instincts drew breath to scream. *Can't trust an Other!*

Which would be sparse comfort when the police discovered her body in the alley. Cold and dead.

But right.

Chapter 3

Dima had been about to pack it in for the night when he caught a whiff of blood on the air, sweet and faintly spicy. It caught his attention and roused his curiosity, but he didn't think too much of it. America, after all, was a violent nation, and blood was shed fairly frequently on the streets of its largest city. It could be a mugging, a murder, an accident, or even an animal.

It didn't smell like an animal, though, he decided, inhaling deeply, and he had definitely not heard a gun or a car crash. And these were the wrong streets for random stabbings.

Following his nose, Dima turned northeast and backtracked across the rooftops to a building a few hundred feet away.

He approached cautiously at first, the reflex too ingrained for anything else. With light steps and careful movements he had covered roughly half the distance to the source of the scent when he heard a terrified gasp and sudden surge of motion. The air stirred as if parted by a knife blade, and Dima knew that only one thing could have made that sound and yet not alerted him with its scent—another vampire.

A rush of adrenaline pumped through him and raised his senses to high alert. He quickened his pace and kept one eye on the street below. This might be nothing more than a vamp with bad table manners, but if it was an actual attack, then Dima couldn't walk away from it; and if it was his lucky day, the attacker might even be someone who could bring him a step closer to Yelizaveta.

His keen hearing picked up the sound of a weight dropping to the pavement with a muffled thump. Cursing, he broke from a trot into a run as he approached the alley where he had deduced the vampire was hiding. He had the sinking feeling his intervention would come too late for the rogue vamp's victim, but he could at least make sure the criminal faced justice. Even in America, the Other authorities could not let such acts go unanswered.

Gathering himself into a powerful coil, Dima stretched out his arms for balance and leapt across the open space between two buildings in his path, landing solidly atop a four-story structure of redbrick and gray cement cornerstones. Because he kept his gaze forward while he was airborne, he quickly sighted a rather large problem—an obviously human woman who strode down the sidewalk from the opposite direction.

She wore elegantly tailored, obviously expensive clothing, and carried a handbag of dark Italian leather; Dima could smell it from a block away. She had the carriage of a dancer and the height of a model, though as a man he instinctively noticed that her figure curved beneath her scarlet trench coat in a way no model's would have. If asked in that moment, he might have said that her figure was her best feature, long and lean and distinctly feminine, but that was before he saw her face.

At once classic and exotic, she had the clear, refined cheekbones of a princess and lightly bronzed skin that reminded him of the sea and the mountains and the Plaça Catalunya. She had the face of an ancient queen—and the bearing of one—as she traversed the block, her pace brisk and her expression distant.

His instincts screamed a warning.

Contrary to all advice for women living in large cities, this one seemed to possess a situational awareness that ranked somewhere close to zero. She'd drifted off into her own little world, and if she wasn't careful, it would cost her her life.

With an audible curse, Dima cast his glance around for the vampire. The rogue lurked in the shadows just beyond the mouth of the alley two rooftops away. Dima knew the instant the creature caught sight of the woman, because he melted back into the shadows just as she reached the far side of the closest building. She would be on top of the vampire in seconds, while Dima still had two rooftops to cross.

He couldn't reach her in time.

A growl welled up in his chest as he poured on a

burst of speed and raced ahead just in time to see
her reach the alley and walk right into the hands of a
killer.

Ava couldn't scream.

The hand clamped around her throat felt as tight
as a hangman's noose, and she couldn't even draw
breath, let alone cry for help. Fighting like a dervish,
she kicked and flailed and snapped her teeth, hitting
anything and everything she could manage, but her
blows seemed to have no effect.

Her fingers curled around her attacker's arm,
struggling to ease the pressure and at least give her
room to breathe. Distantly, she felt the slide of metal
as the clasp of her necklace broke and the mesh collar fell to the ground. Shock, adrenaline, fear, and
anger were combining with the lack of oxygen to make
her head spin, and she wanted to keep it on straight
just now. Ava might know perfectly well she was going down, but she'd be damned if she'd go down
without a fight.

The walls of the alley seemed to close in around
them as her attacker dragged her deeper into the
shadows and fully out of sight of anyone passing by.
Out of the corner of her eye, she caught sight of
something lumpy and motionless heaped against the
wall farther inside the narrow space. A body. The
son of a bitch had already killed someone and
he couldn't be satisfied with just one victim. Talk
about greedy.

She tried digging her heels into the pavement to
slow them down, but the jerk holding her didn't even

have the decency to pretend he noticed. He just kept dragging, leaving Ava with visions of the heels of her boots shredding against the rough asphalt.

Thousand-dollar European-made Gina boots, and they were going to look like crap when her body was found. *That* pissed her off.

Her need for oxygen was growing critical, but struggling to loosen the man's grip on her throat wasn't doing her any good. She had known, had sensed, that her attacker wasn't human the minute he laid hands on her. He was just too fast and too strong to be a garden-variety mugger. Ava pegged him as vampire, damning herself for having spent enough time around Others to even hazard a guess about their species while one of them was trying to kill her.

Claws grabbed at the knot of hair on the back of her head, piercing through the thick strands and digging into her scalp. She heard the vampire pant in excitement as he jerked her head to the side to expose her throat.

Vamp or shifter, she thought as she squirmed and kicked and fumbled in her pocket for the can of pepper spray she always carried, *you will still die bloody, chica, so stop whining and philosophizing and make the bastard pay for this!*

Releasing her grip on the hand at her throat, Ava momentarily abandoned her search for the small spray tube, fisted her hands together in front of her, and drove her right elbow into the vamp's solar plexus with as much force as she could muster. It nearly made him grunt. Back when Ava had taken her self-defense classes, the instructor hadn't thought it would be necessary to factor in being attacked by someone with the approximate physical strength of the boy from Krypton.

Panic began to join the other emotions crowding Ava's mind as her lack of oxygen became critical. She could no longer tell if her eyes were open or closed. Either way, a sort of misty darkness began to fill her vision, punctuated by brief flashes of fiery orange light. The sounds of her struggles took on a distant, echoing quality, as if they were bouncing back at her from the bottom of a great chasm; yet they registered at a high volume, so that every shift of fabric as her coat bunched and rustled sounded as if a microphone were amplifying the noise.

Without her vision, her other senses seemed to fill her awareness. She still couldn't draw breath, but she knew her attacker smelled of old, oily blood, rotting flesh, and heavily composted soil. The odor settled on her tongue and choked her as surely as the hand at her throat.

The vampire leaned closer, his cold, hard body pressing tightly against hers and sending her stomach into a roiling knot of fear and revulsion. It felt as if the nausea had allied itself with her killer to choke her from a second direction. And it didn't help that she could feel his breath, hot and damp and tangibly fetid against the sensitive, bare skin of her neck.

In the last moment of consciousness, before her brain mercifully shut down at the sharp, burning pain of hard fangs ripping through skin and muscle and flesh, Ava knew she would die. She knew she would be found in an alley like a common prostitute instead of like the near-legendary modeling executive she had made herself into. She knew she would be remembered by her friends more fondly than by the little family she could claim.

With the last of her strength, Ava lashed out and sank her own teeth into the arm that held her. As the world went gray, her last wish was that the bastard would wear the scar for the next ten thousand years.

But even if he did, she knew her friends still wouldn't acknowledge that she had been right all along. She wished bitterly for one last chance to say, *I told you so.*

Then she died.

Chapter 4

A cry of fury bellowed from Dima's chest as he flew across the last rooftop and leapt down into the alley below. He had his long knife in one hand and a short, heavy-headed *bulawa* in the other, and he descended on the startled rogue like vengeance.

His first blow with the Russian mace caught the vampire unaware. It struck the side of the rogue's face and knocked him off of his victim, smashing his cheekbone and sending him reeling to sprawl against the pavement for an instant. Dima used the time to place his body between the woman and her attacker, shifting his grip on the bludgeoning weapon and surveying the damage it had caused with grim satisfaction.

The right side of the vampire's face looked as if it had been run through a trash compactor. The weight of the blow had shattered his cheek and jaw into thousands of tiny fragments and the edge of the knob at the top had caught on the skin, ripping open a six-inch gash through which several white shards of tooth and bone protruded. The attacker's lower right jaw hung slack, dislocated from the joint that no longer existed. His face was covered in blood, both his own and that of his victims, and in his eyes, pain and hatred warred. He stood stunned for the space of a single heartbeat before he launched himself at Dima's throat.

The enforcer sidestepped the blow, using the handle of the *bulawa* to block his enemy's clawing hands and sliding the top of his knife—a long, lethally sharp *poyasnie*—between two ribs.

It was almost too easy. The rogue had no idea how to fight or how to defend himself. He just reached out, all teeth and claws, and tried to plow through the opposition, as if acting like an idiot was supposed to frighten his opponent into submission. Of all the frightening things Dima had seen in his nearly eight centuries, this moron didn't even make the list. Obviously no one had trained him for battle, but who had made him? And when? No vampire over the age of five should be walking around so incompetent.

Disgusted and unwilling to prolong the fight, Dima braced his mace hand across the rogue's throat and prepared to draw the *poyasnie* free. He'd been careful not to pierce the heart, so the vamp would recover, given enough time and enough blood. Dima intended to use that time to ask him a few very important questions.

"Who made you?" Dima growled, pressing the handle of the mace against the rogue's throat. "Name your sire."

"Fuck you!"

"Not just incorrect, but unoriginal as well." Dima

bared his teeth in a feral grin and twisted the hilt of the knife, shredding skin and muscle with the double-sided blade. "Try again."

The rogue growled something unintelligible and spat in Dima's face.

Dima lifted the mace from his opponent's throat just long enough to slam his fist into the rogue's ruined jaw.

The vampire screamed.

"Name. Your. Sire," Dima snarled, snapping off the words like bullets. He wasn't prepared for what the rogue did in response.

Mad, bloodshot eyes locked with Dima's for an instant before the vampire grasped the knife hilt in his own hand, tilted it down, and thrust the length of the blade upward straight into the center of his beating heart. He continued to stare at Dima, the remaining working half of his mouth curving into a chilling smile as he rotated the blade in his own hand.

"*Yob tvoyu mat.*"

Dima tensed. This rogue was American; his accent and appearance made it obvious. So why was he telling Dima in Russian to have an inappropriate relationship with his mother?

The knife twisted and tore through the thick meat of the man's chest, shredding the life-giving organ within. Dima saw the instant the beating stopped, saw the life drain from the rogue's eyes, saw the corpse go limp and slide from the tip of his blade to fold like a science lab skeleton on the damp asphalt.

Dima cursed and knelt to check for a pulse. Nothing. The stupid rogue had committed suicide, damn him, and robbed the enforcer of the opportunity to find out what he might know about Yelizaveta's presence in the city. And he'd left a mess that Dima felt in no mood to clean up.

He wiped his blade and *bulawa* clean on the rogue's clothes, checked quickly to confirm that the vampire's first victim was indeed dead, then turned to crouch beside the body of the woman in the red coat.

Despite her struggle with her attacker and the manner of her death, the woman retained a regal bearing as she lay still and pale on the pavement. The belt of her coat had come untied and a button was missing, but other than that and the bite wound on her neck, she appeared almost to be sleeping. Only the unmoving contours of her chest belied the picture she made.

Dima reached out thoughtlessly and brushed the backs of his fingers against the curve of her cheek. He suddenly needed to know if that pale, dusky skin felt as cool and silky as it looked.

He jerked back and stared down at the dead woman.

Her skin burned with fever.

He pushed the thought aside. It was impossible. Humans—and most other creatures he'd encountered—went cold when they died, the inevitable result of billions and billions of cells suddenly ceasing to function. He knew it had only been a few minutes since the rogue had attacked her, but the woman should be starting to cool. She had stopped breathing. That meant she was dead.

A thread of unease crawled slowly up his spine, and Dima experienced a very unpleasant kind of premonition. The kind that told him he'd stepped into a very big pile of trouble.

Slowly, sending up a rusty scrap of prayer, he reached out a second time and laid the pad of his thumb against the woman's painted lower lip. A tiny bit of pressure shifted the curve down and exposed a set of even white teeth. Not a trace of fang peeped out. The teeth looked entirely human, but Dima wasn't reassured. Parting her lips farther, he nudged her teeth apart and groaned at the faint pink staining he saw on two of the pearly surfaces.

Blood.

The woman had bitten her attacker. Normally, Dima wouldn't have blamed her. He fully supported a person's right to use any tool or weapon at her disposal during a fight for her life, but in this case, the sequence of events had gone all wrong. She must have bitten the rogue after he had drained a good deal of her blood, and she had tasted his in return. Only a few drops, it seemed, but a few drops was enough to start her transformation.

She was turning.

In a sick sort of way, that was the good news, despite it being an involuntary turning perpetrated illegally by a vampire who clearly had intended to drain her and leave her for dead. The bad news was that being actually dead would probably seem like a blessing to the woman before the next few days were out.

The rules involved in transforming a human into

a vampire were abundant and complicated. They had been created millennia ago in an attempt by the earliest of their kind to safeguard their existence from frightened humans who believed vampires were soulless monsters who should be killed in excessively gruesome ways in order to cleanse the sin of evil from their souls (and, no, no one seemed to see the contradiction in that).

At that time, so many hundreds of years ago, strict population regulation of the vampire race had been necessary. When settlements had been small and populations scattered, indiscriminate blood exchanges could have led the unwise among them to convert all the inhabitants of a village into vampires, leaving no convenient food source available. And, of course, during the epidemics of plague that had swept through Europe during the Middle Ages, food itself had occasionally become scarce through no fault of the vampires. Today, such matters caused less of a concern, but traditions died hard, and the recent surge of suspicion from humankind, which had accompanied the Unveiling of The Others, gave the European Council of Vampires, at least, plenty of reason to take the old Laws seriously.

Then, of course, came the concerns raised by the method of transformation itself. First, while most vampires and many humans considered vampirism to be a gift, the Laws had laid down many years ago that the involuntary turning of a human was a crime punishable by death. The theft of free will, identity, and familiarity that accompanied the act of forcing vampirism onto another being ranked among the most heinous crimes of their people.

The vampires who committed such crimes had likely been the ones to give the transformation such a bad name throughout so many centuries of human folklore and literature. In fact, one could almost liken the process of turning a human to elective surgery: Done properly, it posed very little risk and conferred on the human a greatly desired result—immortality—but done improperly, or by the hand of a careless vampire, it could cause agonizing pain at a level that could, quite literally, drive the human mind to insanity.

Although turning did not require the death of the human, it did require the mortal's organs and metabolism to adapt to a completely new physiology. The difference between absorbing the nutrients in a roast chicken and those in a pint of blood meant more than the need for fangs. A person's internal anatomy actually changed during a vampire transformation. If the person had a responsible sire, the kind who tended to seek permission first, the initial few drops of blood that sparked the change would be followed by regular infusions from the same source over the next several hours or days.

Just as infants of most species found it difficult to digest any diet other than mother's milk immediately after birth, so the fledgling vampire found it difficult to digest anything other than her sire's blood for the brief time immediately following her turning. Had this woman's change been voluntary and well planned, she would have had an uneventful and likely painless transition.

Unfortunately, the woman had been shoved forcefully through door number two, and now Dima had to make a decision of his own: Should he try to save her, or end her life now and spare her the misery of an agonizing turning and the wrath of a disapproving ECV?

If he had been at home, Dima knew which he would have chosen. As cold as it might sound, in Europe it would be better for her to die before she suffered any pain than it would be to live under the constant eye and antipathy of the ECV. Some of its members had lived for almost two millennia; they knew how to make a girl's life difficult. But this was America, and from what he'd heard of the local Council of Others, its Feline leader had been called a fair and generous man. While the speaker may very well have meant that as an insult, it indicated that things might be different over here. Maybe in this country, orphans—fledgling vampires abandoned by their sires—were not looked upon with such scorn.

He hesitated for a moment, watching the woman's skin drain of color even as the first few beads of blood-tinged sweat broke out on her forehead and trickled across that impossibly smooth skin into her hair. She looked like a marble statue clad in the latest fashion, a Bernini angel stretched unmoving across dirty pavement, but something told Dima she had not been sent from heaven. As he understood it, angels did not walk unescorted through the streets of New York in the wee hours of the morning.

A faint aroma caught his attention, and Dima lifted his eyes from the woman's body. He could smell more rain in the air, but more worrisome was the fact that he could see it as well. Dawn was still far enough away for there to be no light in the sky, but the darkness had begun to lift, to soften. At his age, even direct sunlight couldn't kill him in less than several hours, but for the fledgling, the first fingers of dawn could amount to a death sentence. He needed to make a decision now.

In the end, it was easier not to.

Operating solely on instinct and well aware that he might very well regret it in the morning, Dima settled his weapons in the sheaths strapped to his thighs and scooped the fallen woman into his arms. He would let the police deal with the other bodies. They would hardly be surprised. In the past three months—since about the same time as Yelizaveta had managed her escape, in fact—vampire attacks in Manhattan had been on the rise.

Imagine that.

Chapter 5

By the time Dima settled the woman on the king-sized bed in the small loft he had rented for his time in New York, he had to tie her to it to keep her from killing one of them. The transformation had hit her hard.

She fought him like a rabid badger, all teeth and claws and no sense of surrender. Operating on pure animal instinct, she snapped newly elongated canines at his neck, and he had no doubt that if he'd been slower to jerk his head back, she would have ripped his throat out and lapped up the blood like a butcher's dog. Fortunately for him, at this stage of her development her bark truly was worse than her bite.

He could see that her reflexes and movements had already gotten faster, and her strength easily exceeded what even an athletic woman of her size would normally possess, but compared to him, she was still a babe in arms. Actually, she was that compared to most vamps over the age of six months.

She had no give in her, though, so he proceeded to wrestle her arms above her head and bind them there with a minimum of fuss. As long as he didn't become suddenly paralyzed while within her reach, Dima knew he had nothing to fear from her, but she posed a very real danger to herself. At this point, she was as likely to gnaw on her own flesh if it got in reach of her mouth as she was to bite anyone else. It would be a while before her senses came back on line and her aim improved enough for her to recall the difference between her body and someone else's. Right now she probably had no awareness of anything other than pain and hunger.

Cursing the rogue who had left her this way, Dima rose and quickly shed his coat, tossing it carelessly into the corner to his left. His weapons he removed with far greater care, leaving his *bulawa* neatly propped near the bedroom door and placing the knife in its scabbard on the bedside table. Since the woman was bound as well as half-conscious, he didn't worry that she could seize it and turn it against him. At the moment, she was too weak to seize so much as a thought.

He let his gaze drift over her as he tugged off his shirt and threw it aside. Fever had flagged her cheeks with bright spots of color, and beads of bloody sweat formed along her hairline as the transformation worked ruthlessly to reshape her human body into a more efficient, more powerful vampire form. He knew that beneath her smooth, pale-gold skin, muscles were shifting and stretching, cells multiplying to create new, stronger fibers capable of lifting small automobiles with the ease of a circus sideshow performer. Beneath her flat belly, her stomach and intestines had begun to slough off their human lining and replace it with cells specialized for the absorption of nutrients directly from ingested blood.

And while her heart attempted to seize up and go still under the insult of the foreign blood invading it, the cells of that invader had begun to override the native electrical pulses and squeeze the muscle like a giant fist, forcing themselves along a circulatory system in revolt.

Damn it. It shouldn't have been this way. Dima sat on the edge of the bed and watched a face of stunning beauty contort itself into expressions of rage and torment. This was why the ECV required their kind to seek permission to initiate the transformation of a human—because if the proper procedures were not followed, this would be the result.

Seeing the woman's obvious pain, Dima cursed the rogue who had attacked her and wished darkly that he had the criminal in front of him again. Rest assured, if given another chance at the creature, Dima would make sure his death did not arrive so easily this time.

Putting his thoughts of vengeance reluctantly aside, Dima turned his attention back to the situation at hand. It might be unfortunate that the woman's change had come about so irresponsibly, but if he wished to see her survive it, he would have to help her through it.

At another time, the enforcer might have laughed at the image of himself playing nursemaid to a recently human woman half his size, but his sense of humor seemed to have stayed behind in the alley with the body of the other human the rogue had attacked. Now, he focused entirely on business.

With her hands bound, the woman on the bed would not be going anywhere, but she continued to thrash and fight her restraints in a way that could prove dangerous to her own safety. God knew what position she might manage to contort herself into and what damage it might cause her. Dima would need to tie her feet as well. Unfortunately, he had used the one length of cotton in his suitcase to bind her hands, and the other rope he carried was rough and utilitarian, meant for functions other than restraining living beings. Not that he hadn't used it for that purpose a time or two before, but never on anyone with such delicate-looking skin, and never on anyone he particularly cared about not harming. If he tied her with the rope he had on hand and she continued to struggle as she was doing, she'd make herself bleed in no more than a few minutes. He needed something gentler.

He could rip strips of fabric from his clothing, he admitted reluctantly, but he hadn't brought that much to spare. When on a mission, Dima redefined the concept of packing light. Laundry facilities were never difficult to find, and in a pinch he could always buy or steal new clothing for himself, but he never knew when he would have to move and move quickly in pursuit of the prey he hunted. Such considerations made carrying an extensive wardrobe impractical.

His gaze swept the room, searching for inspiration and finding nothing. The loft had come unfurnished, and he hadn't bothered supplying it with more than the basic necessities—the bed, a chair and a desk that held his laptop computer, and a beat-up and marvelously ugly old sofa he had picked up along with an outdated television at a local charity shop. Neither of the last two items had any but the most basic, functional features, and both suited his purposes perfectly. The sofa was longer than the average, allowing him to stretch out on its surprisingly comfortable cushions while he watched pirated cable service on the television's twenty-three-inch screen.

Dima might be a vampire on a mission, but he was still a man, and he still needed to relax occasionally. His favored method of doing so between October and April happened to be watching the televised coverage of America's NHL season. With luck, the Wings would take it all the way again this year.

The woman beside him jerked violently and twisted her body hard to the side, nearly throwing herself off the mattress to dangle over the edge by her bound wrists. Shaking off his thoughts, Dima scowled. He couldn't leave her this way. He had to secure her feet before she found a way to flip herself backward over the headboard and strangle herself on her own forearms. A quick glance at the skirt riding up her slim thighs gave him an idea.

Swiftly he bent and located the zippers on the insides of her tall black boots. Releasing them, he pulled the footwear off and tossed it out of the way. Beneath the leather, he saw what he'd hoped for— the subtle and familiar sheen of tightly woven black silk.

Dima slid his hands under the wrinkled wool of the woman's purple dress and reached for her waistband. His fingertips found nothing like the elastic waistband of modern panty hose. Instead, he felt a smooth band of silk settled just at the flare of very feminine hips.

Frowning, he slid his hands over the soft curves and told himself the idea that touching an unconscious human in the midst of a painful, forced change couldn't possibly make his skin prickle like a low-voltage shock. He had probably just mistaken the heat of her fever for something else. Still, his jaw clenched as he skimmed his hands down her hips and found matching vertical bands of rough-silky elastic.

Dima reared back and scowled down at the woman's legs, still covered by columns of dark silk.

Ebyona mat' [I'll be damned], he thought, and possibly meant it literally.

Of all the human women in Manhattan, the rogue had to pick the last living one who still wore a garter belt with her stockings?

Unbidden, sharp images of white skin and black stockings, curved thighs and dark folds, invaded his mind and filled his vision. His senses rioted at the possibility of satin skin and woven silk catching on the harsh stubble on his cheeks. He saw his own head bent, his shoulders holding her long legs open as he feasted on the sweetness between them. . . .

Pizdets! [Fuck!]

He was losing his goddamn mind. There was no other excuse for this line of thought. He couldn't even say he'd been too long without a woman. Sure, he was in the middle of a mission and it had been a few weeks, but he'd gone much longer without sex before. Frankly, after seven centuries, sex could no longer be called one of his top priorities. He'd had plenty of time over the many years of his life to do just about everything and everyone who had piqued his curiosity. At this point in his immortality, he gave sex approximately the same amount of attention that he gave to scratching an itch and less than he gave to personal grooming or finding a good bottle of vodka. When he needed it, he got it, but he never spent much time worrying about it. He certainly never spent time thinking about it when he should be focusing on what needed to be done, as opposed to what his dick might be suggesting they do.

Gritting his teeth, Dima clenched his hands into fists, blew out a deep breath, and stripped the woman of her garter belt and stockings so fast, he had to duck to avoid the backlash of her left foot, which was aimed at his head when it sprang free of the confining silk. Then he had to work very, very hard to ignore the fact that in his haste to see the deed done, he'd unintentionally stripped off her panties along with the garter belt.

Dermo. [Shit.] He'd fallen into a perverse comedy of errors.

A few quick tugs freed the stockings from the garter fasteners. Dima worked quickly to use the lengths of silk to bind her ankles together and secure them to the bed frame. Tying them apart was decidedly *not* an option. When his fingers inevitably brushed against her ankles, he gritted his teeth and tried to think of England, but neither the cold and rainy weather nor the cold and reigning queen managed to dampen the spark that leapt between the woman's bare skin and his. All he could do was rush through it and step back from the bed as soon as possible. When he did so and he got a glimpse of her long, luscious body stretched out and bound across his bed, he swore again and turned quickly for the kitchen.

The woman would need more blood, and soon, which meant that Dima himself would have to eat for two for the next few days. Thankfully, he kept bagged blood in his refrigerator in case of emergency. If the current situation didn't qualify him to break into that stash, nothing ever would.

He retrieved two bags quickly and returned to the bedroom with them in hand. Even with her bound, he didn't like the idea of leaving the woman alone for any longer than he had to. With a little mental sleight of hand, he could almost convince himself the only reason for that was because he was afraid of her harming herself, not because she had legs like a dancer and skin like a courtesan.

Dragging a straight-backed chair to the side of the bed, he settled his long frame into the seat and bit through the first packet of plastic. He swallowed reflexively, draining the liquid in record time and reaching for another.

Dima fed like a man doing chores, experiencing none of the enjoyment he usually felt while feeding, but then, bagged blood offered none of the allure of a meal from a living donor. Live blood coursed hot into the mouth, rich with the energy and vitality of the human who gave it. It trickled thick down the throat, coated the stomach with the fire of aged whisky, and sent pulses of electricity through the body. When a vampire fed from a live donor, it felt almost as if he consumed blood and spirit in equal measure.

Bagged blood, by contrast, tasted flat and cold in ways that had nothing to do with refrigerated storage. It had more to do with needles and distance and anonymity, not to mention preservatives. It would keep a vampire alive, but not even a confirmed ascetic would care to consume only bagged blood for long.

Dima had never claimed to be an ascetic. It would have been a hard thing to accomplish, growing up as he had, the son of a rich warrior-merchant who had made a fortune trading in exotic spices from the South, rich silks from the East, and thick, plush furs from the North. Even in a world before electricity and modern comforts, when a wise man slept with a sword by his bed and a friend at his back, Dima's people had taken their luxuries seriously. What they had the technology to produce, they produced, and what they had the fortune to consume, his wealthy family had consumed. Dima could admit to having grown accustomed to the modern luxuries of the twenty-first century, but something inside him still longed for the days when a man could sleep buried in a pile of thick winter pelts without hearing the cries of animal rights activists echoing in his dreams.

A glance at his guest's face told Dima that whatever currently haunted her dreams must be equally unpleasant. Her brow had furrowed, her lips drawn back in a grimace of pain, and he could see where two sharp new canine teeth had begun to emerge from inflamed pink gums. Her breath sawed out of her chest in hoarse, pain-filled moans like those of a trapped animal, and her flesh seemed to ripple over her bones as if something inside her struggled vainly to escape. The change was riding her hard, and even though Dima couldn't cure the agony completely, he could at least ease it a bit.

Tossing aside the second empty blood bag, Dima leaned forward and snagged the tip of his knife on the skin inside his thick wrist. Blood welled almost immediately, dark and shining like garnets against the gold of his skin. Shifting from his chair to sit on the side of the bed, he moved closer to the unconscious woman and used his free hand to grasp the back of her head and guide her mouth to the nourishment he offered.

She latched on like a barnacle, her entire body arching and twisting as she tried to curl around the source of the blood. The ropes around her wrists quivered but held. Thankfully, she still hadn't come into her strength, or he would have been picking splinters of metal out of his skin when the bed frame shattered under the pressure. As it was, she drew strongly at his wound, urging the blood to course faster down her slim throat. She almost reminded him of a newborn kitten rooting at its mother's nipple, whimpering and straining, frantic to fill its belly and dull the unfamiliar pangs of hunger.

His feelings for her, however, were far from maternal.

If he hadn't known better, hadn't been able to feel the slick slide of liquid from his veins to her mouth, he'd have wondered when she planned to begin drinking. What he didn't have to wonder about was whether he had sufficient blood to nourish her, since he apparently had enough to let her suck it down even while a not-insignificant volume of the stuff began to pool behind the zipper of his trousers. The damned woman had brought him fully erect without a word exchanged between them, without him even knowing her name. Normally, he could claim a bit more restraint than that.

Then again, what about the current situation could be called normal?

Clamping down on the lust that surged through him with every pull of her mouth, Dima let her feed for a few more minutes. Not until he could feel some of the rigidity of her body ease did he begin to pull away. His blood had begun to do its work. Already it would be coursing through her, easing the pain of her transformation, healing the violent damage her unwelcome crossing had produced.

She should slip into a more restful sleep now, he judged as he drew his wrist from her lips and closed the wound with his own saliva. Less pain would allow her mind to rest while her body underwent a kind of internal nanosurgery. When she woke—maybe tomorrow night, maybe the morning after—she would be fully vampire, stronger, faster, and more powerful than she had ever imagined. His old blood, seven centuries old, would ensure it.

She was lucky, really, he mused. Dima guessed that the rogue who attacked her had been no more than twenty or thirty. Probably even younger. If he had followed through on her siring, he would have created a vampire even weaker than himself, and compared to Dima, a thirty-year-old equaled a veritable babe in arms, barely able to control his strength, let alone read the thoughts of strangers or influence weaker minds. With Dima as her sire, this woman might very well be her attacker's equal within a few days of waking.

Lucky, indeed.

Of course, she would need time to adjust, Dima acknowledged, especially since her crossing had not been of her own choosing. When she first woke, she would likely be confused, even angry. If she remembered the attack, fear would be there as well. Dima would need to make sure he stayed close so that he could talk her through it, gently explain to her what had happened, what she had become, what she could expect of her new life.

Sighing, he stood and gazed down at her. Wasn't there an old Eastern adage that once you saved a person's life, you became responsible for it? Maybe he should have thought of that before he had jumped into that alley. He had enough responsibilities already and a mission that was both personal and professional to worry about. He should be devoting all his time and energy to that, but instead, he would be playing mentor to a newborn vampire who would have to learn an entire life from scratch—how to eat, how to find food, how to stay out of the spotlight and offend neither the human population nor the reigning vampire authorities.

That last thought made him wince. Technically the vampire authorities in Europe would be less than pleased if they discovered what Dima had done. This woman's turning had not been approved. For aiding her Dima could find himself with a great deal of trouble from his employers.

What on earth had he been thinking?

He hadn't been, of course. He'd been reacting. After seeing the woman struggling to cling to life in that alley, Dima couldn't imagine leaving her there. While her turning had not been approved, neither had it been requested. She had been victimized by the rogue, but Dima would need to find a way to satisfy the ECV if he wanted to prevent her further harassment. Fortunately, he had not turned anyone else during his nearly eight centuries, and that might weigh in his favor. It would weigh more heavily, he was sure, if he presented the entire matter to a council already softened up by his successful completion of the mission to which he'd been assigned.

Giving himself a mental kick in the ass, Dima turned away from the bed and stalked back toward the living room and his laptop. It was too late for regrets now. He was stuck with the woman, at least for a few more days, so he should take advantage of her unconsciousness while it lasted. A few hours in front of the computer might not be as effective a hunting tactic as patrolling the streets and shaking down random rogues for information, but it was better than nothing.

He'd try reminding himself of that every few minutes, he decided, settling into the desk chair. If he was lucky, he might start to believe it.

Chapter 6

Ava woke from the nightmare, her heart pounding, her brow covered in cold sweat. She hadn't dreamed that vividly in years, not since she'd taught herself to step back from her nightmares and will them away. This one had been a doozy, all dark shadows and sharp pain and something cold and powerful staring down at her with eyes the color of an arctic sky. It was almost enough to make her reconsider her true need for beauty sleep. Blowing out a deplorably unsteady breath, she reached out to preemptively silence her alarm clock.

Or she tried to.

She couldn't move her hands.

Her eyes snapped open and presented her with the unwelcome view of an unfamiliar ceiling, high, pale, and crisscrossed with the exposed steel beam work of an urban loft. She had never seen this place before in her life. And she couldn't move.

Panic began to well. She tugged sharply on her hands and attempted to sit up, only to find her feet similarly secured. Aghast, disbelieving, she craned her head around to confirm what her instincts had been trying to tell her even while she'd been asleep: She was a prisoner, bound hand and foot to a strange bed in a strange apartment in what she hoped to God and all his angels was not a strange city.

She'd been kidnapped.

Every synapse in her brain seemed to fire at once, attacking her with an explosion of pain and confusion more intense than anything she had ever experienced. Memory flooded back, dearly drowning her. She felt like she was watching a movie montage— seeing herself at the girls' night party at Reggie's house, staring into the powder room mirror, walking home with her anger keeping her company, passing by an alley she'd walked in front of a million times before. . . .

Then the film went cockeyed, a handheld camera tumbling to its side. She saw the flash of movement on her right, felt the stirring of air and the overwhelming, inhuman strength of the thing that had grabbed her, grabbed her and dragged her deeper into the alley. She saw the slick, dark brick, smelled blood and rot and sick coming from the body that lay in a lifeless pile against the alley wall, smelled it on the breath and the skin and the empty soulless void of the monster holding her. She felt its arm around her neck, corded with muscle and hatred, cutting off her air, leaving her choking and gasping for breath. She felt its hot, fetid breath against her skin, felt the sharp tear of fangs against flesh, and her welling panic took the freeway exit straight to the blind, instinctual, animal imperative to escape.

Gathering her breath, Ava opened her mouth to

scream and threw every ounce of strength in her body into breaking the bonds that held her. She got out no more than a short, sharp whistle before a large male hand clamped over her mouth and cut off her cry.

Her gaze shot to an unfamiliar face, one that hardly looked like it could belong to the stink in her memory. This man looked like death, but not the kind of death that snuck up behind a woman in a dark alley and bled her dry—more like the kind of death that knights had once faced on the battlefield, strong and quiet and rigidly calm. He had features as sharp-edged as stone, intensely masculine and far too heavy to admire. Ava worked every day with models who epitomized the modern sensibility of male beauty, and if this man had walked into her office, she'd have turned him around and sent him right back out again.

Or rather, she'd have called security—and maybe a SWAT team—and had him *escorted* out again.

Beautiful he wasn't, not even with the slightly too-long hair that framed his face in a dozen shades of blond, from warm toffee to cold platinum (Ava had clients—both male and female—who would pay thousands for that hair and never quite be satisfied), but something about him compelled. Maybe it was the eyes—sharp, intent, and the pale blue-gray of an arctic landscape. Or the way those eyes watched her with the quiet, frozen patience of a hawk just waiting for the moment to strike.

It was that uncanny stillness that tipped her off. His lips were firmly closed, so she couldn't see any fangs, and experience had taught her that the horns these guys should have sported to clue in the unwary never did show. The outward trappings of evil didn't matter, though. Ava could tell. Only one kind of man could be so still, so strong, and so bloody silent. He was a vampire.

Shaking off the spell that seemed to have gripped her at the sight of him, Ava narrowed her eyes and prepared to bite the hand that silenced her.

He moved too quickly, sliding a broad thumb under her jaw and pressing hard to keep it closed. "I wouldn't advise it," he rumbled in a voice deep with gravel and spiced somehow with the hint of a place far from Manhattan. "It's too soon for you to be able to control your reaction if you draw blood."

Ava simply glared at his nonsense and began to tug against her bonds once more. She had absolutely no intention of ending her life as an hors d'oeuvre for a fiend from hell. Or Transylvania. Wherever the bloodsucking bastards came from.

"That's not a very good idea, either." His free hand stretched up and pressed against her joined wrists, his strength casual and overwhelming. "You might be strong enough to break free, but I'm afraid it would be a very literal break. The bed is iron and will hold together. Your bones, on the other hand, are less forgiving. They would snap long before the rope did."

Her eyes told him to go to hell. And that was only because her mouth was unable to tell him something far fouler. For some reason, she trusted his warning, but that didn't stop her from trying to get away. Now, instead of pulling against her bonds, she began to run her fingers over the rope, searching for knots or weak points. She had read somewhere that no rope bondage was entirely escape-proof. If that was true, she intended to prove it.

Those cool, predatory eyes looked down at her. "I can take my hand away, but I'm afraid I'm going to have to ask you not to scream."

I'll be as silent as a howitzer.

"We're in a warehouse district and it is three in the morning, so I am not worried about someone hearing you," he explained, reading her mind with obnoxious ease, "but I have very sensitive ears. I much prefer the quiet."

And I much prefer not being tied to a bed and held prisoner by strange vampire perverts with lousy senses of humor. Too bad we can't always get what we want.

Ava saw the surprise spark in his eyes and felt a new wave of anger swamp her. The bastard was reading her mind. She *hated* when they did that! She made a mental note to watch what appeared in his eyes when she planted the pointy toe of her boot in the middle of his scrotum. With excessive force.

"That seems a bit harsh to me," he said. Anyone else might have edged the observation with irony, maybe even humor. This one's expression never changed from its harsh, granite lines. "I did, after all, recently save your life."

"Umphd gy mphygph?" Shock made her forget the hand over her mouth, but the garbled noises she made in place of words didn't seem to faze him.

"Saved your life," he repeated, nodding. "You'd been attacked and left for dead. Do you remember any of it?"

She said nothing. Obviously. When she'd realized he was a vampire, she had assumed—not unreasonably, she assured herself—that he'd been the one to attack her. His words unaccountably made her rethink. This monster might be just as evil as the one who had tried to kill her earlier, but at least he looked clean. He didn't smell anything like the other one. No way could Ava ever forget that scent. But if the giant wasn't her attacker, who was? And more important, where was he? Because Ava intended to prosecute him to the fullest extent of the new human protection laws.

"You look like you remember something, but I'm guessing you're fuzzy on the details." He waited for her to nod. He could wait a goddamn lifetime as far as she was concerned. She had no plans to do this jerk any favors. "You were attacked as you were walking past an alley. Do you usually go for strolls through the city alone? In the middle of the night?"

As if it was any of his business what she did. Ava continued to glare at him silently and search for a knot.

"I would encourage you to take up a new hobby. You were completely vulnerable to the attack. A rogue vampire came up behind you and dragged you into the alley, out of sight. Polite, but probably unnecessary. I doubt anyone else would have passed at that hour. He had already killed another woman. You would have been second if I hadn't found you."

Well, yipdee—frickin'—doo. You're my hero. I'll try to leave your corpse some dignity, she thought, but this time she tried to keep her thoughts to herself. He might not like that particular plan.

"I picked you up and brought you back here. You needed some . . . medical attention. I patched you back up and decided to let you sleep."

"Knphah mnaph zphnst—" She broke off to glare at him.

He watched her for a long minute before he so much as blinked. "Only if you promise not to scream. If you do, I'll knock you unconscious again, and this time I'll gag you before you wake up."

If he hit her, he'd have to kill her before she woke up, Ava thought, mental shields firmly in place, because she would eviscerate the man who laid a hand on her that way. She didn't care how securely she was tied. She would get free eventually, and she had a very long memory. Still, she nodded. If he kept his hand clamped over her mouth and jaw any longer, she'd have bruises no amount of three-hundred-dollar foundation would hide.

Ava nodded once.

Satisfied, he let his hand slide away, moving slowly, as if ready to slam back into place if she should draw too deep a breath. Somehow the feathery brush of his calloused fingers over her skin sent a wave of heat rushing through her. Disgusted with herself, Ava made very sure to stuff that away where no one would find it. What kind of sicko got turned on by a touch from a vampire who'd tied her to a bed?

Okay, Regina, maybe, but that was beside the point.

"I said, why didn't you just call an ambulance and let the paramedics give me whatever medical attention you thought I needed?" Her voice came out low and hoarse, as if she'd spent the evening before screaming her way through a rock concert. Frowning, she tried clearing her throat, but it didn't help. "Wouldn't that have been easier?"

"Much." Again with the lack of irony. "But from what I hear, the emergency responders in this city have been having a hard time adjusting to the treatment of unusual patients."

Unusual. That was one of the new "polite" words for The Others, but Ava saw no point in prettying up her language. A monster was a monster in her book.

"Yeah, well, it wouldn't have mattered. They could have treated me just fine. I'm human."

The giant shook his head. "Not anymore."

A hollow buzzing noise exploded in Ava's head. Her chest tightened as if someone had strapped a belt around her lungs and cinched. She felt the jittery buzz of a caffeine overdose with none of the creamy, latte accompaniment. She shook her head to clear it, but it didn't help. "Excuse me?"

"Your attacker was a vampire. You've been changed."

The feeling she now recognized as panic bled down her throat, burning like ice-cold whisky and jolting her heart into overdrive. She could practically see the adrenaline needle sticking out of her chest.

"That's not possible," she rasped out. "I'm human, and I'm not stupid. I know what it takes for a person to cross over to vampire. You have to exchange blood. No way on earth am I dumb enough to do something like that. You couldn't pay me enough to drink blood, let alone drink blood from a vampire."

The vampire's expression remained impassive, not a shred of sympathy in evidence. Then again, he showed no shred of deception, either. She didn't plan to trust him, but some unfamiliar thing that squirmed in her gut told her she didn't have to take his word for it. Not when she already knew. Deep inside.

A knot formed in Ava's stomach, pulled tight. She struggled for denial. "I wouldn't do that," she repeated.

The man blinked. "You know he bit you. He nearly tore a chunk out of the side of your neck. You remember that, don't you?"

Her hand went instinctively to the spot, felt a small amount of scabbing, a little dried blood. Nothing like the injury that should have been there. "Sure, but one bite wouldn't do it. He could drink me dry and I wouldn't turn unless I'd drunk from him, too. Which I definitely. Did. Not. Do."

He inclined his head just a fraction. "Not intentionally, I'm certain. I believe you would not have planned to do so."

"I wouldn't have done so at all. I *didn't* do so."

"You fought back." When he paused, as if waiting for a response, Ava nodded. "You kicked, elbowed, stomped, hit, clawed."

Another nod.

"Bit."

The knot in her stomach unraveled, along with every nerve and muscle in her body. Despite her prone position on the bed, dizziness overwhelmed her. She raised her eyes to the ceiling and watched the beams overhead dance the tarantella. The entire room was moving around her, and her heart threatened to race the contents of her stomach to see which made it out of her throat first. She fought for breath like a winded marathoner and nearly gagged at the sharp memory of copper heat flooding her mouth.

Santa María, what have I done?

"It wasn't supposed to matter." Her voice was a murmur, weak with disbelief, grief, shame, fear. She wrapped her fingers around the ropes over her head and held on as if afraid she might fall. "He was going to kill me. I know he was going to kill me. It shouldn't have mattered that his blood got into my mouth, because I was never going to make it out of that alley."

He looked at her. "You made it out."

Shaking, Ava stared at the ceiling and unclenched her fists from the ropes, all of the fight draining out of her body. "That's it, then. I'm going to turn into a vampire. I'm going to be one of the monsters." She tore her gaze from the ceiling and turned it on her captor. "Tell me how long I have."

He frowned. She could tell because his brows drew together all of half a millimeter. "What do you mean?"

"How long do I have before I transform?" she demanded, thinking that he might be compelling, but he seemed to be dumber than a catfish in a frying pan. "Before I go all fangy. How long do I have?"

The frown did not ease. If anything, it got even deeper, almost recognizable. "I'm not certain I understand—"

"It's very simple, Sherlock," she snapped, a little of herself coming back to her. If only for a moment. "I want you to tell me how much longer I have before I'm officially one of the liquid diet crowd. I've been around this scene for long enough to know that the last thing I want to do is live the rest of my life as a bloodsucking monster. I'll kill myself first, and damn the Church."

For an instant, Ava thought she saw something almost like sympathy in those arctic eyes, but it passed so quickly she couldn't be sure. When he spoke, he sounded as cold and disinterested as ever.

"You have no time," he said. "This is not a matter of waiting for your membership card to arrive. He drank, you drank, the end. You are vampire. It is done."

The finality of his words accomplished what the fear and dread and panic inside her had not. It froze the last living spark of her hope, leaving her as cold and desolate as those wintery eyes.

Monster, she called herself, and fought the wave of nausea that accompanied the thought. Then something even worse occurred to her. All this time she'd spent resenting her friends and hating their husbands, and now she had become just as bad as they were. She had become the thing she hated most in the world.

The thing she feared.

The thing on which she had been able to focus all of her rage at the father who had abandoned her and her mother, the mother who had loved and hated her husband so much that she had no emotion left for her only child, the industry that had stolen her childhood, chewed her up, and only failed to spit her out because she had left before they got the chance.

All those things that had gnawed at her, that had fueled the silent, agonized scream deep inside her belly . . . For the past five years she had been able to ignore them all by concentrating not on them but on the anger and loathing they made her feel. For five years, she had been able to cope with it all by hating the monsters—the Lupines and Felines and demons and witches and changelings and Faeries.

And vampires.

And now she was one of them.

Fate, she decided miserably, had a sick, vicious sense of humor.

Chapter 7

Shock could have accounted for Ava's silence, but she'd been shocked more than a few times in her life and she'd never before found herself at a loss for words. But there was a difference, she supposed, between being shocked when a younger girl with a big nose and no breasts got the cover of *Vogue* instead of her, and finding out that she had just gone over to the Dark Side of the Force without so much as catching a glimpse of a YOU ARE HERE sign to warn her of the possibility.

Either way, something kept her quiet and malleable while the man looming over her untied first her feet and then her hands from where they had been bound to the frame of a very large iron bed. When he finished, she rubbed absently at the raw, scabby rings of red skin around her wrists where the rope had bitten into them. Lifting herself into a sitting position, she looked down at the marks and frowned.

"You had to tie the rope that tight? I'm surprised my hands didn't turn blue and fall off," she bitched, just because it gave her something *else* to focus on. Something other than the truth.

"I used the softest rope I had, and it wasn't very tight." His eyes weren't on her but on the rope in his hands as he coiled it into a neat bundle. "I left it as loose as I could, but it was on for almost twenty-four hours. You fought hard."

The idea offered Ava little comfort, and neither did the note of admiration she heard in his voice. "I fought? What did I fight? What did you try to do to me while I was out?"

One tawny eyebrow arched. "Relax. I have no taste for forcing myself on women who remain unaware of my presence. I tried to keep you from harming yourself. That is all."

She kept her eyes on him, still suspicious, and slid toward the side of the bed to stand. Her skirt rode up her thighs with the motion. Absently she reached down to pull it back into place and froze. Her gaze shot down to her legs and back to the blond giant's face.

"That's all?" she demanded, her raspy voice bordering on a screech. "That's *all*? If that's all, then *why the hell aren't I wearing my stockings*?"

He looked up, blinked, shrugged. Then he pointed at the foot of the bed. "I ran out of rope."

"You— . . . I— . . . What— . . ."

The fury swamped her, cutting off her power of speech and leaving her gaping up at him like a landed carp. That was okay, though. She's rather have the fury than the fear. Any day.

Energized, she leapt to her feet and . . .

. . . folded like a house of cards on the small bedside rug.

". . . body still needs time to recover," she heard him say through the tinny buzzing in her ears. "You will need to rest and take care for a few more days."

He had scooped her up from where she'd fallen, which was good, because Ava didn't think she had the strength to do more than a bad impression of a sea cucumber. But when he bent down to place her back on the bed, she stiffened. He paused.

"You have been in bed for quite a while," he said, turning toward the bedroom door. "You might feel better if you sat up in the other room. Besides, you should have something more to eat. It will help to build up your strength."

Ava didn't bother to protest as he carried her through a nearly empty apartment decorated in early modern bachelor–cum–charity shop. All except for the computer equipment, which figured. Men and their toys.

Of course she thought about struggling, but after weighing the possibility for all of a second and a half, she discarded it. The man was built like an overly tall gymnast, at least three inches over six feet, with a deceptive leanness that distracted from the mind-bogglingly well-developed musculature padding his long frame. He had lifted her as easily as a scrap of paper and looked like carrying her through the apartment was causing him about as much strain as flossing his teeth. Struggling, especially when she could barely stand on her own, wouldn't do her any good. Better to save her strength for more important things.

For making plans, and carrying them out.

He deposited her on a worn-out sofa with surprising gentleness. Before she'd so much as smoothed her skirt, he had already walked away. She wasn't used to people walking away from her, not even vampires who intimidated her and held her prisoner.

Because she was so off balance, Ava frowned and searched for something to say to get his attention, to stop him from walking away. "I thought you said you were going to feed me."

"I am."

She watched as he opened the door to a small refrigerator and reached inside.

"You're giving me leftovers?" she demanded, infusing her voice with outrage. Outraged was how she would react to such a plan under other circumstances. Normal circumstances. "The least you could do is order out for Thai. I'll have something spicy, with the really thin rice noodles. Shrimp, no pork."

He returned holding something, but the back of the sofa blocked her view of his hands. He detoured to neither the compact oven nor the built-in microwave above it. He didn't even hold whatever it was over a hot plate.

"I'm warning you, if you try to make me eat cold pizza straight out of the refrigerator, I will throw it up all over you. That kind of thing will just ruin your stomach."

"Not to mention my upholstery," he retorted, rounding the end of the sofa and nudging her knees aside to perch on the edge next to her. "Don't worry, it is not cold pizza. Nor is it Thai food, which, I would like to point out, would also not sit very well with you at the moment."

"What is it then?"

He took her hand in his, turned it palm up, and placed something slick and cold against it. Confused, Ava glanced down and felt a new wave of dizziness threaten to overcome her. She jumped back, her spine hitting a particularly worn spot in the arm of the sofa. The bag of blood he'd given her bounced once off her knee before landing on the floor.

"No."

He sighed, reached down, and retrieved the bag. "You need to drink it," he said, his voice calm and level. She wanted to slap him. "Not only does your body need it to help you regain your strength, but since it's the only thing you'll be eating for the rest of your newly extended life, it would be better that you become used to it sooner than later."

Ava shook her head. "No. I'm not drinking that. I'm *not* drinking blood. I'll find another way."

That blond brow arched again. "There is only one other way, and I doubt you would find it pleasant."

"What is it?"

"You could kill yourself."

That flat, hard tone assured her he spoke the truth. His gaze never wavered from hers, and his expression did little to convince her that he cared about her decision either way.

The question was, did Ava? No matter what she considered in the heat of the moment, did she actually want to die? Or more important, to be dead?

Completely dead, as opposed to whatever degree of dead she might be at the moment.

"You are a vampire now," he continued, "and for a vampire, blood is life. Without blood, you cannot survive. If you will refuse to feed, you would be better served to end your life now. Not only will it spare you from suffering through the hunger; it will save me from having to kill you once you go mad and begin to attack humans indiscriminately. Is this what you would choose?"

She narrowed her eyes at him. "I don't like either of those choices."

"That is too bad, for they are the only ones you have."

"What about—"

He sighed, a sound so put-upon, she wondered if he filled in for Sisyphus on bank holidays. "I will make you a deal," he offered, his tone disturbingly pleasant. "If you agree to drink that bag, I will agree not to use force to ensure that you do so."

"Force?" Ava felt her spine straighten almost involuntarily. Her eyes she narrowed quite willingly. "Exactly what kind of force do you think you're going to use on me, Goliath? Because I warn you, if you try to hold my nose and pour it down my throat, you'd better tie me up again first. And hide your kitchen knives before I castrate you. Maybe the spoons, too."

"That would not be necessary. I would not need to resort to such crude physical tactics." He watched her, his eyes glinting with both challenge and confidence. Ava felt herself drawn into those eyes and clenched her jaw against the sudden urge to lean toward him. He saved her the trouble and shifted closer, running a callused fingertip over the curve of her jaw. "All I would need to do," he purred, a new, decidedly unfrozen animation lighting his harsh features, "is ask. If I asked you, *kralya,* you would do anything for me. Wouldn't you?"

She leaned into him like a flower toward the sun, compelled to follow his movements. His words, spoken low and soft and seductive, made perfect sense. Of course she would do what he asked. Anything he asked.

Her lips parted, agreement trembling on the tip of her tongue, until he brushed that warm fingertip over the blade of her cheekbone and flicked the tip of her nose. She blinked and jerked back as if someone had suddenly turned on the lights in a pitch-black room. For the first time, Ava looked at the stony giant and saw real amusement on his face. A slow, creeping lava flow of fury ignited inside her.

"You manipulative fucking bastard," she breathed, much, much too angry to shout. "You got inside my head and manipulated my thoughts. You fucking *mind-raped* me! You can't do that!"

He lifted his brows. "I believe I just demonstrated that I could."

"No, I mean you *can't do* that. You aren't supposed to be able to. You're not the first vampire I've ever met, Fang, and I have it on very good authority that vampire mind tricks do not work on other vampires."

"*Usually* do not work on other vampires," he corrected.

She scowled. "And how did I become the exception to the rule?"

"I think it is more that I am the exception. Or perhaps that we are." He shrugged. "You are barely one day old, *boi-baba*. I have nearly eight hundred years on you. I can do many things other vampires cannot do."

Ava worked hard not to blink at that news. Even she knew that eight hundred was a fairly impressive age for a vampire, especially in Manhattan, which confirmed what the giant's accent had told her: he wasn't from around here. But even if he was the second-oldest vampire she knew of—Reggie's husband being the oldest, and only by a decade or so—she had learned enough from her friend to know that his explanation wasn't the whole truth. From what Reggie said, even when there was a huge age gap between vampires, the elder should have had to put a lot more effort into controlling the mind of the younger than she'd seen Goliath exert.

"Bullshit," she called, glaring at him. "That's not the real explanation, and you know it. There's something else going on here, and I want to know what it is. Now."

Not a woman used to being gainsaid, Ava crossed her arms over her chest and prepared to stare the vampire into submission. It took a few tense minutes, and even then, a part of her wasn't sure if he'd submitted or just decided it was easier to tell her than to come up with another half-truth.

His brief nod acknowledged her point with something less than good grace. "It is not the entire explanation, no, but it is the simplest one. The whole truth is more . . . complicated."

She stared back at him. "I'm a smart girl."

Another put-upon sigh. "Vampires who are unrelated to each other have very little mental influence over each other's thoughts or actions," he admitted. "It is much easier to mold a human mind, and even then, some vampires have a real talent for it and some do not."

"You?"

"I do well enough."

Ava rolled her eyes at his false modesty.

The giant continued. "When one vampire is much older than the other, of course he has an advantage over the younger one. Experience, practice, inherent differences in power—all those things play a part. The problem is that all of a vampire's power comes from the blood, and the blood can be a kind of conduit for that power. Even when attempting to influence humans, this is much more easily done when the human is one from whom a vampire has previously fed. That blood connection strengthens the bond between their minds."

She pursed her lips. "So vampires from the same bloodline would have more influence over each other than, say, a vampire from Argentina and one from Canada."

"Yes."

"But how are we connected? Forgive me for saying it, but you're clearly not from around here. Are you trying to tell me that the vampire who attacked me just happened to come from the same neck of Eastern Europe that you do?"

He looked surprised. "How do you know where I come from?"

"I don't, but that accent isn't from Brooklyn. I made a vague guess." She waved the subject off as unimportant. She wanted her real question answered.

"It was a good guess. And I do not know where your attacker came from, but judging by his age, I would assume it was somewhere local. He was too young to have traveled far."

"So, again, I'm asking . . . how are we related?"

His stony features actually managed a real expression—a rather forbidding scowl. "The rogue who attacked you did not mean for you to survive. His intent was to drain you and leave you for dead. When I became involved, I prevented that from happening, but not before you had accidentally ingested his blood. The change had already been initiated. There was nothing I could do to stop it, aside from killing you. That I was not prepared to do."

"Appreciate it."

The giant ignored her sarcasm. "Your transformation was . . . unusual," he said, looking not quite comfortable with the word he'd settled on. "Most of the time, when a turning is done voluntarily—with preparation and care—it is a painless and relatively simple procedure. Blood is exchanged, and while the transformation begins, the sire keeps a close watch on the fledgling, providing him with whatever is needed, from blood to water to moral support. But in your case, the rogue who sired you had done so unwittingly and had no intention of staying around to nurse you through the change."

"I wish you wouldn't call it 'the change.'" Ava winced. "It sounds like you're talking about menopause. But does the sire really need to be there? I mean, once a person starts turning into a vampire, it's not like it can be undone. Can it?"

Her voice came out more eager-sounding than she'd intended, and she was sure he could read her disappointment when he shook his head.

"No, the process cannot be reversed. And I suppose the sire would not technically have to be present for the ch—I mean, for the process to continue, but it makes things very much easier for the fledgling."

"How so?"

"A vampire's blood is very powerful," he explained patiently. "Only a few drops are necessary to pass the vampirism on to a human, but because the blood is what a vampire's body uses to heal and power itself, much more is required to fuel the actual changes that vampirism makes to the human body."

Ava frowned. "And what happens if the, er, fledgling doesn't get enough blood from the, er, sire?"

"The transformation will be very painful. The vampirism will consume all of the human blood available and then begin to attack the body in a search for more. In essence, if insufficient blood is given to the fledgling, his body will begin to consume itself from the inside out in an effort to complete the turning."

Ava recoiled. "That's disgusting."

The giant shrugged. "It's physiology. Every living body in every species wants to preserve its own life and will go to extraordinary lengths to ensure its survival. This is only one more example."

The ramifications finally began to sink into Ava's overwhelmed psyche and she felt a renewed sense of dread. "Didn't you say that I only got a little bit of blood from the vampire who attacked me? I mean, I only bit him by accident, so I couldn't have gotten more than a few drops, right?"

He nodded.

Ava looked down at the marks on her wrists. Already they were fading, but she could still see them clearly. "That's why you had to tie me up, then. I was fighting because the change was so painful. Because I didn't have enough blood."

Another nod.

Closing her eyes, Ava made the final connection and felt her heart sink into her polished toenails. She had to ask the question, but inside, she already knew the answer.

"So why aren't I dead? If my body turned on itself looking for more blood, why didn't it just eat itself to death?"

He didn't answer at first, not until Ava opened her eyes and met his gaze with her own. It was as if he'd been waiting, as if he couldn't or wouldn't say the words until she could watch him saying them and know them for the truth.

"Because when I brought you back here, I gave

you my own blood," he told her, his voice low and dark and full of something Ava couldn't define, something that sounded almost like possession. "The rogue may have started your transformation, but I completed it. In essence, I crossed you over. I became your sire."

Chapter 8

Ava had endured plenty of bad days in her life, but until now, none of them had actually counted as a disaster.

Staring up into the face of her giant blond hero-cum-tormenter, she wondered briefly if this, all of this, was a direct result of having missed confession for the last few Sundays.

Okay, the last few *years* of Sundays.

"That's why you can influence me," she said finally, her voice sounding nearly as dazed as she felt. How much shock could one woman take and still stay functional, after all? "Because you're my . . . my . . . sire"—she had to force the word out—"you can get inside my head no matter what. Right?"

He nodded, his gaze searching her face intently. Ava didn't know why he bothered. Why look for clues to what she was thinking when he could just slip inside and ask?

"At the moment, that is correct. But it does not always have to be that way. I can show you how to set up shields against unwelcome intrusions. In fact, it is my duty as your sire."

"Can you? But you'd always be able to get past any shields I set against you, wouldn't you? If we share blood, you'll always have a path in."

"I will have a path, yes, but I will respect your wishes if you choose to keep me out."

She looked doubtful. "How can I be sure of that?"

He shrugged. "I suppose you cannot, but it is the truth nonetheless."

"I'm not sure I'm willing to take that on faith."

"My ability to read your thoughts or influence your mind is no different from my ability to overpower you with my strength, or the ability of one lover to break the heart of another. There is never a true equity of power between individuals, but we learn that we can trust those close to us not to abuse their strengths."

Ava thought about Reggie and Dmitri and frowned. She supposed it was unlikely that they had stayed together all these years due solely to that kind of manipulation, but the possibility still made her uneasy. "I don't like that."

"I cannot force you to believe me, but if you want, I can show you how to read my thoughts in return and how to set up defenses that would make such an effort to manipulate your actions very much more difficult, even for me."

She snorted. Her brain felt so overloaded it might explode at any minute. Not to mention that this entire conversation still seemed surreal. This entire *experience* still seemed surreal. Maybe it would turn out to be a nightmare after all. . . .

God, if only she could be so lucky.

"Oh, I want, but there are quite a few things I want. And at the moment, number one on that list is that I want to go home." She swung her legs to the floor and pushed herself up off the sofa. "I think I've had about as much of this as I can handle for one day. I need to get back to my own apartment for a while and . . . process. Or whatever. I need to be by myself."

Ignoring her lack of shoes and her missing purse, Ava turned and headed straight for the apartment door at a brisk pace. When she reached it, he was already leaning lazily against it and shaking his head.

"I'm afraid I can't let you do that."

"Is your name Hal?" She adopted her bitchiest tone, the one that could stop a model's tantrum in the blink of an eye and make the men on the bar stools next to her suddenly remember a childhood desire to devote themselves to the priesthood. It sounded almost as frosty as the man's eyes looked.

"No. My name is Vladimir, but most know me as Dima."

"Ava Markham. Charmed, I'm sure." Sarcastic? Who? Her? The odd thing was, though, that while he blinked as if her name meant something to him, he showed no real recognition, and no inclination to glom onto her because of her fame, present or past.

"But you're apparently not a sci-fi fan. Whatever. The point is that I'm an adult with the right to make my own choices. And for the first time since the Equal Others Protection Act passed, I'm actually happy about that right being granted to people with fangs. So get out of my way before I call the police and exercise those equal rights of mine."

He shook his head. "I cannot. It isn't safe."

"I'm a grown woman. I can take care of myself."

He opened his mouth to object, and Ava had to tamp down the urge to close it with her fist. That would likely cause more trouble than it was worth. Not to mention that she had a feeling his jaw was a lot harder than her hand. Instead, she used a sharp stare and an upraised palm.

"Despite the unfortunate events of last night, yes, I *can* take care of myself. And even if I couldn't, that would be my problem, not yours. If I choose to disregard my own safety, that, again, is my right."

He pushed away from the door to loom over her like a gargoyle. "It isn't your safety I am concerned with," he informed her mildly. "It is everyone else's."

She lowered her palm but didn't dull her stare. Frankly, she wasn't sure if she could.

"You were turned, violently, only a little over twenty-four hours ago," he continued. "You know nothing about your new powers, cannot control your strength, are unprepared for the possibility of someone's stray thoughts interfering with your own and triggering an unintended outburst, and you have refused to feed, so are vulnerable to your own hunger. If I allowed you to leave this apartment, it would be like sending a rabid dog out onto the street. You might appear perfectly normal, but if a human were to get in your way or the hunger were to strike you, you might not be able to stop yourself from killing them. I refuse to be responsible for such an atrocity."

Only a lifetime of practice allowed Ava to conceal the way his words shook her. If she really was capable of those things, she had been right all along; vampires really were monsters. "I'll take precautions. I'll lock myself in a silver coffin if I have to. Just get the hell out of my way."

He grasped her shoulder, turning her away from the door when she tried to brush past him. He touched her only as firmly as he needed to, but she could feel the leashed strength behind his grasp. If he chose to, he could hurt her very badly.

The thought tempted her.

Ava's mother, when she had bothered with her daughter at all, had raised a good Catholic girl. The Church said suicide was a sin, but if she didn't actually take her own life, would it still count? Did it matter anymore? She was a vampire now. Wasn't she already condemned to hell?

Did she really want to die?

"If you really wish to leave my presence," Dima said, "the only way to do that is to convince me that you are ready to live on your own."

She ground her teeth together. "And how am I supposed to do that? Is there a manual I need to study? An exam to pass? I neglected to bring my number two pencil."

"You could eat something. That would make a good start."

"If I eat, you'll let me leave?"

"No. But it will bring you one step closer to that goal."

"How many steps are there?"

"A few."

She glared at him. He remained unmoved.

"How long will it take me to reach all of them?"

"If you put your mind to it? Not very long." That almost-smile quirked the corner of his mouth again. "I imagine there is little you could not accomplish, if you put your mind to it."

Ava lifted her chin and gave the laugh that had been known to make grown men cry in fear. "Mister," she said, her smile a travesty completely devoid of humor, "you have no idea."

He didn't budge. "Does that mean you will agree to feed?"

She stared at him stonily. "I can't be the first person in the history of the universe who was turned into a vampire against my wishes. This must have happened before. So what are the alternatives? Someone must have come up with some before now. Tell me what they are."

He didn't answer right away, but Ava didn't care. She could wait. For pity's sake, she could out-stubborn a Missouri mule without smudging her manicure; she could damned well wait out an inconsiderate bastard with a boss complex and a thoroughly bitable chin—

She stuffed that thought away—*God, where had that come from?*—and focused her scowl back on her adversary. It would be no trouble to wait him out. After all, it appeared that she now had literally all the time in the world.

Finally, he heaved another of those sighs and tightened his jaw. "There are only two ways to feed; you can bite a bag, or you can bite into flesh. Those are the choices. Either way, you *must* consume blood or you will die. End of story."

"But . . . ?" she prompted.

"But there are three types of blood that can sustain you," he admitted with obvious reluctance. "The blood of a living human is by far the most preferable. It provides the most nutrients, is the most readily available—especially in a city like this—and it is what your physiology was designed to process. With it, you run the least chance of becoming weak or ill, and it will help to extend your life for the longest possible period."

"But . . . ?" she repeated.

"But you can survive, if forced to it, on animal blood. It is less complete, less nourishing, and so you would need to consume much greater volumes of it than you would if you drank human blood. With human blood, you will require only a couple of pints per day, less as you age. With animal blood, that figure would easily be doubled. At that point, it becomes dangerous. Only very large animals can give so much without risking injury to themselves, beasts like cows, horses, moose, if you can find them. Also, the sensation of drinking so much at one time can be so uncomfortable that the few who try such restrictions usually end up taking many small meals over the course of the night, grazing like the animals they feed upon. Of course, feeding multiple times in one night requires finding multiple donors, or making room to keep an enormous animal with you through the night, which is often easier said than done. Unless, perhaps, you intend to eschew city life and move onto a dairy farm?"

His sarcasm went unappreciated.

"What's the third blood source?"

"I know less about that one, and I have not tried it myself, but a laboratory in California has supposedly perfected a form of synthetic blood that can provide essential nutrients without requiring the donation of actual blood."

Something tight inside Ava's chest began to loosen. "That sounds a lot more reasonable to me than munching on the neighbors. I'll do that."

"Will you?" He pursed his lips and looked doubtful. "From what I understand, the product is not yet available outside of California. Also, at present, the cost is said to be prohibitive for all but the oldest vampires, those who consume the least."

Ava shrugged. She'd never worried much about money, not after she began modeling, and certainly not after M had taken off. "How much can it cost? I don't mind paying more if it means I don't have to give hickeys to total strangers or to their donation packets. And I'm sure that whoever makes it must be able to ship it. I mean, why else did God give us FedEx if he hadn't wanted us to have guaranteed overnight deliveries?"

"The prices I have been quoted begin at seven to

nine thousand dollars per pint and go up from there. At your age, that would amount to a minimum of ninety-eight thousand dollars per week, or a little less than five-point-one million dollars per year."

Okay, maybe she could learn to worry about money.

He must have read her second thoughts in her expression, because the corner of his mouth twitched upward by almost two millimeters. On anyone else, it would have looked like an involuntary muscle spasm. On this man, she thought it might actually count as a smile.

"Come on. It won't be so bad." He held the blood bag out to her again. "You don't even have to taste it if you don't want to, though I promise it would not taste anything like you remember. Even your taste buds have changed now."

"Right. A-positive now exhibits the spicy piquance of a good pinot noir on my palate."

Her threshold of tolerance had never been very high, and this man had overwhelmed it long ago. She *had* to get out of this place, go home and pretend that this had all been a horrible nightmare.

She opened her mouth to make a graceful—and desperate—exit, only to be cut off by an unexpected noise coming from just behind Dima. Someone was pounding on the loft door.

She shot a quick glance upward. Judging by the look on Dima's face, he hadn't been expecting guests. In fact, he clearly hadn't been expecting anyone.

He grabbed her by the upper arm and urged her away from the door. "Go into the bedroom," he ordered. "Wait there until I tell you to come out. If you disobey me, I will beat you until you bleed. Do you understand me?"

His tone sounded as dire as the apocalypse, but for some reason, Ava felt not even an inkling of fear. She didn't believe a word of his harshly delivered threat.

"Who is it?" she demanded, digging in her heels and refusing to move. "Why are you acting like it's the Gestapo at the door? *Is* there some sort of vampire Gestapo? Did you break the law? Are you in trouble? Can I watch them cuff you?"

Dima growled and gave her a slightly more forceful shove. "Get in the other room, *kurva*. Do not come out until I come for you. Go!"

She opened her mouth, fully prepared to continue the argument, when an enormous crash made her protests moot. In the time it took her to draw her breath to speak, the door to the loft crashed open as if forced by a medieval battering ram. Dima spun to face the intrusion, and Ava found herself trying to peer over the shoulder of a six-foot-three-inch guard dog.

Damn it, she wished she still had her boots on. Without them, he was just a smidge too tall for her. She rose onto her tiptoes and prayed for balance.

What she saw silhouetted in the doorway made her jaw drop.

"Reggie?!?!?"

Chapter 9

Dima mentally cursed himself for relaxing his guard so far that neither his *poyasnie* nor his *bulawa* was close to hand. The knife remained in the bedroom where he'd used it to cut Ava's ties, and the mace sat atop his computer desk where he'd been working when he'd heard her begin to stir toward wakefulness.

He glanced across the room toward the desk, measuring and judging whether he could cross the distance before the intruders were upon them. He had nearly decided to risk it when he felt Ava stiffen behind him and heard her gasp.

"Reggie?!?!?" she shouted, stepping to the side and exposing herself to attack like a little fool. "What are you doing here? How did you even know where here is?" The question seemed to strike her and she shook her head. "I don't even think *I* know where here is."

Dima looked from Ava to the doorway and guessed she must be addressing the small, curvaceous woman who stood there. *He* had already fixed his attention on the enormous masculine shadow lurking in the hallway behind her. He knew the woman called Reggie was vampire, but she was young—and female. He had instinctively prioritized her as less of a threat than the man behind her.

"What am *I* doing here?" the woman in the doorway demanded, sounding irritated in the way only friends or family could become. "I think it's more important to hear what the hell *you're* doing here, Ava. You who have been *missing* for over twenty-four hours! Do you have *any* idea how worried I've been? Do you have any idea how many people are out looking for you right now?"

Ava blinked for a moment, a fleeting expression of regret shadowing her features before she managed to stuff it behind her customarily arrogant mask. She stepped completely out from behind him and glared at the other woman, ignoring the hand Dima put on her shoulder. "The last time I checked, I was a thirty-two-year-old woman, Regina. As I mentioned earlier, I don't need to be walked home from school."

"How about from the after-school program?"

The shadow behind Regina stirred and stepped forward, filling the doorway and making Dima's palms itch for his weapons. He could smell the man from here—Lupine. From the looks of him, he was no omega wolf, either. This one screamed alpha, and judging by the way he hovered over the third figure in the doorway, he wouldn't hesitate to kick ass if anyone threatened the women he'd accompanied.

"Just hold it, Graham," the woman named Regina ordered, shifting so that the light caught and glinted off her dark red hair. "You can have a chance at Ava when I'm done with her. I think I deserve an explanation, and I want her to give it to me before we go any further."

"When *we're* done with her," the second woman corrected. Her tight tone contrasted sharply with her soft, sweet features and baby-perfect skin. "We've all been worried, Reg, and I want to hear this explanation, too."

"It's good to want things." Ava nodded, raising her brows. "In fact, I myself want a few things, like the reason why you two are here, not to mention how you found here at all. Did you have Graham follow my scent like a bloodhound?"

Dima expected the Lupine to take offense to that. Instead, the man just arched his eyebrows and looked resigned. Annoyed but resigned.

The second woman, the soft, mousy blond one, laid a hand on the Lupine's arm and frowned. The instant their skin came in contact, it became obvious they were mates. "Of course not. We were really worried something might have happened to you. We brought Graham along for muscle, nothing else."

"We didn't even need him to track you down," Reggie said. "He just wouldn't let Missy come unless he came, too. Finding you wasn't hard, just time-consuming. We tracked your cell phone via GPS. But since you're not a wanted criminal and you hadn't been gone long enough to file a missing persons report, we couldn't just call the phone company and ask for your location. We had to get creative. It took Misha's assistant all night to hack into the system!"

Dima stiffened at that, but Ava just tilted her head to the side and batted her lashes. "Oh, well, let me just apologize for the time it took your husband's personal assistant to commit a felony. I don't know what I was thinking."

"I wondered about that myself, Av, though for completely different reasons. You see, for some reason I got all upset when I found out this morning that my best friend somehow managed to plant herself at the scene of a homicide last night when she told me she would be safe walking home on her own!"

Ava blinked. "What did you say?"

"You heard me," Regina dismissed. "What? Did you think no one would notice? That while routinely patrolling the city, the Silverbacks wouldn't spare a glance for two dead bodies, one of whom was Other and the second of whom had been obviously munched on?"

"Noticing that stuff and cleaning it up is kind of what the pack does, Ava," Missy threw in.

"And of course when they found a woman and a vampire murdered in an alley along the route everyone knows you usually take when you walk home from my place, Graham thought Missy and I should know. The scouts said your necklace, the one Bertie North designed specifically for you, was found at the scene."

Fingers instinctively reached for her throat. Finding it bare, Ava looked confused for a moment. Dima hadn't noticed her wearing a necklace last night, but he had been a bit preoccupied. If one had been there, he wasn't surprised to hear it had gone missing. She had likely lost it while she had fought with her attacker. It would make sense if the clasp had broken in the struggle.

"And you think I had something to do with killing those people?"

"No! Frankly, we were afraid the necklace was all that was left of you! I nearly had a damned stroke!"

A flash of guilt crossed Ava's face, but it was gone so fast, Dima couldn't be positive he hadn't mistaken it. It was replaced with decided irritation. A more natural reaction for her, he was sure.

"I didn't ask you to wait up for me," she snapped. "I didn't ask for either of you to babysit me or act more like my mother than my goddamned mother ever did."

"That's not fair, Av." Missy's voice had softened and she reached out to lay a hand on her friend's arm. "We were worried about you. How could we not be? We love you."

Dima saw the way the Lupine—who he was guessing was the same Graham he had heard led the city's largest pack of werewolves—pulled a face at that comment, but he was more interested in Ava's expression. She appeared distinctly uncomfortable with such an outward show of emotion. Regina apparently noticed it as well.

"Yeah, and we proved it by not letting Rafe tag along tonight." She injected a note of irony into her voice, clearly trying to lighten the mood. The look of panic had faded from her eyes.

"Why would Rafael want to come with you? I would think he'd be pleased at the prospect of my possible demise."

"He wanted to come in a professional capacity," Graham said. "As the head of the Council of Others, he felt responsible for looking into the accusations." That statement ended in a grunt as his mate jabbed a sharp elbow into his stomach. He frowned and rubbed the area. "What? Did I lie?"

"What accusations?"

"One of the bodies found in that alley you left *wasn't* human. That makes the murders Others business."

Two of the women looked uncomfortable. Ava just looked baffled. "I must be missing something. . . ."

"The council can place you at the scene of a double murder. The first victim, a human, was obviously killed by the second victim, a vampire," the Lupine explained. "It's the second victim that concerns them. The council knows he was stabbed and died as a result of massive trauma to the heart, one of only two ways to kill a vampire. They feel there is a possibility that the vampire's killer committed the act after becoming enraged over the human's murder. That it was a sort of vigilante act."

Ava shook her head. Dima could see that she understood the implications, but that wouldn't make them easy for her to accept.

"We know you didn't murder anyone," Missy rushed to reassure her. "It's obvious that as a human, you don't have the strength to have killed a vampire even if you wanted to."

Regina sighed and eyed her friend soberly. "But the council knows how you feel about vampires, Av. You haven't exactly kept it a secret. Everyone on earth knows you think we're monsters, so you shouldn't be surprised that the council might think—"

Ava cut her off with a humorless laugh. "That in my spare time I do double duty as Buffy the Vampire Slayer?"

"What?" Regina scoffed. "Are you going to deny it? Are you going to tell me you *don't* think vampires are—and I quote—'the filthiest scourge on earth since the bubonic plague'?"

Teeth clenching, Ava turned away from her friend and swore. "Yes, well . . . maybe I've changed my mind."

Dima kept his expression carefully bland. "I suppose you could say that, couldn't you?"

"Shut up."

"No," Regina protested. "What does he mean by that? And come to think of it, who the hell is he, and why are you in his apartment? I'm assuming this is his apartment?"

"That's a bit of a long story. . . ."

Missy folded her arms across her chest. "We're not going anywhere until we hear it, Av."

Dima tried to suppress his urge to cause Ava trouble, really he did, but he failed miserably. It only seemed fair. She had already caused him a great deal of trouble, and he had a distinct feeling this was just the beginning. "Would you like me to tell them for you, *diva*?"

"Tell us what?"

Regina's eyes narrowed at his casual use of the endearment. She looked from him to her friend, but it was obvious from Ava's expression that she had no idea she'd been referred to as a beautiful fairy-tale heroine. She seemed to take all his endearments in stride. He should be grateful for that, since he seemed to slip and use them more often than he should. And since one or two of them hadn't quite been endearments. Few women felt dear when a man called them *kurva* (a shrew), which he had done, or *damochka* (an arrogant little woman), which he'd certainly thought of doing. *Kralya* (regal beauty) he figured she would take as her due.

He ignored Ava's glare, her loud protests, and the hand she tried to slap over his mouth. At her height, it was in easy reach, but Dima was quicker.

"Tell you that Ava is finding it just a bit difficult to hate the thing that she has herself so recently become."

Ava shut her eyes when the bomb dropped. He guessed she didn't need to see her friends' faces to know that shock had widened Missy's eyes and made Regina's freckles stand out in even sharper than previous relief against her milk-pale skin, but Dima found the sights fascinating.

"You bastard," Ava muttered, aiming the insult in his direction. Even if she missed, he doubted she would regret it falling on anyone currently in the room.

"You can't be serious," Regina said, her voice breathless with shock and disbelief.

Missy gaped. "Are you telling us . . . Are you saying that . . . you've changed? That you're a . . . vampire?"

"Newly fledged," Dima answered cheerfully, ignoring the foot Ava slammed into his shin. It likely hurt her more than it hurt him anyway. "Shall we have a toast?"

"Well, well," Graham said, a smile slowly blooming across his face, "Ms. Ava Markham has become a vampire. What *is* the underworld coming to?"

It took twenty minutes to get their visitors out of the loft, and Ava only managed it by promising to show up at Vircolac—Graham's Other nightclub and the site of the chambers of the Council of Others—at the crack of dusk the day after tomorrow. On the penalty of death. Permanent death.

"That's as much time as Rafe can give you," Graham had said. "The council's meeting on Tuesday, and they'll need an explanation by then."

Which left Ava approximately—she glanced at her watch—approximately thirty-six hours to flay Dima alive, cut him up into little pieces, and display him on spikes along the city walls.

She leaned against the loft door for a minute, struggling to recover her energy after the onslaught of her friends. She knew they meant well, as they always did, but she'd been overwhelmed enough for one night. Her head was pounding, her hands were trembling, and she felt as if she hadn't slept or eaten in a week. All she wanted was to crawl back into the bed she'd been so eager to get out of a couple of hours ago and sleep until this nightmare had run its course and she could get back to her normal, sane, *human* life.

Was that really so much to ask?

A deep breath and a concentrated surge of will-power gave her the strength to turn away from the door and fix Dima with her special reserve Ice Queen Bitch from Hell Death Stare (patent pending).

"I would like very much to know," she began in a tone as even and silky as good dark chocolate, "exactly who the hell you think you are and what you think gave you the right to meddle in my affairs by telling *my* friends about events in *my* life that are entirely *my* business?"

"You know who I am." Dima didn't budge, not even when she began to stalk toward him like a lioness intent on a kill. "My name is Dima. Vladimir Rurikovich. I am your sire."

"I don't care if you're my *goddamned inner beach bunny,* you had no right to do that." Her volume didn't increase, but neither did her intensity decrease. Ava wasn't sure if she was just too tired to shout or if she'd reached an entirely new level of anger never before experienced by woman. It could be both. "It was *my* news, and they were *my* friends. I deserved the opportunity to tell them at my own pace in my own way."

"And when would that have been? When your hunger became so overwhelming that you bit your friend with the Lupine husband, who would have needed only a fraction of that excuse to chew on your heart? Or would you have first attacked your vampire friend, the one who may not be more than a few years old, but who could still have snapped your neck like a birch twig before she remembered to pull her punches out of love for you? Which of those would you have preferred?"

Ava felt herself pale, but no way would she let him see that he'd scored a hit. "I wouldn't have done either of those things."

"You have no idea of how powerful the hunger can be, Ava. You have no idea what it can make you do." He leaned forward as he spoke, making her sharply aware of his heat, his size. She knew he was tall and powerful—he'd carried her like a feather pillow, for pity's sake—but she tended to dismiss those qualities in men. After all, very few men in the world could literally tower over her, at five feet, ten inches. Dima, in fact, only bested her by five inches— less than half a foot. But when he stood this close, when she could feel his breath on her skin, smell his musky, spicy scent, see the pulse beating in the side of his throat, she began to realize that it wasn't his height that made this man so overwhelming; it was his presence.

He had alluded to his age, eight centuries, which would put his birth somewhere in the Middle Ages. Judging by his appearance, he would have been around thirty when he crossed over, and unless she needed her vision checked, his physique suggested a career as a warrior, hours spent training with heavy weapons and utilizing that training on the brutal battlefields of the past. Unlike men of today who honed their muscles with weight reps and built their endurance with active cardio, Dima's physicality was part of who he was. He was fit because fitness had meant survival, strong because strength had meant success. He'd been forged at a time when Darwin would have ruptured a blood vessel from the excitement of seeing his principles at work.

Ava frowned. This "him Tarzan, me Jane" thinking was really not like her. Most men who tried that attitude with her ended up swinging through the jungle without a vine. So why was she standing there staring at him, practically drooling, when thirty seconds ago she'd been imagining pulling a Salome on him and demanding his head on a silver platter?

His eyes locked on hers and held, the connection between them vibrating like the strings on a cello, while he raised his hand to his throat. Ava saw the movement in her peripheral vision, but she couldn't seem to break away from the icy grip of those cool predator's eyes. Then, he touched the skin just above the collar of his dark shirt, and she couldn't look at anything else. She saw his finger press hard, digging into flesh, piercing skin with a nail that couldn't possibly be so sharp, could it? But it sliced like a razor, a small bead of claret blood welling up at one end of the short slash, and like a camera effect gone horribly wrong, Ava watched her vision narrow and fill with red until all she could see was the contrast between the taut, golden skin and the dark, rich, shimmering, beckoning blood.

Everything else ceased to exist. Her brain shut off. Her breathing quickened, each inhalation bringing with it an intoxicating scent colored with musk and spice and earth and sweetness. Her mouth went suddenly dry, and she swallowed reflexively, only to find, in the space of an instant, a flood of saliva rushing forth. She swallowed again, breathed again, and her stomach cramped with hunger for the first time since she'd put her modeling career behind her.

A cacophony of drumbeats sounded in her ears, a deep, steady, bass rhythm overlaid with an erratic, ragged tempo that clawed at her already-frayed nerves. Something rasped in low counterpoint, dull and uneven, like scratches heard through cotton wool, punctuated by a sound like the whimper of an animal in pain.

Around Ava the room receded, the world receded, everything receded but the blood. The blood was everything.

The blood was life.

Chapter 10

Dima saw her eyes glaze over, pupils dilating until the black void all but swallowed the surrounding dark brown of the iris. The hunger had her.

He knew it, had counted on it, and stubbornly pushed away the faint twinge of guilt that tried to creep into his consciousness. He knew she was too young to control it, too young to even understand what the hunger meant, what it could do to her, how it could take her over until nothing of Ava remained—just the need, intense and gnawing and all-consuming. That had been the problem. As long as she denied the hunger, she could never learn to control it, and as long as she couldn't control it, she couldn't be allowed out of his sight. He'd taken on the role of her sire, and that meant it was his responsibility to teach her the rules of her new life. The first rule was respect the hunger.

The second rule was know how to feed.

Dima tried to tell himself that his enthusiasm for teaching that particular lesson had nothing to do with the way his body tightened at the image of her lips against his skin, her tongue cleaning the blood from his flesh, her teeth biting deep and drawing strength and life from within him.

His self just laughed.

Ava swayed toward him, her gaze locked on his throat, her slim figure trembling with need. Ignoring his own, different, need for the moment, Dima curled one hand around the back of her neck and slowly drew her to him.

She latched on to him with a desperate whimper, shaking like an addict. He expected to feel the burn of fangs ripping through flesh without regard for finesse or restraint. Few fledglings managed anything else the first feeding after their change. In the beginning, the hunger ruled, and the hunger had no time for niceties. But it didn't happen that way.

Instead, he stiffened in surprise at the gentle pressure of her lips and nose and chin nudging his skin, like a kitten preparing to nurse. His breath froze in his chest as, for a long, painful moment, she seemed content to breathe him in, to absorb his essence through her skin instead of through the nourishing warmth of his blood.

Dima gritted his teeth. He had known Turkish sultans and Romanian princes who had never thought of torture so devious. He tried to pretend that it was circumstance that set him afire, that the connection of the blood they shared forged an unwitting bond between them and intensified the normal sexual attraction between two healthy adults.

The trouble was that he'd been an adult since the middle of the thirteenth century and he had never, in all his existence, felt the way he felt when this arrogant, stubborn, manipulative woman before him reached out her soft, pink tongue and dragged it over the surface of his throat. He had been inside women and felt less arousal than he felt now, with both of them fully clothed and fed up with each other and no contact between them but for his hand at her nape and her face buried against his neck.

This was a very bad sign.

Quickly he debated pulling her away from him and forcing her to drink from a bag of preserved blood, but his body seemed to have a mind of its own and it reacted with violent denial at the very idea. His fingers tightened reflexively, drawing her closer, and he felt a vibration very like a purr just before she sank her fangs into his flesh and began to feed.

His eyes nearly crossed in his head.

Last night, her feeding from his wrist had been all about survival, a primal instinct based entirely on the nerve signals firing deep in the reptilian core of her brain stem. It had been about as erotic as donating to the Red Cross, and still he'd become aroused. This time he was lucky he didn't come in his pants. The jolt of lust that hit him nearly knocked him on his ass, but frankly, he didn't care if he kept his feet or not, just so long as he got Ava off of hers. Once he got her off her feet, he could turn his attention to her legs, to spreading them and lifting them and sliding between them and—

"*Dermo*," he swore.

While he had been distracted by the idea of how

it would feel to get his hands on that lean, lush body, the source of his consternation had been making herself busy.

Her mouth never moved, too busy drawing in his essence for anything else, but her body was another thing entirely. It shimmied closer, pressing full length against Dima's larger frame, her arms snaking up around his neck to hold him in place. Then she began to shift, twisting and rubbing against him, not kittenish anymore, but as wild and wanton as a she-cat in heat. Urgent little moans hummed against his skin, driving him crazy, but nothing could compare to the eye-crossing torment inspired when she arched her hips, fitting the soft vee between her legs directly against the bulge in his trousers, and then rolled forward like a tidal wave. If they had been naked, the motion would have sunk him inside her to the hilt.

"Zayebis'!"

Dima groaned. He couldn't do it. He might want her like hell burning, but at the moment Ava had no idea what she was doing. She was operating on pure instinct, unaware of anything but the first enthralling waves of hunger, and that was a big problem. In a couple of months, a few weeks even, she would learn to control herself, and the hunger would no longer be able to drive her into the kind of feeding frenzy that bled over from the need for food to the need for sex. It was something all vampires had to learn to untangle, but until she got the hang of it he couldn't touch her like this. It would be like taking advantage of her when she was drunk.

Maybe even in a few days she would at least understand how intertwined the two needs could be and would be able to make a decision about whether she cared which one was currently driving her. Not now, though. For now, she was entirely under the control of her most primitive instincts.

Reluctantly, he slid his hand from her nape and grasped her by her upper arms. "*Kralya,*" he rumbled, his voice sounding even rougher than normal. "*Kralya,* that's enough. You're finished."

Not even a flicker of an eyelash suggested she had heard him. Her tongue continued to rub against his skin in time with her drawing suction, and her body slid over his in an enormous, sensual caress.

"Stop."

She whimpered and pressed closer. One dainty hand released its grip in the hair at his nape and slid over his shoulder and down his chest, fingers curving to allow her nails to drag across his nipples. His breath shot out in a hiss.

"Ava, enough!"

Her hand moved, quicker than he would have thought she could this soon, and before his brain, sluggish with arousal, could catch up, he heard a rasp and felt a tickle of chill air. His pants were open and her hand around him when he finally processed the input from his overwhelmed senses. Then all he could do was groan at the feel of her slim fingers curled around his cock, cool and firm against his overheated flesh. She slid her hand down to the base, then back up to the tip, milking him with sure, feminine strength. When she reached the end of the shaft, she slid her thumb over the tip and flicked the edge of her nail lightly against the sensitive bundle of nerves under the glans.

Dima's whole body rocked with a shudder. In another fifteen seconds, the decision would be entirely out of his control and—ironically, given their track record with each other so far—he thought she deserved better than that. When he finally got inside her, he didn't want her to regret a second of it.

"*Enough*," he managed again, forcing the word through gritted teeth. He grasped her hand in both of his and carefully pried her fingers from his cock before pressing her forcefully away from him. When her mouth left him, he felt oddly bereft and had to bite back a sigh. "That's enough. You don't want to do this now."

Ava licked her lips. Her tongue caught a few stray trickles of blood, and her eyelids drooped as she savored the taste. Her cheeks were stained red, flushed with blood and excitement, and she looked like nothing so much as a woman well and recently fucked. One who would like nothing so much as to repeat the experience.

"I want more." She swayed closer, her gaze fixing on the scratch at his throat, now dotted with two slightly uneven puncture wounds. "Tastes so good."

She looked and sounded like a drunk, drunk on blood and desire, but she also looked soft and warm and infinitely inviting. And if Dima ever wanted to get his dick back inside his pants, he needed to stop looking at her for a minute so things would have a chance to calm down.

"You've had enough." He sounded harsh, harsher than he'd intended, but Ava didn't flinch at his words. Instead, she ignored his bark and stepped forward.

"Want more."

Dima turned his back and fisted his hands at his sides. "No."

He fixed his gaze on the windows and wondered if it would help if he pressed his dick against the cold glass for a few minutes. Better yet, maybe he could just shove it in the freezer. Though the way he felt right now, he could encase the bloody thing in six inches of clear glacial ice and it wouldn't make any difference. He burned for her.

He could see her reflection in the window. She stood behind him, heavy-eyed and frowning, flushed with desire. The elegant bun at the back of her head had started to come loose—hardly surprising after all she'd been through—giving her a disheveled look that only made him wonder how long her hair would be when she let it down. When he spread it across his pillow, would it frame her face like a halo? Or would he be able to wrap it around them both, blanketing them in silky darkness as he rode heavily in and out of her slick, tight—

God help him, but even Russian might not have sufficient curses to get him through the next few minutes!

Dima closed his eyes against the image of her hovering behind him and fought hard for control. His muscles pulled tight around him, making his body feel two sizes too small. In fact, the only thing about him that didn't feel too small at the moment was his damned dick, and that was the thing he most needed to have taken in.

Taken in. He groaned. Holy hell, but he had to stop thinking in metaphors.

Breathe deeply, he instructed himself, and shifted his shoulders as he fought to blank his mind and bring himself back under the control he hadn't lost in a literal age. He could do this. He'd faced Vikings and Huns, Cossacks and Saracens, and defeated them all. He wouldn't allow himself to be brought low by a recently human woman with the bearing of a queen and the temper of a rabid badger.

After a moment, Dima's breathing finally began to slow, and he allowed himself the luxury of a small smile. He had known he could do it. Vladimir of Novgorod was too highly trained a warrior to be defeated by—

A mouth, hot and wet and silken, gliding over the head of his cock. Tongue flicking, rubbing, cajoling. Lips gliding, teeth and fangs carefully pulled back, as she drew him deep, deep, deep inside her and held him there like a taste of rare ambrosia.

"Bozhe moy [My God]!"

His eyes flew open, his gaze slid down, and he blinked, disbelieving, at the sight of this woman kneeling before him, her dark head bent, her red lips stretched around the shaft of his penis, a look of intense excitement on her beautiful face.

Inside him, demons roared, demanding that he welcome her attentions. He had forced nothing on her, had tried to stop her, they argued. She was doing this of her own free will, and his conscience could just sit down and shut up and no one would have to get hurt!

But in spite of his urges, Dima was not a stupid man. He knew what would happen if he didn't stop her. Oh, he would enjoy it in the meantime, but afterward, she would hate him. She would tell him that he had taken advantage of her while she was weak, while the hunger controlled her, and he wouldn't be able to deny it. He might have the satisfaction of one amazing night, but if he took this one, he doubted there would be any others.

He very decidedly wanted for there to be others. God help him.

Scraping up the last of his strength, Dima savored the feeling of her mouth on him for one more minute, then grasped her head in his palms and growled her name. Slowly, her lashes parted, and she looked up at him, her eyes dark and dazed and hungry.

"Ava," he growled hoarsely, watching her to be sure she understood him. "This is not you. This is not what you want. You have to stop."

She blinked, pulled back slowly, her lips sliding off of him and into a frown. "Stop?" she repeated, and he saw a glint of something like herself in her eyes. Her gaze slid from his face to his dick, lingered as if confirming it was indeed attached to him, and back again. The glint brightened. "You can't want me to stop."

He choked out a sound that might—just—have passed as a laugh. "Want has nothing to do with this. You need to stop. You are not thinking clearly. The hunger is in control now. You are still too young to be able to control it."

Ava pushed slowly to her feet. Her frown tightened and her eyes—noticeably clearer now—narrowed. "You're going to want to get out of that habit you have."

"What habit?"

"The one where you're always telling me what I want and what I can do."

"I am your sire. It is my responsibility to make sure you come to no harm and to teach you how to adjust to your new life."

Ava peeled back her lips and used the tip of a perfectly manicured finger to test the sharpness of one of her new fangs. Then she wiped a tiny trace of blood from the corner of her mouth and raised her eyebrows at him. "As far as I can tell, I seem to be adjusting just fine on my own."

This time, Dima was the one frowning, because he could see that. No trace of the haze of hunger remained in her eyes or her expression. She looked utterly calm and utterly confident and utterly in control of her own actions. And damn it, he'd just pulled her mouth off his dick. Was he out of his mind?

No, he reminded himself. Forcefully. He'd had to stop her. No vampire her age—barely over a day— could possibly have that much control over her own hunger. It took most vamps days' worth of feedings, all carefully supervised by their sires, before they could keep from killing every human they fed on. And once they learned to control the bloodlust, it was usually another week at least before they got a handle on the regular lust. The hunger for blood and the hunger for sex were intimately entwined, and there was no way Ava could have gained control over both of them in the space of one supervised feeding. Things like that just didn't happen.

Things like fledglings and women turning their backs on him and walking calmly away before he was finished with them didn't happen, either. But Ava did it anyway. He moved to follow her, swore, paused, and refastened his pants. By the time he entered the bedroom, she was sitting on the edge of the mattress pulling on her stockings.

"What are you doing?"

She gave him the kind of look people usually reserved for slow children and senile old men. "I'm putting on my stockings."

"Why?"

"Because I hate wearing boots over bare feet." She wrinkled her nose. "It feels somehow unhygienic."

He scowled. "You don't need boots. You are not ready to leave."

"Oh, trust me. I'm so ready."

Ava slid off the mattress, knelt, and located her boots where they had landed under the bed. She pulled them out and resumed her seat.

Confusion was not an emotion with which Dima had much experience—none, actually, that he could remember over the last five hundred years. He disliked the feeling it gave him. "Normally, a fledgling will stay with his sire for at least the first month or two following his turning—"

"First, and I'm not quite sure how you missed this before, I'm not a 'he.'" She zipped up the first boot, slid her foot into the other. "And second, there is absolutely nothing about the current situation that counts as normal, not in my book, and I'm guessing not in yours. I don't know what the rule book you carry around in your head says about being a vampire"—she held up a hand when he would have interrupted—"and I don't care. No matter what anyone else says about it, this is my life, and I intend to go on living it exactly as I please."

When she stood, he stepped in front of her to block her path to the door. "There is no rule book, as you so disdainfully put it, but there are certain things about being a vampire that you need to know, for your own safety, as well as for the safety of our entire race."

She pursed her lips. "You know what? You can shoot me an e-mail."

He grasped her arm when she tried to step around him. "You act as if this were a kind of joke and if you play along for a little while, you can go back to normal as soon as the laughter dies down."

"Do you see me laughing?"

"No, I see you behaving as a spoiled little girl who has been told she must finish her chores before she can go and play with her friends."

She jerked her arm from his grip. "I was *never* a spoiled little girl, as you so gallantly put it," she informed him, all but spitting fire, "and I finished my chores a long time ago. In fact, I did a few other people's chores while I was at it, and I made up my mind years ago that I wouldn't waste any more of my time worrying about other people's rules. I make my own, and I play by them. And if anyone you know has a problem with that, you can tell them to confront me themselves."

He watched her stalk toward the door and fought the urge to grab her and shake her. How could anyone who counted a vampire as a best friend be so ignorant about what it meant to live in their world? Had she learned nothing from that Regina woman? He needed to make Ava understand that, as of the previous day, she was now a very small, very weak fish swimming in an ocean full of sharks.

"If someone comes after you, Ava, a confrontation will not be what you get from them," he said to her retreating back, and something in his tone must have penetrated that stubborn hide, because she paused in the doorway to the living room. "You're living in a whole new world now, *damochka*. Things are not so neat and tidy as they were before. You are no longer safe."

She turned around and laughed in his face. "I'm *no longer* safe? Like I was safe when I walked by that alley and got attacked by something that wanted to suck out all my blood and leave me there like an empty candy bar wrapper? Spare me the dire warnings, Dima. At least now if someone attacks me, I have some strength to fight back."

"It's true you are stronger. Faster, too. At least compared to the average human. But what about the average vampire?"

He saw the small furrow between her brows and knew she had not thought about her situation from that perspective. She had considered herself powerful for so long that she could not fathom herself in any other light.

"Our population grows slowly, *kukla*." He pressed on. "That means that it will be rare for you to encounter a vampire who is not much, much older than yourself, and an older vampire is a more powerful vampire."

"Now you're trying to scare me?"

He shook his head. "Merely warn you."

"About the boogeyman under my bed?"

"About the price for infringing on another vampire's territory, or feeding from his servant. Or interfering in a dispute between two vampires. Or disrespecting a vampire's line. Or underestimating his age. Or—"

"Kissing the wrong cheek of his ass?" she asked sweetly. "So far, the dangers you're telling me about sound a lot like the ones I faced when I started my own modeling agency. Just substitute the word 'agent' for 'vampire' and 'model' for 'servant' and I've already been through all of that." She paused. "Come to think of it, modeling agents and vampires are starting to look eerily similar to me."

Dima bit back a growl. "This is not a laughing matter!"

"That's too bad, because if I stop laughing at it, you're not going to like my backup response. At the moment, that one begins with me screaming at the top of my lungs and then possibly burying my boot heel in your left eyeball. So which one would you rather I go with?"

"*Lapushka*," he gritted out, "your fangs are not yet sharp enough to be snapping them at me."

She smiled as sharp as broken glass. "Why don't you put your dick back in my mouth and we'll see about that?"

So this was what could drive a man to strike a woman, mused a small voice in the back of Dima's mind, *perhaps even to strangle her.* With those choices in mind—kiss or kill—he took the only path left to him. Eating the distance between them with two long strides, he reached out, cupped the back of her head in his hand, and sealed her smart, sarcastic, suicidal mouth with his own. Judging by the way he currently felt, by the time he worked off his mingled fury and arousal in her body, either she would be too weak to speak, let alone cause more trouble, or he would be dead and Ava Markham would have become someone else's problem.

He just couldn't decide which outcome to hope for.

Chapter 11

She should protest, Ava knew. She should beat her fists against his chest, or dig her thumbs into his eyes, or slam her elbow into his solar plexus, or do something else to let him know that this was no way for him to win an argument. He'd done it once already, using his strength to force her to drink from him, and as far as she was concerned, she still owed him for that one. She wasn't about to start running him a tab.

The problem was that her body refused to obey the commands issued by her mind. It was too wrapped up in the feel of him: hot, hard muscle, strong, callused hands, focused, predatory intent; the scent of him: musk and spice and rich, dark earth; the taste of him: coffee and vodka and decadence. Her body didn't care about the arguments between them or the ones they would undoubtedly have once they returned to their senses. It just cared about getting as close to him as possible and staying there.

Of course, it did care a little that they'd wasted the time between when she'd been on her knees in front of him earlier and now. That was a lot of time wasted when they could have been doing much more interesting things than fighting. And it was a lot of steps for them to retrace. If only there were a shortcut.

He seemed to read her mind, or perhaps the way she met each heavy stroke of his tongue with one of her own and then strained closer, eager for more. Rather than wasting time wooing her, he touched her as one sure of her welcome, his hands stroking over her sides, cupping and kneading her breasts, following the plane of her stomach and the curve of her hip, sliding down to grasp the hem of her dress and tug insistently upward. Bless his enterprising heart.

Realizing her hands were gripping his biceps in a veritable death grip—enjoyable but hardly helpful— Ava unclenched her fists and reached down to help him strip off her clothes. It was important to her to get rid of them yet equally important that he not damage the expensive designer dress. She might be blinded by lust, but she hadn't completely lost her mind.

Brushing his hands away was easy once he realized she only meant to redirect them from fabric to skin. He gripped her thighs, groaning into her mouth when his thumbs found the straps of her garters and began to stroke. He seemed to appreciate her choice in lingerie. Leaving him momentarily content, she crossed her arms, grasped the bottom of her dress, and with a long tug and a well-timed shimmy, had it up over her head and tossed into the corner before he'd traced the length of the first garter strap up to the belt and slipped underneath.

She felt him stiffen—in more ways than one—as their lips parted to allow her to pull the dress over her head. His pale blue eyes burned, looking more like blue flame than glacial ice as he ran his gaze over her nearly nude form. He lingered on all the usual places—the swell of her breasts beneath the black lace of her bra, the dip of her waist, the flare of her hips and the satin-and-lace-covered mound between her thighs—but in no way did he make her feel like an anonymous sex partner. Not when his gaze then slid up to her throat, her lips, and he reached a hand out to cup her face reverently in his palm.

"Nenaglyadnaya," he murmured, leaning down to brush her lips with his. *"Kak ya tebya hochu."*

She didn't need a translation to recognize his appreciation of her body, nor his desire, not when she could match it breath for breath. She had never wanted a man so much, certainly never wanted a man like him—a man too strong to control, too powerful to dismiss. Her first career had taught Ava that sex was a commodity, something that could be parted with more pleasurably than money and that conferred as much benefit on the giver as on the recipient. Provided, of course, that the giver remained in control.

With Dima, Ava did not feel in control, at least not completely, but somehow it didn't seem to matter. For the first time in her life, intimacy didn't feel like a transaction or a battle. It felt like a partnership, each of them giving and taking in equal measure, each leading and following in easy rhythm. Maybe it was because lust had left her completely mindless, but she couldn't care less about control with Dima. All she cared about was touching him and being touched in return.

He seemed to have no problem with that. Sliding the hand on her face around to her neck to urge her closer, his other made itself useful by stroking across her body, leaving trails of gooseflesh in its wake. Everywhere he touched her felt electric, as if some kind of power traveled from his body to hers through skin-to-skin contact. When his callused fingers skimmed her belly, she felt the surge of energy all the way to her toes, but when they skimmed beneath the soft fabric of her panties and garter belt and dipped into the secret space between her thighs, her toes curled up and died, along with approximately half of her brain cells.

His touch made her want to shout, but that would mean taking her lips from his, and he tasted too good for her to try anything so foolish. Instead, she moaned and shuddered and flexed her hips toward him, urging him to touch her. His large, clever fingers rifled through her neat curls and pressed lower, parting the soft lips of her sex to find the hidden treasures within. Rough fingertips traced the length of her slit, teasing the wet silk of her most intimate skin, making her tremble. They circled the tight ring of her entrance, probed, teased, then drifted up to scissor around her clitoris, making the little nub pulse and ache.

Ava moaned into his mouth. If he had felt anything like this arousal while she'd had her mouth around him earlier, how had he found the strength to pull her away from him? Why the hell had he wanted to? Never in her life had she felt this fire. He had been so insistent on impressing upon her the power of a vampire's hunger for blood, but this was the urge she felt could more easily become an addiction. If drug addicts felt like this when they pumped chemicals into their bodies, it was a wonder any of them ever came down off a high. To feel like this forever, Ava would be willing to do many, many things she had never before considered. Including lower her guard even a tiny bit.

Then his fingers shifted again, lower, pausing at the entrance of her body until she thought her heart would stop if he didn't come inside her; then one finger pressed forward, penetrating her, and it did.

Their lips parted, her head falling backward as if her neck could no longer support it. Only the warm, heavy hand cupping her there kept the back of her skull from bouncing off her shoulder blades. She let out a whimper, a low, husky breath of sound, and her eyes began to drift shut.

Simultaneously, the finger inside her was joined by a second, stretching her, and the hand at her neck tightened, pulling her forward until her forehead came to rest against his and his breath filled her mouth with his scent.

He shook her gently and flexed his wrist, sending his thick fingers sliding deeper within her. "Open your eyes," he ordered, his voice dark and ragged. "Look at me, *kralya*. Watch me."

She shook her head. She couldn't. The feelings were too intense. If she could see him watching her while he touched her like this, she would come undone, and more than a climax would be at stake.

"Look at me."

His mouth touched hers, a quick brush, sweet and

tender; then she felt something sharp nipping at her lower lip. He took the plump flesh between even, white teeth and bit down until she gasped at the faint sting. A second later, he crooked the fingers buried between her legs and dragged his nails across the front wall of her sheath. Against her will her eyes flew open and her body jackknifed, instinctively seeking to escape the overwhelming bolt of pleasure. He held tight, controlling her with the hand on her neck and the one in her pussy as he pressed pleasure upon her. His gaze captured her, blue flame consuming her, leaving her self-control cindered in little mounds at her feet.

"No," she moaned, the incoherent protest garbled not by his unrelenting grip on her lower lip but by the intensity of her arousal. She couldn't speak, could barely form the words in her mind, let alone on her tongue, but it didn't matter. She had no idea where the protest had come from. She wasn't trying to make him stop—God, if he stopped, she would die, right after she killed him—but she had no other language to express how unbearably intense the sensations he pressed upon her had become. She had no way to tell him that watching him watch her as he forced her higher and higher toward climax was going to shatter her, that when the smoke cleared, he would find her lying in little tiny pieces at his feet and, like Humpty Dumpty, the damage to her would be irreparable.

But she couldn't say any of that, so she panted and she moaned and she began to chant the word *no* like a mantra, even as she pressed herself harder against his fingers, trying to coax him closer to her clit, and her hands clawed at his shirt, ready to shred the material like confetti if it would allow her to touch the smooth, hard skin beneath. She thought briefly about demanding that he strip, quickly, but that would mean asking him to take his hands off of her, and there was no way she could bring herself to do something so foolish.

Taking matters into her own hands, she reached for the hem of his shirt with both hands, intending to yank it over his head with a minimum of fuss and a maximum of speed. To her surprise, the shirt didn't just lift when she pulled; it split all the way down the middle until she could shove it back over his shoulders, completely out of her way. She paused for barely a millisecond, stunned by the new strength in hands she had thought she knew so well; but if this was what she could do as a vampire that she hadn't been able to do as a human, maybe her new life wouldn't be all bad. There was something to be said for being able to strip a man in under thirty seconds.

She decided right then to go for the record. With his shirt out of the way, she turned her attention back to the pants she had already unfastened once before. This time she wasn't so careful with his zipper, but then again, this time she wasn't having to sneak up on him. He grunted his approval when he felt her hands grip his waistband and shifted to grant her better access. Once again, she had his zipper down and his shaft in her hand before he remembered to breathe, and if she fisted the length a little abruptly this time, well, he had only himself to blame. The stroke she had meant to tease him with coincided with a particularly devious flick of his wrist, one that had her melting all over him like hot, sweet syrup.

Dima didn't complain. Instead he grunted and pushed his leg forward, spreading her thighs until he could insert his own between them, making a place for himself close to her center. If that was what he wanted, Ava was happy to oblige him. Pressing herself closer to him, she rubbed her lace-covered breasts against his chest and curled one leg around his, locking her ankle on the inside of him and then yanking forward without warning. The unexpected movement threw Dima off balance, and he tipped backward, his bulk conspiring with gravity to land him flat on his back on the floor of the bedroom doorway.

Grinning maniacally—and definitely relieved that he'd released his grip on her mouth before he went ass over elbows—Ava followed him down, landing on his chest with a breathless thump.

Dima cursed and blinked up at her. One arm had curled around her back instinctively to cradle her protectively as they fell, but the one between her legs had jerked away to flail vainly for balance. It had taken her panties with it. He tossed them aside and reached for her again, but Ava was already ahead of him. Bracing both palms on his chest, she levered her lower body up until she could straddle his hips like a cowgirl. Staring down at him, grinning, she acknowledged to herself that this was the most fun she'd ever had during sex, and thank God, they were still far from finished.

"I think I like this position," she purred, pressing

her hips down so that her bare pussy brushed teasingly over his straining erection. She still wore her bra, her garter belt, and her stockings, and while she'd gotten Dima's shirt mostly off, he still wore his pants. Mostly. The fly was open and the material spread like wrapping paper around a highly anticipated gift. Ava couldn't wait to play with it.

Bending down, she pressed her lips to his and circled her hips, spreading her own moisture along his overheated skin. His eyes glinted, then narrowed, but she read the warning in them too slowly. Before she could move, his hands slid down to clamp on her hips like twin vises. With a grunt, he thrust his hips up while at the same time tugging her down hard against him, filling her with one fierce thrust.

She shrieked breathlessly in surprise, the sound quickly going soft and broken as she registered the feeling of his body inside hers, thick and long and incredibly hard.

"Now," he rumbled, a slow smile lifting the corners of his chiseled mouth, "so do I."

Laughing, breathless, Ava pressed a fierce kiss to his mouth and then sat back to enjoy her ride.

Through narrowed eyes, Dima gazed up into Ava's beautiful, laughing face and gave thanks to whatever gods were listening that lust had not yet rendered him completely blind. It might have been a near thing, but it would have killed him to miss seeing her poised above him while her body clamped around his in a hot, snug caress.

He felt her shiver around him, felt the rippling

contractions of her sheath milking him, and he gritted his teeth against the need to drive blindly and feverishly into her. If he gave in to the impulse, he knew he wouldn't last more than a few minutes, and he wanted to draw this out as long as possible. He'd never felt anything more perfect than this.

She tried to shift her hips above him and lead him into a rhythm, but he gripped her hips tighter and held her still.

"Move," she ordered, her smile slipping a little, turning darker as the need drove her.

"Not yet."

He wasn't quite ready. First, he had a few final details to see to.

With a warning squeeze, he released her hips and reached up and around to the bun at the back of her head. A few quick tugs and a handful of pins went flying, leaving her hair to tumble down her back in a thick, heavy curtain the color of rich espresso. Even having spent so long in its confining twist had barely left a wave in the straight strands. They swung past her shoulders, the ends falling to her shoulder blades in back and swinging forward to frame the sides of her breasts.

Which were next on his list.

He felt her watching him, felt those dark, chocolate eyes intent on his while he ran his hands over her loosened hair, fascinated by the soft silken texture and the way the color stood out in stark contrast against the pale, dusky tone of her skin. He met her gaze, held it, slid his fingers from her hair to trace the design of the fine black lace cupping her breasts. Beneath the fabric, her nipples were already pebbled tight. He could feel the hard little nubs pressing against their confinement, but he could not see them, and Dima really wanted to see them. And taste them.

Carefully, he gathered her hair in two large handfuls and pulled it back over her shoulders to drape across her back. His hands stroked one last time over the soft strands, then burrowed under them and flicked open the clasp at the back of her bra. Ava didn't wait for him to pull it away from her. She shrugged out of it herself, an act of which Dima thoroughly approved, because it let him focus all his attention on the sight of those two pretty mounds meeting his gaze for the first time.

Her breasts drew his hands like magnets. The lace of her bra had barely dropped away before he reached up and cupped the soft curves in his palms, weighing and cuddling them, savoring the way they gave against the slightest pressure of his fingers, then sprang back into shape as if eager to greet him again. She was neither large nor small, but sweetly swelled and perfectly proportioned to her long, slim torso, with delicate nipples in a deep, dusky mauve. He couldn't have imagined anything more beautiful, and he rewarded her perfection with two carefully placed flicks of his tongue.

Simultaneously, her arms curved around his elevated shoulders, cradling his head to her body, and her sheath clenched tight around him. It felt as if she feared he might slip away from her, and she wanted to be sure she gripped him too tightly to lose him. He could have spoken and reassured her that he had no intention of leaving, but he had much more satisfying plans for his mouth, like closing it over the tip of one soft breast and drawing the hard nipple and tightly crinkled areola inside with a deep, heavy suction.

She tasted like candy, not insubstantially airy like spun sugar, but heavily, richly sweet, like butter toffee or thick, dark caramel. He scraped his teeth over her skin and felt her body jolt, every shift a heady massage to his deeply buried shaft. With that in mind, he repeated the caress again, and again, until she tugged insistently at his hair, forcing his mouth away from her.

Lowering her forehead to his, she adjusted her balance and spread her legs wider, pressing herself more firmly down upon him, taking him another fraction of an inch deep until he swore he could feel her heart beating against the head of his cock.

"Dima," she breathed, and he could smell her sweetness on her breath, feel it drifting over his skin in another teasing caress. "I love having you inside me, all huge and hard and thick. You make my toes curl and my brain melt. . . ."

Ava paused, shifted, moaned as he probed deeper and hit a spot that made her breath freeze in her chest.

"You make me crazy," she whimpered after a moment, when she could finally open her eyes again and lock that chocolatey gaze onto his. "But if you don't stop teasing me and start fucking me in the next fifteen seconds, I don't care how long it takes me; I will find a way to kill . . . you . . . ugly. Do you understand me?"

Dima laughed. He couldn't remember the last time he had laughed during sex. Had he ever? Had it ever, *ever* felt this good before?

"Hold on, *lyubushka,*" he ordered, and grinned.

Gripping her around her rib cage, he levered himself into a semi-sitting position and twisted, flipping both of them over bodily and reversing their positions so that Ava lay on her back beneath him, his hips still wedged between her thighs, his body still clasped tightly in hers.

She gasped in surprise, blinked, then scowled. "I liked it better when I was on top."

"I imagine you did. But I have something else in mind."

He ignored her muttered insult and spread his legs, drawing his knees up until he knelt on the cold hardwood floor with Ava's thighs parted obscenely wide and draped over his. Before she could open her mouth to issue another complaint, he straightened his torso and lifted her hips until only her shoulders remained on the floor, with the rest of her body elevated and his grip supporting her weight.

The position drove him even deeper inside her, bringing a moan to her lips.

"Christ, would you hurry up already?"

She reached out to him, her hands finding his thighs and gripping hard until he could feel her fingernails biting into his skin through the heavy cotton fabric of his trousers. Then her stocking-clad legs curled around his waist, gripping him like a vise. She attempted to use the little leverage her hold gave her to thrust her hips against his and initiate a steady rhythm of mating, but Dima wasn't quite ready for that.

"Ah-ah," he scolded. "Not yet, *lapushka*."

Fighting for just a few more minutes of control, he took one of her legs and unwrapped it from around his hip. He grasped it behind the knee and straightened it, lifting it until the back of her calf pressed against his shoulder and her delicate, high-arched foot pointed straight up at the ceiling. Then he stripped the stocking off that leg, returned his hand to her waist, and leaned forward, forcing her leg to bend at the hip and her channel to accept another breathtaking fraction of an inch of his arousal. The high, breathless cry that shuddered from her made him feel as powerful as a god.

"Now," he growled, bending to brush his lips over hers. "Now I'm ready." He turned his head, pressed another achingly gentle kiss to the back of her knee, and met her desperate gaze with a smile. "Are you?"

Before she could even think to answer, his lips parted, erect fangs glistening above her for a moment before he sank them deep into the tender white flesh at the back of her knee.

Ava screamed.

The sound echoed in his head, driving him faster, deeper, making him crave to get closer and closer to her. If he could have melted against her, merged them into one, he would have. He could imagine no future so glorious as remaining inside of this woman for eternity. Her blood flowed into his mouth, hot and thick and sweet, and he could feel himself getting drunk on her taste.

Ava, however, appeared to care less about eternity. She used every muscle she could, every new strength she could find, to throw herself against him. She arched her body like a drawn bow, body curving toward his like an offering. But she was no meek virgin giving herself in sacrifice; she was the mature goddess-queen of her people, using her fully realized sexual power to subdue the beastly threat, ensure the bountiful harvest, and ensure the safety of all the future generations of her people. Dima might be physically stronger, might have her pinned to the floor beneath him, but he had lived a long life. In that time, he had grown wise enough to realize that for all the apparent male dominance of his position, he had been conquered the moment he first felt the tug of her lips on the head of his cock.

Mindlessly, they strained together, instinct and need in motion. He felt his orgasm building in the base of his spine, heard the rhythm of her breathing change, grow sharper, shallower. He threw himself desperately against her, caught her when she followed suit, let his body flow into hers as her blood flowed into his mouth.

Let the two of them flow together, joined, mingled, bound to each other, two bodies clinging together as the world exploded around them, leaving them weak and breathless and changed. Forever.

Chapter 12

Morning-after regrets had nothing on the ones that hit a girl after dark, Ava discovered when she opened her eyes to stare up at the loft ceiling.

The apartment around her was silent and tangibly empty, as was the bed next to her. Turning her head on the pillow that had materialized beneath it sometime between when she passed out from sexual overload and now, she confirmed what her instincts had already told her—Dima had already risen and made himself scarce. Thank God.

A slip of color on the white pillowcase caught her attention. Frowning, she reached up and found a small sticky note propped up and waiting for her. The sum total of its contents consisted of two words scrawled in a barely legible masculine hand—*Stay put*.

My, such a charmer.

Ava tossed the note back where she'd found it and sat up with a scowl. If he honestly thought that he'd get a positive response from her with that kind of tactic, the man not only had no idea who he was dealing with; he was out of his little Eastern European mind. Nearly as dangerously unstable as she had been when she'd thrown aside every single one of her beliefs and values in the wee hours of the morning and let lust, rather than logic, make her decisions for her.

Lips firming, Ava threw back the blankets and climbed out of the bed. She had only the vaguest memories of how she'd gotten into it—dim recollections of her limp body being scraped off the floor and placed gently between the sheets before the man responsible for her condition climbed in after her and proceeded to worsen it—but the how didn't matter right now. She was too busy mentally smacking herself upside the head for the why.

She should have known better. In fact, she *did* know better, and that was what really had Ava steamed. Steamed and scared in ways she didn't even want to contemplate.

She wasn't the type of woman who let her libido make the decisions. She had always believed herself too smart and too savvy to take that kind of chance, with her health or her heart. Sex, she had decided early on, was a very pleasant activity that worked best when she approached it from a point of cool, careful consideration, but she'd known none of that wisdom last night. Hell, she'd barely shown any sanity. She had leapt on Dima like a sailor on shore leave, not a thought in her head other than doing something to assuage the empty ache between her legs. Just the memory of her behavior made her lip curl in distaste.

Finding her dress draped carelessly over the back of the single chair in the room, Ava grabbed it and tugged it on, not bothering to search for her lingerie first. Strapping herself into a bra wasn't nearly as important as getting her armor back on, and she had a vague recollection of her panties fluttering away in half a dozen pieces anyway. And God help her, she didn't think she would ever wear stockings with a garter belt again as long as she lived. As nasty as they might be, she would become a panty-hose girl from now on. Even if it killed her.

Searching for the rest of her belongings gave her a good enough excuse not to think about the other reason she regretted last night so strongly, but she had no intention of lingering on those particular thoughts. Those led to even darker thoughts, ones that pointed out how she hadn't been herself last night.

Those were the insidious thoughts, because they started out all soft and sympathetic, telling her it was all right, that she shouldn't blame herself. None of it had been her fault, those thoughts pointed out. After all, it had been the hunger making her decisions, not Ava herself. Ava hadn't been in control. The hunger had controlled her.

Shit, shit, shit.

She shoved that thought ruthlessly away, not just refusing to deal with it but completely denying its existence. At least for now.

Suppressing a shudder, Ava damned all stockings to the black pits of hell and pulled her boots on over her bare feet and legs. The feeling of leather directly against her bare feet made her nose curl, but she gritted her teeth and pulled the zippers high. No way would she let disgust with her footwear keep her a prisoner here. When she got back to her apartment, she would call a cobbler or somebody and send the damned things out for a thorough cleaning. The important thing right now was getting home and never coming back to . . .

Ava frowned. Where the hell was she, exactly? Considering that she'd been unconscious when Dima carried her back to the loft, she hadn't gotten a chance to make note of the address. Moving to the window, she pushed back the heavy, light-blocking drapes and peered outside. She had known it would be dark—duh, being a vampire now, she couldn't have woken up before dusk if she'd tried—but she hadn't expected it to be quite as pitch-black outside as it appeared. It looked like she'd completely bypassed dusk and headed straight into full-on night. A glance at her watch confirmed it. It was nearly ten o'clock, which wasn't late for Manhattan—heck, it was practically still lunchtime—but the sidewalks below the loft were surprisingly bare. And surprisingly bright.

Ava blinked and craned her head until she could see the end of the block just a few yards away. The street lamp on the corner was nearly burnt out, but even in the dim brownish light she could read the street signs posted there as easily as if it had been high noon.

She could see everything outside quite clearly despite the dark, which kind of weirded her out. It didn't look like it did during the day, precisely, and maybe that was what made her so uneasy about it. It made sense that vampires would be able to see well in the dark, and if she'd thought about it, she would have realized that meant that now she could see well in the dark, but she'd never before stopped to wonder what the nighttime looked like to a vampire. Now she knew.

It wasn't like looking through night-vision goggles so that everything looked eerily green, nor was it like looking at a photo negative of the world, with lights and darks reversed on the spectrum. And it wasn't like seeing in black and white, either. Things looked essentially normal if she didn't linger on them too long. It was just that she could *see* the darkness.

She shuddered just thinking about it. She didn't mean that she could see where the shadows lingered in the streets and doorways; she meant she could see the darkness as if it were a thing, as if it were a veil of transparent black fabric that draped over certain spots in the environment, shading but not hiding their contents. It made the hair on the back of her neck stand up. If this was what Regina had been looking at since Dmitri had transformed her, it was no wonder she hadn't told her friends about it. Ava would have freaked.

A thought occurred to her, and Ava glanced around the bedroom, taking in the sparse décor and complete lack of personal effects lying around. It had vaguely occurred to her last night that she hadn't seen her purse since she'd woken up after her attack, but at the time, she'd been preoccupied with other things, like learning she'd been turned into a bloodsucking fiend. A missing purse hadn't seemed like a priority in her life. Now, a day later, it had taken on an entirely new level of importance.

Her purse was where she normally carried her

cell phone. The cell phone in which she kept programmed the number of the livery company she used to hire cars for herself and her models whenever they were required.

Cursing aloud, she stalked through the living room, double-checking to be sure she hadn't missed seeing it. But no, her purse was definitely missing. And Dima apparently used a cell exclusively for his own calls. Or maybe he relied on smoke signals and mind control. Whatever was in vogue for vampires these days, it didn't matter, because there was no landline phone in the apartment.

Her cell phone rang again. After a quick glance at the caller ID, Ava shoved it back into her pocket unanswered. This time, Missy was calling, of course.

Ava was sprinting back into the bedroom before the memory could slide back into her subconscious.

Dima had tossed her coat on the floor on the far side of the bed where you couldn't see it unless you actually went all the way around to the other side of the mattress. She scooped it up and quickly patted the pockets.

Yes!

Digging the sleek silver toy from the coat's left-hand pocket, she flipped it open and scrolled through her contact list. A push of a button—and a verbal slap to a young new booking agent who had never dealt with Ava before—had a car on its way and gave Ava just fifteen more minutes to freak out before she'd be on her way home and officially one step closer to forgetting her current nightmare. Although she didn't know the exact address of the building, she wasn't about to let a little thing like that prevent her from making good her escape. She gave the dispatcher the names of the cross streets that she'd been able to read off the signs outside and figured she would just walk down there to meet the car.

She would happily walk to Istanbul to meet the car. Whatever it took to get back to a place—and an existence—she could understand.

Carefully, she steered her mind away from last night. At least, she told herself to do so, but the scary thing to her was that the entire experience of being attacked, nearly killed, and turned into a vampire didn't shake her composure nearly as much as what had happened between her and Dima.

The sex—no matter how earth-shatteringly good it had been—wasn't really the problem. Ava was thirty-four; she'd had good sex before. She'd even had *fantastic* sex a time or two, but it had never affected her the way this had. No man had ever gotten into her mind before, beneath her skin and into what made her Ava. No one had ever been allowed to do that, not the mother who had tried nor the father who hadn't bothered.

So how had this man—this *vampire*—who was practically a stranger to her, managed it?

She wrapped her arms around herself, huddling her shoulders against an internal chill as she gazed out the loft window. She hated this unaccustomed feeling of vulnerability. Ava had worked long and hard to brick up all the little cracks and chinks in her defensive wall. That had been how she'd survived her first career. She'd learned to smile not just for the camera but for all the agents and editors, the designers and paparazzi, who each felt they deserved a tiny little bite of Ava and her success. Smiling had kept them from understanding that the face and figure they schmoozed and sucked up to had been as far removed from the real Ava as she had been from herself. The real Ava had been tucked up inside her head piloting herself around like a puppeteer in the rafters above the stage.

Ironically, it had also satisfied her mother, who had believed herself the real one in charge. Ava had never been able to decide if her mother's obsession with her aristocratic bloodline had made her more or less likely to know those smiles had been false. On the one hand, Isabella de Castille had been the one to teach her daughter that a woman should be pretty and happy on the outside so that people would love her, so a person would think Isabella would know that appearances could be deceptive. But then again, Ava's mother hadn't cared about much other than appearances; her father hadn't cared about much other than himself.

Isabella had been royalty, or at least a third cousin, twice removed from it, and the man she'd married— briefly and histrionically—had certainly seen himself as royalty. Tristan Markham believed that a successful multi-national company such as he ran conferred on one a state near godliness, and he'd been determined that both he and his immediate family should behave themselves as befitted their positions, even after he'd decided he no longer wanted to be a husband or father. He couldn't completely hide Ava's existence; therefore he felt he had every right to control her behavior. Weakness he would not tolerate, nor would he countenance anything other than a bright façade of father-daughter devotion. Love had had very little to do with either of Ava's parental relationships.

Self-defense had therefore molded Isabella and Tristan's daughter into a consummate liar, the kind of woman who carried herself like the queen of the universe even when she'd had the self-esteem of an outcast lemming. Ava had learned to act as if she ruled the world and to plow through pain wearing a smile and a ten-thousand-dollar haute couture gown. "Vulnerability" had been erased from her vocabulary before her fourteenth birthday.

Sucking in a deep breath, she forced her arms to drop to her sides and deliberately straightened her spine.

Chin up, hips out, hands loose, she reminded herself. Sex could not make her vulnerable, and neither could Dima; even discovering herself to be a newly turned vampire couldn't do that as long as she refused to allow it. She just needed a little time alone, a few hours in her own home to get her bearings and figure out what she would do next. Once she had time to think, she felt certain everything would make more sense.

Please, God.

Her course of action set, Ava stepped away from the window, slipped on her coat, and tightened the belt around her waist. Reflexively, she reached for her purse, cursing mildly when she remembered she'd lost it during the attack. She knew there was no hope in hell she'd get it back—even in a good neighborhood on the Upper East Side, a Kate Spade packed with luxury leather goods and high-end accessories, once out of its owner's hands, was gone forever.

Ava sighed as she made a mental note of the problems losing it would force her to deal with. She'd have to report her credit cards as stolen, of course, and start the process of getting a new ID. Living in the city, she didn't drive and so used her passport as her primary photo identification, which would turn out to be a mixed blessing; while she wouldn't have to deal with the interminable lines at the DMV, she would just be trading them for the interminable red tape of the State Department.

The small leather notebook, sterling silver Tiffany pen, and other assorted frills she carried with her could all be replaced, of course, and her PDA was backed up on her office computer, so once she bought a new one, she wouldn't be losing any of her data. Still, she hated the bother of having to shop for new items when she'd been perfectly happy with the old ones.

As she checked her watch and headed for the door, on her way to meet her car, one final task occurred to her. Just to be safe, she should have the locks changed at her office and her apartment, so instead of getting copies of her keys, she would just get totally new ones from the locksmith when they completed the changes—

"God damn it," Ava hissed, stepping into the hall outside of the loft and slamming the door shut behind her. She had no keys! She was locked out of her own bloody apartment!

She uttered an indecipherable sound of frustration and located the building's converted freight elevator at the end of the hall. So much for her fantasies about going home and locking herself into the familiar, safe cocoon of her own home. Without her keys, she would never be able to get inside. The super in her building was an unbending petty dictator, and despite the fact that he had known her for the last seven years, the lease stated he could not let her inside without seeing photo ID, which she no longer had, and she knew better than to ask him to bend the rules. He'd just as easily bend the beams of the Brooklyn Bridge with his bare hands.

Madre de Dios, could anything else go wrong for her? Being turned against her will into a vampire hadn't been enough; now she would have to go begging for assistance from friends who were already pissed at her. She didn't even bother to consider going to Danice or Corinne to borrow their copies of her keys; they each spent more time away from home these days than at it, and tracking them down in Faerie was not something she knew—or wanted to know—how to do.

It would have to be Reggie or Missy, which meant it would have to be Missy. Even though Ava knew both of them were upset with her at the moment, Reggie was more likely to take Dima's side and yell at her for not obeying his orders to stay in his loft where she was safe.

Well, that was not quite true. Missy would probably

take Dima's side as well—she was the wife of a council member, after all—but at least she was less likely to yell about it. At the moment, Ava had to take whatever infinitesimal advantages she could get.

With a very resigned sigh, she met the sleek black Town Car that stopped for her at the curb, and gave the familiar company driver Missy's address before she let him help her into the backseat. Allowing her head to fall back against a cushion of black leather, she closed her eyes and prayed that things please, *please* start going her way for a change.

I mean, wouldn't the law of averages say they'd have to? she asked herself, feeling a headache begin to stir behind her temples. *How long can one person's streak of bad luck really last?*

Chapter 13

"I had to ask," she muttered when the door to Missy's house swung open, pulled not by Missy, but by her larger, hairier husband.

Graham scowled down at Ava, clearly less than thrilled to find her standing on his front doorstep at 9:22 on a Monday night. "Ask what?"

"Nothing," Ava dismissed. "I was talking to myself. Is Missy here?"

"Of course she is. She just finished putting the boys to bed."

When he said nothing else, just stood in the door and continued to frown at Ava, she sighed and gave him a pointed look. "Well, can I talk to her?"

"About what?"

"Graham! What on earth are you doing? You can't just leave people standing on the doorstep. Let her in, for goodness' sake."

Childishly satisfied at getting to hear Missy scold her obnoxious husband, Ava raised her chin and stepped haughtily around the Alpha Lupine and into his front hall. She just barely resisted the urge to chant

Nyah-nyah-na-nyah-nyah under her breath as she stepped past.

Missy stood on the stairs to the second floor, one hand on the banister and the other planted on her hip.

"Don't look so smug, Av," she said, her lips firming. "I have the same question for you. I thought Dima said tonight would be too soon for you to go out and that you wouldn't be able to make it here to talk to the council until Tuesday?"

The pointed question halted Ava in mid-step. She had forgotten that motherhood had given Missy a decided talent for maternal scoldings. It was like some kind of strange side effect of the hormones.

Straightening her spine, Ava looked up at her friend, pointedly refusing to turn around and glance at Graham. It didn't matter. She didn't need to see him to know that he was smirking behind her back.

"I feel just fine," she said coolly. "Dima was being overly cautious, but I didn't come to talk to the council."

"Then why did you come? You don't usually like to visit when you know Graham might be home."

When isn't he home? Ava wondered sourly. The man's job was running the private club for Others that just happened to occupy the building next door, which used to be part of the same mansion as the house they currently stood in. Even when Graham was at work, he was still right there, hovering.

"It's a bit of a story," she hedged, superconscious of the werewolf at her back. "I don't suppose you'd like to offer me a cup of coffee?"

Graham brushed past her, not bothering to hide the fact that he was rolling his eyes. He paused at the bottom of the steps, his wife's position on the third placing them eye-to-eye for a change. "Don't mind me," he said sarcastically. "I'll just check on things next door. Just buzz the staff line if you need me."

He kissed her, the kind of sweet, affectionate kiss husbands gave wives all over the world every day, so Ava wasn't quite sure why watching it made her feel so uncomfortable. Maybe it was because even in that tender gesture, she could see a flash of heat spring between the couple.

Or maybe it was because even the heat was clearly tinged with a strong mutual love.

Or maybe she was just overtired.

She kept her eyes on Missy, who kept her eyes on her husband until he disappeared behind a concealed door in the wall adjoining the club.

"It's too late for coffee," Missy said when she finally turned back to her friend. "That much caffeine will keep you awake all night."

Ava's mouth twisted. "I don't think I need to worry about staying awake all night anymore, Melissa."

"Fine. Then it will keep *me* awake all night. But I made some hot cocoa for the boys earlier, and there's still some left. I'll heat it up."

She didn't really want cocoa—she hadn't wanted coffee, either—but she still followed Missy to the back of the house and into the large, well-appointed kitchen.

"I assume this is when you tell me what you need," the woman said as she flicked a knob on the gleaming stainless-steel stove. "Somehow I get the feeling you didn't come over for a little girl talk."

Ava pulled out a stool from its place at the center island and slid onto it. Fatigue was making her shaky. She needed to sit down. "I got locked out of my apartment, and I don't have my ID on me, so my nitwit super won't let me in. I need to borrow the spare key I gave you."

"Ooo-kay. I'm thinking there's more of a story here than that. . . ."

"You already know it. I got mugged, killed, kidnapped, and changed into a vampire. Somewhere along the way I lost my keys and my ID. The end."

"But why do you need to go back to your apartment tonight? Dima said you'd be staying with him until you . . . got a better handle on things." Missy's eyes narrowed. "Come to think of it, where is Dima?"

Ava ignored the question. Answering it would only lead to an argument, and her head already hurt too much to deal with that. "Dima taught me how to— God, I can't believe I'm saying this—drink blood, so what else do I need to learn? The secret vampire handshake? I think I can manage without, thanks."

Missy set a mug down on the counter with a hint too much force. "Ava, where is Dima?"

God, Ava's head was pounding. And frankly, the smell of the warming chocolate was beginning to make her a little sick. She swallowed. "He said something about going out to work for a few hours tonight. He's on some kind of mission or something. He wasn't very forthcoming with the details."

"And he told you it was okay for you to go back to your apartment without him?"

"What, is he my father?"

"Based on what you both told us last night, yes, he is."

"Don't be cute with me, Melissa. You know that wasn't what I meant." Ava had aimed her tone at dismissive, but she missed by a few inches, landing instead at bitchy. Whatever. She couldn't concentrate well enough just now to worry about it. "I'm a grown woman and I don't need a vampire mentor to tell me how to live my life. I'm a capable, intelligent woman. I can figure things out just fine on my own."

"When it comes to trading stocks or following a recipe for bouillabaisse, maybe, but this is a little more complicated than that, Av. There are rules that you need to know about, and they aren't always the kind of thing you'd think of if you—"

Without thinking, Ava slammed her palms down on the butcher-block top of the kitchen island, leaned in menacingly toward her dear, sweet friend, and snarled loudly. "Fuck the rules, Melissa," she hissed, pulling her lips back to expose teeth that suddenly felt too big for her mouth. "I'm fucking sick to death of hearing about the rules! Do you understand me?"

Missy froze, her warm brown eyes widening, her breath freezing in her chest for a long, tense moment. Then, calmly, she took several steps to her right without ever taking her eyes off of Ava. Blindly, Missy reached for a slim black telephone, lifted the receiver, and pressed a single button from memory.

"Hi, Sam," she said, her voice sounding as sweetly calm and even as always. "Can you do me a favor and grab Graham? Tell him I need him next door right away. . . . No, nothing's wrong. But ask him to bring along a bottle of Nosferatu, okay? Thanks."

Ava stared at her for another minute, then closed her eyes and slumped back on her chair. Wearily she bowed her head and raised a hand, pressing the heel of her palm hard against the smooth plane of her brow just between her eyes.

"I'm sorry, Missy," she mumbled, feeling the anger drain out of her as quickly as it had flashed, taking with it every ounce of energy in her body. "Please forgive me. I don't know why I snapped at you like that."

"It's okay. I do."

Ava opened her eyes and frowned. "What?"

Missy didn't answer. Instead, she edged around the far side of the counter, placing herself between it—and by default, Ava—and the door to the hallway. Missy reached her chosen spot just in time to stop her frantic husband from leaping through it and onto her friend.

"Are you all right?" Graham snarled, grabbing his wife by the arms and running a searching gaze over her from head to toe, as if looking for injuries. "Did she hurt you? Do you need a doctor? A bandage? What?"

"I'm fine," Missy soothed, grasping his elbows in turn.

He ignored her and turned his eyes on her friend.

They had murder in them. "I want her out of here. Now. Either throw her out now or I'll do it myself, and I will *not* promise to be gentle."

Startled, Ava stared at him. She knew perfectly well that Graham had never liked her—frankly, the feeling was entirely mutual; he'd never been good enough for Missy—but he'd never before threatened to throw Ava out of his house.

"No," Missy said, her voice firm and just a bit louder than usual. "Will you calm down? Graham, listen to me."

At another time, Ava might have indulged in a chuckle at the sight of her petite, curvy friend grasping her enormous, supernaturally strong husband by the arms and shaking him to get his attention. At the moment, though, Ava was afraid to. She had the disturbing feeling even such a gentle sound and accompanying motion would either split her head wide open or send her stomach shooting out of her mouth to land inside out on the stone-tiled floor.

"Graham, I'm fine," Missy repeated. "Ava didn't touch me. She just got a little grumpy, that's all. Did you bring the Nosferatu?"

He stared down at her. "Are you kidding me? She threatens to bite you and you want me to feed her? Are you out of your pretty blond mind?"

"She's here, and she clearly needs to eat something. Do you want me to send her outside without her dinner and let her find it on her own?"

Graham swore, creatively.

"Exactly. So either buzz Sam again or go back to

the club and get a bottle before she passes out or rips one of our throats out. And I'm warning you, I do plan to use you as a Lupine shield."

Her husband grumbled. "I don't have to buzz Sam. There's a bottle in the back of the pantry. I try to keep some on hand for Misha and Reggie."

Ava had long since given up trying to follow the conversation. She heard the words, but they just buzzed around her head like so much white noise.

God, she felt so weak. So tired and sick. She needed to lie down. Somewhere far away from the smell of that hot chocolate. Her stomach lurched and she moaned softly.

She heard the sounds of footsteps on the tiles, fabric shifting, a cabinet door opening and closing. She also felt unfamiliar arms pull her off the stool and scoop her up with zero ceremony and barely more gentleness. A few moments later, she felt herself placed on a low, soft surface.

A cool hand touched her forehead, surprising her with the knowledge that she had somehow spiked a fever in the last five minutes. Was that even possible?

She heard a sound like liquid pouring and someone pressed a glass to her lips.

"Drink," she heard. The voice sounded like Missy's. "It will make you feel better."

Ava thought of the cocoa, and her stomach immediately clenched in protest. She tried to turn her head away, but the glass followed.

"Drink," Missy repeated, gently but insistently.

Ava tried to turn away again, but a hand—far too

rough and large to belong to Missy—grasped her lightly by the chin and held her still. Some of the liquid splashed onto Ava's lips, and instinctively she licked it off. Every cell in her body wept with pleasure.

Blood.

Distantly, she heard a sound like a whimper, and she refused to believe it could possibly have come from her. Especially not when she had already opened her mouth to the press of the glass and taken her first greedy gulp.

Missy slid an arm beneath Ava's neck and helped her raise her head so she could finish the glass. As soon as it was empty, Graham refilled it to the rim, and Ava drained that as well. Slowly, the horrible, debilitating weakness began to leave her, and she blew out a shuddering breath. She opened her eyes carefully and had to squint against the light of the table lamp beside the sofa where she lay. They had carried her into the den, she realized, and pushed herself dazedly into a sitting position.

"Welcome back," Missy murmured, pursing her lips. "Did you have a nice trip? Because I have to tell you, from the way it looked to me, I'd be asking for my money back if I were you."

Ava just blinked at her friend. "What happened?"

"You passed out. From hunger," Graham snapped. She looked up to find him looming over her, a dark wine bottle in his hand and a fierce scowl on his face. "Right after you nearly leapt on my wife like a rabid dog. Have you forgotten that already?"

Shock and fear blindsided her. Sweet Mother Mary, what had she nearly done?

"I would never hurt Missy!" Her voice sounded unwaveringly certain, and probably loud enough to be heard in Queens. But she remembered being in the kitchen with her friend, remembered them talking and having Missy give her the same annoying lecture Dima had already subjected her to a million times. Sickeningly, she remembered the swelling of impatience and anger that had accompanied the roiling in her stomach and made it so hard for her to focus. "I snapped at her, sure, and I apologized, but it wasn't like I attacked her!"

"No, thankfully, she recognized what was happening before things went that far and called me to intervene."

"That's just bullshit. I would kick the crap out of *myself* before I'd lay a hand on Missy!"

Ava tried not to think about whether she was trying to convince Graham and Missy . . . or herself.

"I know you wouldn't have wanted to hurt me," Missy said gently, "but I don't think you even knew what you were saying, Av. When you yelled at me, it wasn't just you getting pissed at me. You were in a rage. Your face was paler than death, but your eyes were practically glowing red, and your fangs were practically dripping with venom."

"My *fangs*?!?"

Her friend nodded. "Like I said, I know you wouldn't have wanted to hurt me, but I don't think you were really in control of yourself, Ava. You had let it go too long. The hunger was making you a little crazy. Not to mention sick as a dog."

Ava felt her stomach clench again, only this time the sensation had nothing to do with appetite or the lack thereof; it was shame, pure and simple.

Maybe with a little panic thrown in. *You know, just for good measure.*

"I'm . . . I don't know what to say. I'm so sorry. I had no idea."

"Which is why you shouldn't be running around the city by yourself," Missy pointed out. "Dima didn't lay down a bunch of rules just to drive you crazy. Av, you really do have a lot to learn about your new life. Like when to eat."

Ava glanced down at the glass she now held and then up at the bottle in Graham's hand. "And what, apparently. I didn't know the Bordeaux region was famous for a liquid other than grapes."

He set the bottle down on the low cocktail table in front of her. "It's not from Bordeaux. It's bottled for the club by a small company in Oregon. The main ingredient is blood—the real stuff, donated, of course—processed to remove the clotting factors, and mixed with pinot noir, spices, and a few other secret ingredients. It's not meant to be a dietary staple, so get that hopeful look off your face. But in an emergency, it can substitute for whole blood until you can get your hands on some."

She blinked. "Thanks."

"You're welcome, provided you never do something so stupid again," he snapped. "You know, I've known you for a long time, Ava, and I always knew you were arrogant, but I never pegged you for stupid."

Missy made a hushing sound, but Graham ignored her.

"While this might be a change of pace for you, it's time you started to think about a bit more than yourself now and then. You can't fuck around like this. Being a vampire isn't all about superpowers and mind reading and petulant fucking pity parties. It comes with responsibilities, one of which is that you take care of yourself by feeding often enough that you don't put innocent bystanders, family, and *friends* in danger because of your hunger. What part of that is so goddamn hard for you to understand?"

Ava didn't answer. She didn't *have* an answer. What she had was an entire boatload of confusion that hadn't been there when she'd stalked out of Dima's apartment, or even the first time she'd awoken inside it. She had, she realized as she stared up into Graham's angry, handsome face, been acting like a spoiled brat for most of the last forty-eight hours. All she had been thinking about was how much things sucked for her. How she hadn't wanted to become a vampire, she didn't want to drink blood, she didn't want to learn a bunch of stupid rules, and she didn't think she should have to since she didn't want to ever spend any time around other vampires anyway.

Seriously, she'd been acting like a three-year-old. So damned what if none of this was what she wanted? It was what she had, and the only way she was going to be able to deal with the rest of her life was if she accepted it and moved on. Which, she supposed, was what Dima had been trying to tell her.

Ugh. She really hated it that he'd been right.

Taking a deep breath, Ava lifted her chin and met the Lupine's narrow golden gaze. "You're right," she said, accompanying the admission with a small, regal nod. "I've been behaving badly, and I apologize."

Graham stared at her. For a full second, he just stared at her, his expression slowly morphing from one of angry accusation to one of faintly terrified confusion. He turned to his wife.

"What the hell does she mean by that?" he demanded.

Missy smiled gently. "I think she means that she's sorry."

He looked back at Ava. Then back at Missy. "Did she fall and hit her head in the kitchen?"

"No."

Back to Ava. "When you were attacked?"

Missy snorted.

"Not that I recall," Ava said, feeling a stirring of amusement.

"We're going to have to go to her apartment." Nodding decisively, Graham reached for his wife. "I'll sniff for gas leaks, and you can check under her bed for an alien pod."

"Oh, go sit on a chain saw," Ava grumbled, trying to hide a smile, and failing when Graham sighed in relief.

"Oh, thank God. It really is you. You had me scared for a minute."

Missy slapped her husband lightly on the arm and

leaned forward to pour her friend more of the Vir-colac club's special house wine. "Have one more glass," she urged. "It should keep you until Dima can get you some real food."

At the mention of her sire's name—and the re-minder of what kind of mood he would likely be in when she saw him again—Ava shifted uncomfort-ably. "Right," she said, setting her glass aside with suspicious care. "I should probably head back to his loft, now that you mention it."

Missy raised her brows. "I thought you said you wanted to go back to your own place tonight?"

"Well, yes, but I wouldn't want Dima to worry when he gets back and finds me missing—"

"You mean you didn't tell him where you were going?" Graham demanded, his expression once again shifting into his thundercloud impersonation.

"He was already gone when I woke up tonight."

"But you left him a note, didn't you?"

Ava glanced toward the door.

"I swear to God, Ava," the Lupine growled, but whatever he had intended to say next was interrupted by a familiar brown head that poked through the open doorway from the hall.

"Sorry to interrupt," Samantha Carstairs-Baker said, her voice as cheerful as her wide, white smile. Samantha was Graham's personal assistant and an-other regular attendee at girls' night. Unlike most of that crowd, she was married to a human. She herself, however, was a werewolf. "I thought I should bring this over. Rogers said it was just dropped off at the back door of the club by a messenger."

Ava looked down at the black bag in the Lupine woman's hands and grinned. "My Spade!" she cried, getting up and hurrying over to take it from her. "Oh, my God, I never thought I would see it again! I had totally written it off. Did Rogers get the messenger's name?"

Samantha shook her head. "I don't think so. Why?"

"Because I'd be happy to give him a reward. My PDA is in here, not to mention one of my favorite pairs of earrings. I really didn't want to have to replace all this stuff."

"Before you go tossing out reward money, why don't you check to make sure all that stuff is really still in there?" Missy cautioned. "Just because someone returned the bag doesn't mean they returned all the contents."

Ava rifled through the purse. "PDA, notebook, earrings, passport, keys . . . I think everything's here."

"Check your wallet," Graham advised.

Pulling out the thick rectangle of red leather, Ava popped the snap and flipped it open. "Well, the cash is gone, of course."

"How much was in there?"

She shrugged. "A couple hundred dollars. Annoying, of course, but hardly surprising." She ran her fingers over the slots and through the compartments. "What is surprising is that I think all my credit cards are here. Will wonders never cease?"

Samantha shook her head wryly. "Apparently not."

Happy to be reunited with her belongings—she'd felt half-naked ever since she'd realized her purse had been missing—Ava put her wallet back inside the bag. When the heavy accessory somehow wedged itself between the covers of her small leather memo pad and several sheets of folded paper, she pulled the miniature notebook out to straighten them. Dog-eared papers drove her crazy.

Smoothing the top sheet into place, Ava saw the dark script on the crisp white surface and frowned.

"What's the matter?" Missy asked.

"This isn't my handwriting."

With a frown, Ava ripped the top sheet from the notepad and placed the rest of her belongings on the coffee table.

"Whose is it? Your assistant's?"

She shook her head. "No. I don't recognize it."

"Well, what does it say?" Samantha sounded intrigued.

Ava skimmed quickly over the text. She felt herself go a little pale. "I'm not quite sure."

Graham cocked an eyebrow. "Is it not in English?"

"Of course it is. But that doesn't mean I know what to make of it. I've never heard of the person who signed it."

"Maybe it wasn't meant for you," Missy suggested.

"I could accept that, if it weren't directed to 'Dear Ava.'"

Samantha gave a lengthy, exasperated sigh. "Well, are you going to tell us what it says or just stand around and be cryptic?"

Ava read, "'Dear Ava, Congratulations on your

recent elevation in the world. As a member of my household, it is your duty to present yourself to me at your earliest opportunity. I receive callers at the address below for two hours each evening, beginning thirty minutes after dusk. Please try to be prompt. I believe your change in circumstances leaves us much to discuss. Sincerely . . .'" She shook her head. "It's initials, I think, but whoever wrote them down needs to have a serious rethink about her calligraphy hobby. It looks kind of like a 'KO.' No, wait, 'YO.' 'YC'? 'KC'? I can't be positive."

Samantha pursed her lips. "Huh. I don't suppose that's any less confusing to you than it is to me?" She glanced at Graham and Missy. "To us."

"Not really. Like I said, I have no idea who it's from. I mean, the language would make me think it had something to do with my . . . turning, but other than you and Dima—and Reggie and Misha—who else would know about that?"

Missy shook her head, then turned when the phone in the corner buzzed. Recognizing the light that indicated the intercom function that connected the house to the club next door was flashing, she pressed the speaker button. "Yes?"

"I am sorry to disturb you, madam," said a very proper voice with an accent that was just dying to be British but couldn't quite manage it. "I wished to speak with your husband, if I might."

"I'm here, Rogers," Graham said. "What do you need?"

"I'm afraid we're having a . . . small disturbance, sir," the club's butler explained after a brief hesitation.

He sounded reluctant to talk over an open speaker line. "There is a gentleman requesting entrance who is not a member. He is being quite insistent."

"Tell him the rules, Rogers. If he wants to join, he can come fill out an application just like everyone else."

"Yes, sir, I did explain the standard procedure to him. He says that he does not wish to join, that he is here looking for someone. He also claims to know you personally."

"What's his name?"

There was a slight hesitation and a muffled noise in the background before Rogers spoke again. "Vladimir Rurikovich."

Ava was certain she didn't make a sound—though inside she was cursing like a dockworker—but she obviously didn't need to. Graham's attention snapped immediately to her and an unholy look of anticipation lit his eyes.

"I'm sorry, Rogers," he said, suddenly full of charm and cheer. "I should have told you about my new acquaintance. Mr. Rurikovich is visiting from out of town, but we're going to be granting him the privileges of a full membership while he's here in town. Dima is also very close with one of my wife's dearest friends, so feel free to treat him as such. In fact, why don't you send him over to the house right now?"

"Very good, sir."

The intercom clicked off and Ava treated Graham to a look she usually reserved for overly persistent salespeople and men who wouldn't take no for an answer.

"I hope you're enjoying yourself, Winters," she snapped, her tone promising a retribution too dire to be put into words.

"Actually"—he smiled, turning to step into the hall in preparation for welcoming his newest guest— "for some reason, my day has just begun to really look up."

Chapter 14

He would begin by shaking her so hard, Dima decided as he stalked through the hallway the very stiff butler of the Vircolac club had directed him to, that he could not help but rattle some sense into her thick, pretty skull. Then he would turn her over his knee and paddle her ass until she thought of him—and his orders—every time she even considered sitting down. For at least a week.

Or maybe he would paddle her first. Then lecture her, then shake her. So, so many options, and at the moment he was mad enough to try every single one of the variations he was considering, just to see which one worked the best. In case this ever happened again.

"If it does, I'll just save us both the trouble and kill her," he muttered, pausing at a closed door and lifting his hand to knock. Before his fist could fall, the door opened and the Lupine he had seen before at his apartment smiled and held out his hand.

"Believe me, if you ever decide to go through with it," the Lupine said, shaking his hand in an almost commiserating manner, "you have plenty of volunteers lined up to help, and to testify on your behalf in court. Or to provide an alibi. Whichever you prefer."

Dima paused, breathed deeply, sighed. "I may need all three. Where is she?"

"Right this way."

He followed his host across a beautifully furnished hall and through an open door into a small, comfortable study currently occupied by three women, two of whom were familiar to him, one of whom he wanted to strangle, and a third he'd never seen before.

"Dima, you remember my wife, Missy," Graham said, with the polished manners of a man hosting a cocktail party instead of eagerly watching in anticipation of a bloody confrontation. "And this is Samantha Carstairs-Baker, my assistant and general right hand."

"Nice to meet you," the brunette said. She had pretty features, a noteworthy smile, and the decided scent of a Lupine. She watched him with avid curiosity.

Dima managed a small, civil nod for her and a grunt of acknowledgment for Missy. Then he turned his focus on the object of his fury.

Who currently sat, pretty as a picture, on the end of a comfortably elegant sofa, with her long legs crossed at the knees and her hands folded daintily in her lap. She nodded to him and offered a small smile.

"Dima." Her voice emerged as regal as ever, but with its characteristic arrogance surprisingly absent. It made him frown. "I want to apologize right away. I wasn't thinking when I left your apartment, and I realize it was badly done of me. I hope you'll accept my sincere apologies and know I will not discard your advice so lightly in the future."

His frown slid into a glower. "Who are you, and what have you done with Ava Markham?"

She made a face. "You're just as amusing as Graham. Why is it so hard to believe that I recognize I behaved badly, and that I sincerely want to apologize for the trouble I've caused in doing so?"

"Maybe because you've never done anything remotely like it in your life?"

"You've known me for two days. How can you possibly draw that kind of conclusion after so short a time?"

"Intuition?" he hazarded.

"He looks like a pretty bright guy," Sam offered.

"We may have let something along those lines slip," Missy murmured.

"You three should take your act on the road," Ava observed sourly before turning back to Dima. "Whatever the case, the apology I'm offering now is sincere. If you don't believe it, that's your problem, but at least acknowledge that I offered it before I'm tempted to shove it down your throat."

"See? She's fine," Graham reassured the other man.

Dima gritted his teeth. He had come here expecting a fight, not an apology, and he was finding it surprisingly difficult to change gears now that she'd swept his rage out from under him.

"Damn it, Ava, what were you thinking?" he snapped, but the question came out sounding more like a sigh than a bellow. There wasn't even much point in asking it, but it had been dancing on the tip of his tongue for so long that it had leapt out before he could stop it. "You could have been hurt, or you could have hurt someone else."

"I know," she said calmly. "In fact, I almost did. If not for Missy and Graham, I would probably have either bitten her or passed out and cracked my head open on her kitchen counter. I was stupid, and I'm admitting it freely. For the last time."

His jaw snapped shut. He looked to Graham. "What happened?"

"Hello? Sitting right here." Ava waved a hand at Dima. "I wasn't feeling particularly hungry when I left the loft, but I didn't realize I needed to do a slightly macabre version of a diabetic monitoring his blood sugar. By the time I got here and was talking to Missy, the hunger had gotten a little out of control. I snapped at her, then nearly passed out, so she and Graham poured some of that down my throat." She pointed to the bottle of Nosferatu on the table, then pursed her lips. "They said there's wine in it. I wonder if I might not be a little tipsy."

Dima didn't recognize the label of this particular bottle, but blood watered down with wine—or even spiked with hard liquor—and enhanced with flavors was a common enough thing. Vampires had existed for as long as humans. It wasn't like they hadn't experimented with developing a sort of cuisine of their own over the millennia.

He grunted. "How much did you drink?"

"Only a couple of glasses," Missy assured him. "We told her she would still need to feed later tonight, but we don't tend to keep a lot of whole blood around, and we generally go through most of that on Friday and Saturday nights at the club. The new stock won't come in until Thursday for this coming weekend."

"I will take care of her." He blew out a breath and looked back at Ava. "Are you feeling all right to leave? You and I should talk, and it would probably be more comfortable for both of us at home."

"Why bother? Everyone here knows you're angry at me, and they know why." She didn't react to his instinctive slip in calling the loft "home" for both of them but couldn't tell if that was good or bad. "You might as well lecture me here. That way if you miss anything, one of the others can chime in."

"Sure, and then maybe you can explain about that note Ava found in her purse," Graham suggested, looking innocent and earning his wife's elbow driven hard into his ribs. "What? Ava said she thought it sounded like it was about vampire stuff. Of course she'd want to share it with Dima. He is her sire, after all."

Ava shot the Lupine a very disgruntled look.

Dima asked, "What note?"

She hesitated a moment, looking uncomfortable; then she sighed and reached into the black handbag on the coffee table in front of her.

"This one." She handed him a small slip of white notepaper decorated with an obviously feminine and very old-fashioned script. "The writing is so ornate that I can't make out the signature at the bottom. I'm guessing it's someone's initials, but as far as I can tell, the first one could either be a *K* or a *Y*, or maybe an *R*, and the second one looks like an *O* or a *C*, but who knows for sure?"

Dima accepted the note, took one look at the initial on the bottom, and swore up and down, using curses in both Russian and English that he'd forgotten he even knew.

"What is it? What's wrong?"

It took him a moment before he thought he could answer Ava's startled question without shouting. Even then, it was a near thing.

"The letters are a *Y* and a *C*," he confirmed. "The note is from a female vampire by the name of Yelizaveta Chernigov, and it implies that the vampire who turned you was a member of her bloodline, which means that you would be as well."

Graham rolled his eyes. "Christ, if I didn't know better, I'd think every bloody vampire in Manhattan had immigrated here from Russia. I thought some of you were supposed to be from Romania, at least."

Ava just furrowed her brow. "Wait, do you know the vampire who wrote me this note?"

Dima's head jerked in a nod. "I do. In fact, she is the reason I came to the United States several weeks ago."

"What is that supposed to mean?"

At another time, Dima might have wondered if the snappish note in Ava's voice indicated jealousy and been pleased, but at the moment he was too busy wondering how he was going to explain this to the ECV.

Yes, my lords, I am aware that it is expressly against the Laws to create a fledgling without your authorization, or to lend aid to a declared enemy of the council by such actions as willfully aiding a minion of said outlaw.

But technically I wasn't the one who created her, and when I lent her aid, I didn't know she was one of the Chernigov woman's minions. Really. I swear.

That would go over well, he was sure.

"It means that I am in New York for a highly specific, and up until now classified, purpose," he said, feeling the reins of his mission torn from his fingers by the laughing hand of Fate. That bitch. "Yelizaveta Chernigov is a vampire and a criminal who has escaped from the custody of the European Council of Vampires in order to avoid a sentence of imprisonment for her many crimes. The latest intelligence we had was that she had fled to the United States and was in hiding. I am a member of the council's division of enforcement of the Laws, and I was ordered to track her down and see that she is returned to prison in Russia, where she belongs."

Dima noticed that Ava looked confused, Missy looked worried, and Graham looked angry. The other woman, Samantha, looked invisible. At some point in Dima's speech, she had left the room. *Damn it.*

"Do you mean to tell me that you came here on official business as a representative of another nation's governing body of an Other population, with the intent of finding and seizing a resident of our jurisdiction," Graham asked, his voice growing slightly louder with each word, "and you didn't bother to clear this with *our* governing body?"

Dima met the Lupine's angry glare head-on. "The members of our council did not feel it was necessary to alert yours. We did not believe we would require your assistance, and we believed the matter would be handled quickly and quietly. It was deemed unnecessary to inconvenience you with the details of my mission."

"Funny, but I think that's more of *our* decision to make. And I'm sure the head of our Council of Others will agree with me."

"I am certain he would." Dima didn't back down and instead let Graham see how he intended to calmly play the next turn of this hand. "From what our sources revealed before I came here, the head of your council is a very close friend of yours, isn't he?"

The werewolf stiffened, his lip curling in a definite snarl. "Are you implying that the head of the council is somehow corrupt and couldn't be trusted to make a sound decision about this Chernigov person's acts because of that?"

In his peripheral vision, Dima saw Missy step forward to position herself discreetly but decidedly within arm's reach of her husband. Dima just wasn't sure if it was so she could interfere if Graham decided to attack or so she could help.

"I imply nothing."

"So you're just going to say it flat out?"

"Perhaps the real reason the European Council of

Vampires concluded it would be wise to conduct this mission under the radar of your council was to avoid discussions and accusations just like this one."

"And perhaps the two of you need to calm down and remember the point behind this discussion." Ava stepped between the men, silencing each of them with a pointed look. "Let's bring it back to me here and ask the really important question: Why is some runaway vampiress I've never heard of summoning me like a debutante being called up for her royal presentation?"

"She says you belong to her house," Dima answered roughly. He looked at Ava while he said it, but part of him was keeping a weather eye on Graham. Just to be safe.

"And in English that translates as . . . what?"

"It means she believes you share a bloodline passed on to you by the vampire who turned you. In Europe, many of our kind still adhere to the system of houses and clans, where vampires who can all trace their lineage to the same set of ancestors form a sort of extended family network among themselves. Each house is headed by a vampire who is usually older and more directly related to the founder of the house than the others. In this case, Yelizaveta was the daughter of the first member of a noble family to turn to vampirism. Her father, Kazimir of Chernigov, embraced the change for himself and then crossed over his only son, Stepan. Stepan later changed Yelizaveta. When the men died, Yelizaveta stepped up to assume control of the house. She has been its head since roughly the fourteenth century."

"Okay." Ava nodded. "I get that. It makes sense, in a feudalistic, very *droit du seigneur* sort of way. But why would she need to meet every single person who's part of her bloodline? If she's really been around that long, there must be thousands of them. Does she honestly think she can keep track of that many people?"

"There aren't really that many of them. Two hundred, maybe two hundred fifty at the outside."

Dima could read the surprise on Ava's face.

"Why not more? Do they have a 'one bite per century' rule or something?"

"No, but they have been a cause of much trouble among the other houses in Europe. Their numbers have been . . . thinned over the years."

Ava's eyes narrowed. "What do you mean by that?"

Dima met her gaze unflinchingly. "Only that when you initiate as much trouble as the Chernigovs have over the years, it can cut down on your population. Or rather, *I* can cut it down."

"So she would want to meet me, why? To recruit me to do her bidding or something?"

"She would want to see if you could be . . . influenced. Yes."

Graham snorted. "Obviously she's new in town if she thinks she can influence *the* Ava Markham to do anything. New, or terminally stupid."

"That is not a word I would use to describe Yelizaveta Chernigov." He shot Graham a quelling look. "But if 'stupid' is a word you use for women who slaughter two of the most powerful vampire princes in Europe and nearly bring both the Russian and Austro-Hungarian empires to their knees at the height of their power, that is a personal choice with which I would not want to interfere."

The Lupine's smirk disappeared. "When and how did she do that?"

Missy put a hand on her husband's shoulder and shook her head. "I'm not sure now is the time to get all those details, honey. You know as well as I do that if there really is a dangerous vampire fugitive on the loose in the city, the council is going to need to know about it. Dima shouldn't have to go over the same story twice."

"Fine," Graham said, his reluctance to wait clear. "I'll call Rafe. The council was going to meet on Tuesday and deal with Ava then, but when they hear about this, they may want to move things up."

In the doorway, the sound of someone clearing her throat drew everyone's attention.

"Actually, sir," Samantha said, a look of sheepish anxiety clouding her features, "the council has been alerted and has already begun to gather."

Graham did not look pleased. "You alerted them?"

"Indirectly, Alpha."

"Explain."

She shifted her weight, pointed her chin down and to the side, and fixed her eyes on the empty space beside the Lupine's upper arm. Dima recognized the signs of one werewolf attempting to pacify another and wondered what else the woman would reveal.

"I recognized the name that Mr. Rurikovich mentioned," she said. "Yelizaveta Chernigov. It rang a bell, but I couldn't quite remember why, so I slipped out to check my files. I was reacquainting myself with an incident at the opera a few years ago involving the then head of the council and a female vampire named Lisette. Apparently Lisette turned out to be—"

"Yelizaveta's sister," Dima finished for her.

Samantha nodded. "She had been targeting the head of the council for retribution for a past slight. Apparently, there was quite a long history between the Chernigov woman and his family."

Dima could have said that a sound caught his attention, some soft footfall in the hallway, or the sound of the latch on the door through which he'd entered earlier clicking open, but the truth was, there hadn't been a sound. All there had been was a change in the air, a slight adjustment in the temperature, a thickening of the ions, an infinitesimal something that was both imperceptible yet unmistakable.

By the time the shadow filled the doorway, his eyes were already locked on it, and when he saw who stood there, he experienced a riot of conflicting emotions, but not one of them was surprise.

"She means 'our' family," Dima corrected, his pale gaze catching a much darker one that emerged from eyes that appeared nearly black in the shadows.

Dmitri.

Misha.

He looked much the same as he had the last time Dima had seen him. Perhaps a little less gigantic, but then, at their last meeting, Dima had been all of fifteen, still scrawny and underdeveloped, and Dmitri Rurikssen had been a man full grown. In a boy's eyes, Dmitri had seemed to tower over everything but the sun itself. But that had been before he left. Before he disappeared and left his people to the fate the Chernigovs had planned for them.

So far, nothing like recognition had shown on the darker man's face, but then, a lot of time had passed. More than eight centuries, in fact.

He wore the years well.

Mouth curving in a smile of little warmth, Dima stepped forward until he could look clearly into the other man's face. *"Moyo pochteniye, bratok,"* Dima drawled, watching as puzzlement flitted across his brother's face, catching in the creases of his brow. "It has been a long time, no?"

Dima saw confusion give way to disbelief as eyes as dark as his own were light traced the lines of his features, swept over his tall, muscular form, took in the fair hair and the hardness wrought in warfare.

"Otets?" Before Dima could correct him, Misha caught himself, shook his head. "No, it is not possible. It cannot . . ."

They stared at each other for a moment in silence.

Then Misha stirred, stepped forward. Behind him, a smaller form stirred, and Dima recognized Ava's friend Reggie from her visit to the loft. So, he thought, his brother had married this hot-tempered redhead, had he? He had been the husband named Misha that the woman had alluded to. Dima had tried to write the name off as a coincidence when he first heard it, but no longer. And it appeared as if their marriage was a strong one, judging by the way his brother gripped the woman's hand like a security blanket. Disbelief had been ousted from his expression and replaced by wonder.

"Vladimir," Misha breathed, halting just before the other man, close enough to touch. But he held back. They both held back. "Vladimir," he repeated, wondering. *"Brat. Eto-vay."*

"Da."

It was anyone's guess how long they might have stood there if Ava hadn't interrupted. Dima felt her eyes on him, but he couldn't tear his own from Misha's face, not after having not seen it in so long. When Dima refused to look at her, she poked him solidly in the ribs.

"What did all that mean?" she demanded. "Was that Russian? Are you Russian, too? Damn it, I was really hoping that was Lithuanian or something you were speaking all those times. Christ, how did I get mixed up with another one of you? Wasn't the one Manhattan already has enough? We needed another one?" She looked at her friend and scowled. "Did you catch any of that? You said he's taught you to speak some Russian. What did they say?"

"Misha called him Brother," Regina said, sounding as confused as her friend. "And he agreed."

Chapter 15

Ava nearly choked on an incredulous gasp. "*Brothers?*" she shouted, stepping back as if they had announced both had leprosy. "You two are *brothers*? Of all the vampires in the world who could have rescued me, I had to be rescued from certain death by Dmitri fricking Vidâme's *brother*?"

Regina made an only slightly less incredulous sound, her gaze traveling from Dima to Misha and back again. "Yes, let's explore this, please. At the moment, I'm really *quite* interested in learning how it's possible that these two are brothers." She looked at her husband and frowned. "When you say that, do you mean 'childhood friends'? Or is it just a 'Yo, bro, 'sup?' Russian cultural thing? Because I know you can't possibly mean 'born from the same womb.'"

"Not the same womb," Misha admitted, not looking away from his brother's face. "The same seed. Technically we are half brothers. My mother died when I was still a child, and my father—*our* father—took Dima's mother as his new wife."

"And you never mentioned this to me in all the years we've been together . . . why, exactly?"

Misha glanced down at his petite spouse, his expression instinctively softening. "*Dushka,* I never thought it would come up. I never expected to see him again, and the whys and wherefores are rather complicated."

"Misha, my idiotic love, so are you."

Ava examined each of the men in question again. "You look nothing alike," she pronounced, still having trouble grasping this revelation.

"Sure they do," Regina said. "They have the same cheekbones, the same jaw. Even their mouths look similar. You can definitely see the resemblance. I think it's the coloring that throws you off at first."

That made sense. After all, Misha had dark hair and eyes so brown they appeared black in all but the brightest lights. His skin was darker, too, with a more olive undertone than Dima's.

"Dima looks like our father," Misha explained. "Eerily so, I must say. For a moment, I thought it was Papa standing before me. I have some of his features, but my coloring comes from my mother. She was a dark-complected Slav from the southern part of Russia, probably with some Romany mixed in. Dima's mother was from Kiev—fair, like our father."

"So you claim him now?" Dima growled. Ava's gaze flew to his face. He hadn't used that dark, threatening tone with her, not even when she'd run away from home and not left a note about where he could find her. "It is eight centuries too late for that, don't you think, Misha?"

"What are you talking about? What makes you think I haven't claimed him all along? Rurik of

Novgorod is as much my father as yours, and I have always admitted this with pride. Why would you think differently?"

Dima stepped forward, his eyes narrowed in anger. "If you honored your father, where were you when he needed you?" His voice shook with such fury that Ava had to steel herself against the urge to back away from him. "Where were you when the stinking Chernigovs waged war against us? For a decade and more we struggled against them, but after Father was slain, our warriors lost heart. With no Dmitri to lead them, they thought the war already lost. And so, lost it was. But *I* remained. I fought on until I, too, fell beneath their alliance with the filthy Turks. But where were you, Dmitri? Why had you abandoned us?"

"Abandoned you?"

Anger flooded Misha's voice as well, and Ava suddenly realized being in the line of fire in this particular little family squabble might not be the best idea. She stepped back.

"Is that what you think? That I abandoned you? My God, I would have given anything to see you again! I left to protect you!"

"Why? Did you believe you were the only reason the Chernigovs attacked us? You could have protected us better if you had stayed and faced them at our sides. Father and I needed you, and you let us think you were dead. Do you have any idea how we felt when we learned differently?"

While Ava was busy looking for a nuclear fallout shelter to climb inside of, Regina planted her hands on her hips and squared off against her newly discovered brother-in-law with the ferocity of a mama grizzly.

"Hey, don't you talk to my husband like that, buster," she warned, displaying the redheaded temper Ava hadn't even known Regina possessed until Misha had come into her life. "If he says he has an explanation for what happened, you owe it to him to listen."

Dima stared down at the fierce pint-sized woman in front of him and snarled. But when he curled his hands into fists, Ava knew it was to keep from strangling Regina, not in preparation for hitting her.

"I owe him nothing," he bit out, turning away from his brother and stalking across the carpet to the wide marble fireplace at the far side of the room.

Ava fought back the urge to follow him, mostly because she wasn't sure where the impulse had come from. She still hadn't decided just what it was they had going on between them, and so far had been planning to go with pretending the sex they'd had last night—the *amazing* sex—hadn't happened. But even if they were now in some sort of strange and disturbing vampire equivalent of a relationship, she wasn't the type to go all melty and protective over a man. Was this unfamiliar desire to comfort him something she was coming up with on her own, or was it another side effect of the blood they shared? And hence another reason to stay the hell away from him so that she could relearn how to think with her brain instead of that alien, unwelcome hunger inside her?

Damn it, she hated this feeling of not being in control of her own damned life. Control was as fundamental to her sense of herself as her intelligence, and giving it up about as alien as shopping in a consignment store. Yet since she had met Dima, the only time she had legitimately been in control of her own actions had been when she had gotten in the limo and ridden across town to Missy and Graham's house. And look how that had turned out. If nothing else, it had very clearly illustrated for her that regaining the control she had always cherished would not be an easy thing to do. From now on, she would always need to remember that her actions affected more than just her and that making the wrong decision could have fatal consequences.

The only way she could shake off the paralysis that threatened when she tried to examine that thought was to put it quickly away and focus on something different. When she considered the obvious problems between Dima and his brother in that light, their argument seemed almost like a godsend.

Slipping on the chic, bored mask she habitually wore, she strolled back to the sofa she'd lain on earlier and sank lazily into the corner. Then she crossed her legs and hooked one elbow over the back.

"Well," she drawled in her best Queen Bitch voice, "I'd certainly like to hear an explanation, if for no other reason than that it's rude to have a conversation when two of the four people in the room are completely clueless about what's actually being said."

Regina shot her a suspicious glance, then smoothed her own expression into one of imperious irritation and settled on the other end of the sofa. "Right, though personally I think it's even ruder to have a conversation in front of one's *wife* about significant family matters that she's never heard of before."

"Where is Emily Post when you need her?"

"Maybe she just never encountered men this rude before."

Misha shot his wife a dirty look. "Thank you, Burns and Allen, for that amusing routine. If you are quite finished . . ."

Ava gave him a toothy smile. "Quite."

"I have no objection to telling the tale, but it seems rather pointless if my little brother refuses to listen."

"I would love to hear what creative excuses my big brother has to offer," Dima retorted, "but I reserve the right to clarify them with the truth."

Misha stiffened. "I do not lie. Especially when I have no reason to do so."

"Then let's hear it, *bratok*." Dima finally turned back to the room, crossing his arms over his chest and propping his shoulder up against the ornately carved mantel. "You perceive me all ears."

Well, ears and bitterness, anyway, Ava thought. She focused most of her attention on Dmitri because she really did want to hear what he had to say, but she kept one eye on Dima all the same. While she might not understand a lot of the feelings she had for him, and might resent a lot of the ones she did recognize, she couldn't deny that seeing him upset left her feeling . . . discontent.

"The explanation is neither long nor complex," Misha sighed. "You grew up in the same world that I did, Dima. Our father's people were good people, but they were products of their time. They had no education to speak of, no knowledge of the world outside their village or their region other than what they heard as tales from travelers or legends told around campfires. They still believed that a witch in the village was the cause if crops sickened and died, and they thought that the *domorovoi*—the local spirits—would be offended if they did not leave offerings in gratitude for their livestock not disappearing in the night."

"You speak as if I do not know all this, but I do not see what it has to do with your disappearance."

"Perhaps that is because while you grew up among their superstitions, you were never the target of them."

Ava watched Dima's face crease in a frown. "What do you mean?"

Misha's mouth twisted wryly. "I remember how relieved our father's people were when he announced his choice of new bride," he said instead of answering the question. "I was only eleven years old at the time, but I remember the cheer that went up in the crowd. They were so grateful to hear that this time he had chosen a local girl, a respectable virgin from a respectable family that everyone knew and liked. After my mother, they all wanted the peace."

Ava could see the question growing on the other man's face, but he remained silent and allowed his brother to continue.

"My mother had been an outsider, brought back by our father from a trading journey he had made to the southwest. He stayed away for nearly a year and traveled further than anyone had expected. In addition to trading the goods he had imported from Scandinavia, he was searching for new items, and he traveled along the western edge of the Black Sea all the way into what are now Hungary and Romania. But in addition to finding trade goods, Papa found himself a bride, a fiery gypsy girl with dark hair and dark eyes. And, so his people came to believe, dark magic."

Dima blinked. "I remember no rumors that your mother was a witch. In fact, I do not recall anyone speaking of her much at all."

Misha snorted. "Of course not. During her life, they believed she would put a curse on anyone who showed her the slightest sign of disrespect. They believed that if they spoke ill of her after death, she would never cease to haunt them."

Ava felt her impatience rising and raised an arrogant brow in the older vampire's direction. "I thought you said this explanation wasn't long?"

That earned her a glare.

"The explanation is not. The backstory is."

She rolled her eyes. "Whatever. Do you think you could do a little judicious editing? I might not be getting any older, but it certainly feels like I am."

"The bottom line," Misha growled, shooting Ava an impatient glance, "is that while our people loved Papa, and by extension loved both of his sons, in the back of their minds, they could never quite forget who my mother had been. They never quite trusted me the way they did Father."

"That is a lie." The denial came swiftly and violently. "I remember how they spoke of you in the same tones they used to speak of God! They worshiped you!"

Dima's brother shook his head. "They feared me. I was thirty years old when I was turned, Brother, and yet I had never married. In that age, such behavior was freakish. By thirty, I should have been looking forward to grandchildren. Indeed, there were whispers that marriage to my mother had unnaturally prolonged our father's life. He had reached his fiftieth year, and yet he could still best any of his men with a sword or an axe. Most men of his age had retired to sit by fires and tell tall tales of their glory days, if they had even survived so long. Our people believed that my mother's magic had blessed Father with long life but cursed me with a taint to my soul."

"I cannot believe this. And even if I did—"

"Dozens of men saw me fall on that battlefield," Misha pressed on. "Seasoned warriors saw the Turk I battled skewer me through the gut. They knew there was no way I could survive such an injury, and indeed, when the battle was over and they claimed a dear victory, they left me for dead where I had fallen. What do you think would have happened if I had reappeared in our father's hall a month later? They would have believed me returned from the dead to haunt them as my mother would have done. And if I had tried to explain that as I lay dying, a woman appeared on the field that night and offered to return me to health, to grant me eternal life in exchange for my aid in avenging the death of her younger sister . . . If I told them that she drank my blood and fed me hers in return, and that when the strange ritual was finished, I watched as the wound in my stomach knit itself back together, leaving no scar and no sign that I had ever wandered so close to death's door?" He laughed at the image. "I would have been cast as the devil, and they would have said it was no wonder, as I had been tainted by my mother's blood."

There was silence for a moment, and Ava watched Dima's face as he attempted to process the story and to reconcile it with beliefs he had held for so long.

"You didn't even send us word," he finally said, and beneath the anger, Ava could hear the confusion of a young boy deserted by the brother he idolized. "We grieved for you until I thought the heart had been cut from my father's chest. He died believing he would see you again in the next world, and I shared that belief for years, until after I had been turned as well, and I traveled to the land of the Bohemians and heard tales of a dark Russian who battled the Mongols with the ferocity of a demon and who never appeared in the light of the sun. It was then that I learned you had betrayed us. All of that time you had been alive, and yet you left us to mourn you and to fight the battles you should have fought at our sides."

"Do you think it was easy for me to stay away? Do you think I enjoyed the isolation? The exile? I would have given *anything,* including my immortality, if I could have returned to you and seen our father again!"

Dima's eyes blazed. "Why didn't you? We would have accepted you. Father would have accepted you had you told him you were the devil himself. And we would have shielded you from any who thought to do you harm out of fear or superstition."

Misha took a deep breath, and Ava saw Regina's hand tighten on his, offering comfort, promising support. "I was going to," he said softly. "By the year you reached your twenty-fifth birthday, I had begun to realize that, and to regret my own foolishness. But then I began to look into what had happened at home, and I learned that—"

"That you were too late." Dima finished the sentence for him, his tone flat and cold, but underneath, Ava could hear the disappointment. "Father had been slain, and with him, your reason for returning."

"No. There you are wrong." Misha shook his head very definitely. "I still planned to come. Even with our father gone, if you remained, I had ample reason to return to Novgorod."

"I cannot believe that. If you had wanted to return, you would have. And it would not have been eight hundred years between our last encounter and this one."

Calmly, Misha waited until his brother turned a challenging stare in his direction. Then he caught Dima's gaze and said quietly, "They told me you had died, too."

"When?" The younger brother's tone echoed with surprise. "Who told you that I had died? The Chernigovs? You would never have been so stupid as to take their word for such a thing."

"No, which was why I sought confirmation from

several sources. I knew better than to trust the bragging of a Chernigov, but I did trust the word of your mother. When Ireniya told me of your death, I believed her, for I saw pain and despair in her eyes of the kind that touches a woman when both her man and her child are taken from her by her enemies."

"That is impossible. My mother knew that I was injured and that the vampire Stepan Chernigov nearly had stolen my life from me, that he had cursed me by forcing an unwilling change upon me, but it was she who cared for me when I crawled back from the battlefield. She knew perfectly well that I survived."

Ava was watching Dima's face carefully, so she saw when the first seed of doubt planted itself in his consciousness, saw when his memories began to shift, and something old and familiar suddenly took on new significance.

"Dima," she prompted quietly when he remained silent. "What is it? What did your mother do?"

He lifted his head, his eyes blindly scanning the room, flashing over the faces of the people around him until they locked on Ava's. She shivered when she saw them, for she had never seen them look so empty, nor full of so much pain. Without thought, she surrendered to the tug they inspired within her, standing and crossing to where he stood beside the empty hearth.

She reached out, hesitated, then let her hand fall back to his side. She didn't know how to touch him. Providing consolation had never been her strong suit. All her life, she'd stood separate from people, even those she loved most, and now, even though her heart urged her with great surges of violent emotion, she couldn't quite bring herself to take his hand or place her own over his heart. A gesture like that would be too much, too intimate.

Instead, she turned so that they stood side by side, facing out from the corner into the room at large. She leaned into him and let her shoulder press softly into his upper arm. It wasn't a large gesture, nor a particularly lover-like one, but it was something. Something to remind him of the connection he had to her, to the present, to people who cared and wanted to know his story.

He kept silent another moment, then let out a ragged breath full of wonder and hurt and disappointment.

"She killed herself," he said, his voice gruff and quiet, as if to say the words too loudly would be some sort of offense. "I thought she had drowned. Everyone thought she had drowned. It had been cold for more than a week, and everyone thought that she had assumed the river had frozen just as they had. They thought she was walking along it when the ice gave beneath her, that the weight of her clothes and the cold of the water overcame her and pulled her to the bottom. But it was a lie. She killed herself, because of me."

Ava saw Regina frown in confusion, the same confusion she felt but did not know how to express.

"That doesn't make sense." Regina's forehead furrowed in confusion. "Why would she kill herself because of you? I mean, if you had died, maybe I could understand. You know, the shock of losing you after the death of your father. But to kill herself after nursing you back from your injuries . . . that doesn't make sense."

Misha squeezed her hand and shook his head sadly. "It would have to Ireniya. She was a devout Christian, much more devout than anyone else in the family, or in the village, where they still prayed often to the pagan gods of the area. She would not have understood Dima's transformation. For him to become a vampire would have amounted to something worse than his death for her. She would have believed that his soul itself had died. It's what she thought of me when I last spoke to her, when she told me Dima had died. It must have been right before she took her own life."

"She never even told me she had seen you," Dima said. "She just went for a walk and didn't return."

"And you were left with no one."

Ava knew the anger she felt had crept into her voice, but she couldn't help it. It was just too much. His older brother's desertion had obviously wounded him, and although she thought Misha was an idiot, she sort of got what he'd been thinking. In a weird sort of way, he'd been trying to protect his family from the taint of being associated with what those around them would have perceived as "evil." Their father's death would have added to that burden of sadness, but death in battle had been part of life back then—devastating but understandable. But for Dima's mother to then go and kill herself was an action that Ava could not forgive.

Suicide was the ultimate act of selfishness, and

she could admit that now as a person who had briefly considered that it would be better to end her life than to live it as a vampire. That, however, had been before she had looked into Dima's eyes and seen the pain that could linger after the act even almost eight hundred years later. His mother had caused him that grief, had caused it by believing that ending her own pain was more important than the suffering she would cause to the son she left behind. Committing suicide essentially said to friends and loved ones and the world at large that you were the only thing that mattered, that *your* problems were hopeless, that *you* deserved to escape from them, and to hell with everyone else.

Suicide was nothing more than a way to look in the eye of the people who loved you and say, *My pain is paramount, and I want it to end. The pain you will feel when I am gone, and the guilt you will experience at not having been able to stop me, do not matter to me. I am willing for you to suffer for the rest of your life so that I can take the easy way out of mine.*

If Ireniya had been alive and standing in front of Ava today, Ava would cheerfully have killed her.

Misha dropped his wife's hand, stepped away from the sofa, and crossed to face his brother in front of the cool fireplace. When Misha spoke, his voice was low and full of regret. Even Ava could hear his sincerity.

"For my part in that, I apologize, *bratok,*" he said, humble in a way Ava had never thought possible, let alone seen before. "I never knew you were alone, for if I had, I would have come to you regardless of the consequences. I know what it is like to feel true loneliness, and it is a fate I would wish on no one, especially not a beloved brother." He reached out, placed his hand on his brother's shoulder, dark eyes meeting blue and holding. "I do not know if I deserve your forgiveness, Dima, but if you were to give it, you would have my eternal gratitude. Either way, you will have my eternal love, from brother to brother."

Ava watched the emotions scroll across Dima's face like slides of microfiche—first denial and betrayal and anger and hurt, then sadness and acceptance, forgiveness and love. The second set lay as a purifying blanket of snow over the first, not washing it away, but softening it and eroding it so that in the spring there would be something new and better that grew from its rubble.

"I have only one brother," Dima answered finally, his voice low and harsh, "and I have just found him after many lifetimes apart. I do not want to lose him again, no matter what pasts lie between us." He raised his own arm, placed his hand on Misha's opposite shoulder. *"Bratok."*

They looked into each other's eyes, searching; then each quirked a lip in a mirror-image half smile.

Regina sniffled. "That's so beautiful."

Missy handed her a box of tissues. "It really is. I love happy endings."

Behind them, Samantha cleared her throat. "Um, so do I. Except that I'm not sure we can actually call this an ending."

Graham glanced at her. "Why not?"

"Because while I was checking my files for information about the connection between Misha and Mr. Rurikovich, I was also making a phone call." She took the inside of her lower lip between her teeth and gazed with fascination down at her feet. "Since he was in town on official business, I figured that I should follow standard procedure."

Graham swore, loudly, but the sound did not drown out Misha's own profanity, this one uttered in forceful, guttural Russian.

Samantha cringed. "I'm sorry. I thought I was doing what I was supposed to."

Missy reached up to grasp the Lupine woman's hand. "It's all right, Sam. You didn't do anything wrong. I think the boys are just grumpy is all. They don't really blame you for anything."

Misha glared in Missy's direction. "Speak for yourself."

Regina smacked him. "She's speaking for *all* of us. Because *none* of us can blame what's going to happen next on Sam. It was inevitable. The fact that she sped it up a little is nothing we can hold against her."

Ava felt a stirring of concern. You know, just a twinge. "What exactly is going to happen next?"

Misha was the one who answered, and his grim expression did nothing to reassure Ava or to quiet the butterflies in her stomach.

"The council. It's time to explain to them exactly what's going on."

Chapter 16

The chambers where the Manhattan Council of Others met were tucked beneath the concealing floors of the Vircolac club and were accessed by a stairway from inside the club that was guarded at all times by members of the Silverback Clan's security team. It also, Ava discovered, was decorated like something out of the imagination of Vincent Price.

She had managed not to goggle when she and Dima were led down into the club's basements and through a series of stone corridors lit with actual torches. Torches! In twenty-first-century New York. Someone involved in this thing was taking the whole "creatures of the night" thing just a little too seriously.

She thought the same thing when she met the actual members of the council itself. They were lucky, Reggie had assured her, to be meeting only the "Inner Council" of a couple of dozen members and not the full council of nearly two hundred. Ava felt sure she would be grateful for that, just as soon as the lot of them stopped staring at her as if she were a particularly rancid-smelling homeless person who wouldn't stop asking them for spare change. As usual, she met any sign of disapproval or distaste with the kind of attitude and appearance that said, *Think what you like, peon. I am too important and perfect to care for the opinions of others. And, by the way, did you step in something, because I detect a whiff of something . . . unpleasant.*

Thankfully, after changing into the clothes Missy had sent for on her behalf, Ava looked good enough to pull it off. She touched the lapels of her slim pin-striped waistcoat discreetly and pretended to care about what Rafael De Santos was saying to the rest of the crowd. Rafe was the current head of the Council of Others and husband of practicing witch and herbalist Tess De Santos. Tess had become a good friend of Missy's and had begun attending girls' nights several years ago.

"There are reasons we do not have rules like that, Preston," Rafe was saying as Ava tuned back in to the debate, his faintly accented voice sounding both polite and completely in control. And as if his patience had begun to wear thin. "Unlike our European brethren, we do not believe we should punish the victim for the actions of the criminal. It is not Ms. Markham's fault that a rogue vampire attacked her and turned her, nor do I think we should fault Mr. Rurikovich for choosing to aid her rather than allowing her to die or to suffer through a painful transformation unaided."

The man to whom Rafe had addressed himself, a portly older man in a wrinkled three-piece suit, opened his mouth as if to launch another protest, but

Rafe cut him off with a raised hand and a raised voice.

"Ladies and gentlemen," the jaguar Felix said, his voice calling all the room to order, "I believe we have strayed from our topic. It is not our prerogative nor our intention to sit in judgment over the actions of either of our guests. Rather, we have gathered so that we may decide what actions need to be taken now that we have heard their news from the European Council of Vampires."

Yes, and the news had been received with all the enthusiasm with which the inhabitants of glass houses received the news of a forecast for hailstorms and the reinstitution of public stonings. After hearing about the rogue who had killed one human woman then attacked and turned Ava; the mission Dima had been sent to New York to carry out; and the communication the female vampire had sent to Ava, the council had acted as if the only matter for concern was Dima's breach in protocol. The only thing they got ticked about was that they had not been alerted of his mission immediately upon his arrival in New York. They thought their right to know trumped the fact that a convicted multiple murderer and violent megalomaniac was on the loose in their city and looking to raise an army of new vampires to help her wage war against most of Eastern and Central Europe.

"I think we have all agreed that we disapprove of our European friends' tactics in this case," Rafe continued, ruthlessly steering the group back onto the track of the discussion, "but that does not help us to deal with Yelizaveta Chernigov."

"She displayed a lack of respect for the laws set down by this council several years ago," Misha said from his seat near the middle of the long conference table—Ava thought it was actually an antique dining table, late eighteenth century, probably English or French. "At that time, she sent a representative to our city with instructions to kill the head of the council and recruit as many new vampires as possible into her house. I have no doubt, after hearing Dima's story, that Yelizaveta is back up to her old tricks. She must be stopped."

There was a brief silence around the table.

"I don't think anyone is arguing with that." This came from a small woman with East Indian features and a certain feline cast to her face. "We are not debating whether or not this Chernigov woman is a threat, or whether or not we must take steps to have her recaptured and returned to the ECV to serve out the punishment they have given her. The question, I think we would all agree, is how should we do it?"

There were murmurs of agreement.

"After all, she isn't really our problem at the moment," said a small man with a sharp, pointy face and whisker-like stubble. His voice was high and, like his movements, tended to dart from one spot to another. "We shouldn't have to risk our people. Why risk our people when she isn't our problem? Contact the ECV, I say. Contact them and tell them to send more men. Let them take care of it."

"If the ECV sends an army," Dima warned, "Yelizaveta will dig in her heels and we'll have an all-out war on your soil. If you think you will be able to remain out of it in those circumstances, I suggest you think again."

"There are those of us already here who would be happy to join in any action the council authorizes against Chernigov." Misha's undertone of eagerness left little doubt that he counted himself among that group.

Dima shook his head. "While I appreciate the support, I have believed all along that stealth is what will triumph over Yelizaveta Chernigov. I have no more desire to raise an army here than I have to send to the ECV for one. I would much prefer that I and one or two others infiltrate the target's resting spot, the place where she will be surrounded by the fewest guards and minions. That way we can get it, take her by surprise, subdue her, and bring her out again with minimum fuss and the least amount of risk for anyone to be harmed."

"If you have such a fine plan, young man, why haven't you executed it already?"

Ava looked across the table at the speaker, an old woman with silver hair and dark eyes and the kind of commanding presence Ava wanted to be able to maintain when she reached that age.

For the first time it occurred to Ava that when she reached that age, she would still look exactly the same as she did today. The thought made her a little wistful that she'd never get the opportunity to be a crotchety old woman. Then she realized that just because she wouldn't look like a crotchety old woman didn't mean she couldn't act like one, and she felt a little better. The element of surprise, she knew, was not to be taken lightly.

Dima turned his attention to the woman and spoke with carefully civil tones. "Up until now, I was unable to locate her. Yelizaveta is arrogant, but she is not stupid. She knows enough not to broadcast her whereabouts to those outside of her own house while she is still being pursued by the European Council."

"Up until now?" The old woman seized on the phrasing like a terrier with a juicy soup bone. "That sounds like you recently made something of a breakthrough. Am I right?"

"You are. Yelizaveta recently made contact with Ms. Markham and revealed her whereabouts."

"Well, then what are you waiting for, you young pup? Go out there and get her!"

Rafe smiled at the old woman, amused but clearly still respectful. "I believe our guest would like to use a bit more finesse than just knocking down her front door, Ms. Berry."

The name clicked in Ava's mind. The old woman was Adele Berry, grand dame of Manhattan Other society and grandmother of another occasional girls' night guest, Cassidy Quinn. Ava had heard that Cassidy, her husband, and her family were very involved in the politics of the council, but she'd never expected to see any of them in action.

Adele made a noise that, coming from any other woman, Ava might have called a grunt, and leaned back in her seat. The change in position made it clear that her right hand rested not on the arm of her chair but on the top of a silver-headed cane she rested on the floor beside her. "That seems like a lot of trouble."

Dima turned away from the old woman and focused on Rafe instead. Ava could almost see him thinking that at least the Felix was likely to speak reasonably. "Thanks to Ms. Markham, we have recently learned of the location that Yelizaveta is using for her headquarters," he said, "but the only information we have is the address. I don't know what the building is like or how many men or guards she keeps on hand, let alone what room or rooms she uses for her private quarters. If we want to take her there, we need to know where they are and when she's most likely to be in them."

"Ah, so you need a plan, then." Adele nodded sagely. "Best look to the women, then. I've never known a man who could strategize as well as an intelligent woman."

Ava had to bite back a smile. Damn, but she could get to like that old biddy. "Actually," Ava spoke up, "I had a thought. I don't know if it qualifies as a plan, per se, but I believe it makes sense to try it."

Dima looked at her, and she could tell from his frown that he was already feeling a bit suspicious. "What are you talking about? What sort of plan have you thought up?"

Next to his brother, Misha scowled. "I have found over the years that it is best to ignore her when she says things like that, *bratok*. Asking questions will only encourage her."

Ava shot Misha a look that might have done Adele

Berry proud, then ignored him. "The reason you know where to find Yelizaveta is because she sent me a note summoning me to meet her there," she reminded Dima. "I don't see why we should waste time trying to come up with some complicated plan involving the cover of darkness and a bunch of gadgets out of a James Bond movie when we already have the perfect excuse to show up at her place and ask for a tour."

"No." Dima's denial was swift and loud, and she hadn't even finished explaining what she intended.

"It's simple," she continued. "I'll answer the summons and go to Yelizaveta's lair. While I'm there, I can make note of all the details you need to know to get inside and then report back. Or if you're worried I might forget something, you can tag along inside my head. Simple, straightforward, and low risk. So what do you think?"

Dima glared at her, and his warning was a silken threat. "I think I'd like to see you try it."

Chapter 17

Dima spent the next day and a half regretting those words. Bitterly.

He had been the only one unimpressed with Ava's idea. The council had thought it was brilliant. No surprise there, since most of them had never met Ava before, and so had no personal feelings for her whatsoever. They wouldn't worry about what could happen to her when she wandered into Yelizaveta's lair, alone and unprotected, and started sticking her nose into the woman's business. If the vampiress even suspected why Ava was there, Yelizaveta would kill her—without hesitation and without mercy.

But Dima was supposed to sit back and pretend that watching it didn't bother him? Yeah. Right.

Tonight he sat in a small sitting room at Vircolac and brooded about the fact that when the sun set again tomorrow, he would be confined to listening in Ava's head while she walked into the den of the lion and prepared to tug its tail. The mood such contemplation had put him in was the reason that he was up here alone instead of in one of the game rooms with Misha and Graham and several of their other friends playing poker to pass the time. They had kicked his sorry ass out for being a "downer." So he had come upstairs, to the small two-bedroom suite Graham had given him and Ava to stay in for the night. Vircolac was closer to Yelizaveta's headquarters than the loft was. Ava remained with her girlfriends somewhere downstairs.

Dima didn't actually enjoy his own company at the moment any more than anyone else did, but he was the only one without a choice. He had to stick around regardless.

Last night he'd had panic, anger, and more panic to occupy his evening, and during most of the day he'd taken advantage of the blessed oblivion of sleep, but at the moment it was 11:00 P.M. and he was about as sleepy as a camp sentry surrounded by a forest full of Turks preparing an ambush. He felt even jumpier than one.

Part of that could come from the way he'd spent the first half of his evening. Just after dusk, once everyone was awake, he had sat down with Misha, Graham, and Rafe, their wives—who refused to be excluded for some reason—and Ava to review the plan for her trip to Yelizaveta's hideout. Ava had wanted to keep things simple. Go in, see what the bitch wanted, poke around, and leave, and she hadn't taken well to his suggestions that things just might *not* go that smoothly. She wasn't used to people who didn't automatically agree with her assessment of herself as undisputed queen of the universe, and the idea that Yelizaveta might be part of that small group seemed hard for her to grasp. It was almost as though, while she understood the words when he said them, somewhere between her eardrum and her frontal lobe, the message got lost or garbled. In her mind, everything would go smoothly because for her, everything usually did.

When he'd reminded her of Friday night, she'd actually gotten a bit offended. He still hadn't decided if it was because she was embarrassed that she hadn't looked at things that way, or because she honestly took offense to the idea of not always having things her own way. With Ava, he had quickly discovered, either was a possibility.

It was also a possibility that she had gotten offended when he had tried to forbid her from taking part in the entire operation.

Dima sighed and flipped idly through the television channels from his spot propped up against the arm of a sofa that was comfortable, but too small for his frame. It needed at least another foot added to the end to accommodate someone his size. Even half-sitting, he had to prop his feet up on the opposite arm to keep from having to bend his knees. He could think of a million other ways he would rather be spending the night, but then again, he'd already thought of at least half of them while he'd been sitting with the others and reluctantly agreeing that Ava's invitation gave them the best opportunity they were likely to get to do a thorough casing of Yelizaveta's building.

Samantha had traced the address on the note Ava had received and provided Graham with an interesting leg up on their inquiries. It turned out that, as befitted her taste, Yelizaveta had not been content to rent an apartment or a building in Manhattan or wait for a place she wanted to come onto the market for sale. Instead, she had decided where she wanted to set up her base—Fifth Avenue—and picked out the building she wanted. Since it wasn't on the market— as few classical town-house mansions in the heart of Museum Mile were—she had simply sent her people to kill their people and moved right in.

A remnant of old Knickerbocker New York, Wadsworth House had been the home of a wealthy early-nineteenth-century industrialist by the name of Russell Morgan Wadsworth II, who had built it for his wife, who had promptly snubbed his gift by dying. It had remained a private home for many years, stayed miraculously in the hands of the family, and wound up, situated as it was between the Cooper-Hewitt and The Jewish Museum, just blocks from the Met and across the street from Central Park, something of a museum in its own right, a privately owned house occupied by a wealthy, aging eccentric with a passion for lending his home for charity functions and then criticizing their catering. Jonathan Russell Wadsworth-Chatham enjoyed equal fame with this magnificent house, and reveled in their notoriety.

Or at least he had. Since about sixteen weeks ago, no one had seen or heard from him at all. Not even when the Avery Foundation for African Refugees had hired Passionate Affair—the company owned by his former lover Geoffrey Orchand—to cater the event and then hosted it just down the street in the "drab, intimacy-crushing echo chambers" of the Metropolitan Museum of Art. That was what Jonathan had called it last time, according to the article in *The New Yorker* that Samantha had cited. His disappearance was the hip new Manhattan murder mystery, and everyone in the city was wondering who'd done it.

Everyone, of course, except for Dima.

He knew perfectly well what had happened to the unfortunate man whose only sin had been to own a piece of property that Yelizaveta had wanted for herself. Dima knew that the man either was now a corpse, drained of blood and disposed of in some anonymous dump site, or had been kept as a mindless servant for the vampire's ease and amusement. Neither fate was one the man had deserved, no matter how sharp his tongue had been.

Now Dima was supposed to let his woman walk into that spider's web with nothing more concrete than her promise to him that she "would be fine." He would rather have faced Yelizaveta himself, naked, weaponless, with his hands tied behind his back.

Dima had to admit it: he'd fallen for the prickly woman with the fierce temper. He had no idea how, and very little idea why, given how badly they'd gotten along for most of the time that they'd known each other, but it didn't seem to matter. Every time he was in the same room with her, his heart and mind went soft, even while his body hardened. Every time he thought she might be in danger, his breathing froze, his blood pressure skyrocketed, and he could think of nothing else until he had found her and reassured himself of her safety.

That was how it had been last night when he had

returned to the loft and discovered her missing. He had been convinced that she had wandered outside and been seized and attacked on the street, by either a vampire protecting his territory or a fundamentalist activist who wanted to see all bloodsuckers destroyed. Then Dima had only imagined her to be in danger. How the hell was he going to cope when he *knew* she was in danger?

"You'll practically be right there," she had said, dismissing his worries with a wave of her elegant hand. "I've agreed—very reluctantly—to let you into my head while I'm in the mansion. If anything goes wrong, you'll know right away and you can send in the cavalry with my blessing. Believe me, I would find myself very unhappy to almost die again, so if the time comes when you need to rush to the rescue, please feel free."

He hoped she had really meant those words, because if he sensed that she would be in danger from Yelizaveta or any of her flunkies, he wouldn't hesitate to tear bodies apart in order to get to her.

This wasn't something he'd ever expected to happen. When a man went through the equivalent of more than a hundred lifetimes without ever finding a woman he could imagine spending eternity with, it tended to make him rethink the idea of a committed relationship. Was something like true love even possible? And if it was, could there really be someone out there for everyone? It had been a very long time since Dima had drawn the conclusion that the fairy tales were, quite simply, bullshit. Love as they portrayed it did not exist.

Actually, now that he thought about it, he supposed what he felt for Ava really did nothing to disprove that. After all, the love in those stories was always pure and shining and self-sacrificial. It made couples content to gaze into each other's eyes and to view their partners as nothing short of perfect. If Dima had been in the throes of a fairy-tale love, shouldn't he have viewed the object of his affections as perfect and sweet and all that was good and loving? A woman like that would bear absolutely no resemblance whatsoever to Ava Markham.

The Ava he loved was prickly, arrogant, rude, stubborn, ungracious, mostly tactless, haughty, and occasionally cruel. And when he listed it all out like that, he decided he had to be completely off his rocker to consider wanting to remain with her for long after he had completed his mission. But then he would remember that she was strong, intelligent, perceptive, decisive, fiercely loyal, and utterly fearless, and he would feel his heart clench in his chest, sending him over the edge once more.

Acknowledging his love for her might have made him happier, he reflected, if he had the faintest inkling of her feelings for him. Unfortunately, in addition to her other faults, Ava kept her thoughts and emotions stubbornly under her own control, and he had kept his word that he wouldn't invade them without an invitation. It felt a lot like having hobbled himself of his own free will. His brain fairly itched with the desire to poke inside her mind, just a little, just for a minute or two, just until he could get a sense of whether she felt anything for him other than the resentment and irritation she generally showed when he was around.

He had thought he saw a hint of something more the night before, in the sitting room next door when he and Misha had been caught up in their emotional reunion. She had moved near him after all, lending him the support of her presence, if nothing else, but from what he could tell, she would have done the same for any of her friends. How could he tell if what she felt for him was any different from what she felt for Missy or Regina?

Well, for starters, I doubt she's ever ridden either of them like a championship barrel racer, his subconscious taunted.

Dima dismissed it. Sex, he knew, was not something by which you could judge the quality of a relationship. The night they had spent together in his loft might have been the most amazing sex either of them had ever had—which was slightly more impressive when Dima said it—but it was still sex. The relationship Dima had decided he wanted needed something a bit more substantial as a foundation if he was to build something lasting upon it.

The problem, he acknowledged, was getting Ava to open up about her feelings—the deep ones that she always kept to herself. He had noticed that she would share the easy ones, the ones on the surface, without the slightest hesitation. She had no trouble expressing anger or impatience or frustration or sympathy, but they were like barriers she held in front of her to keep from exposing the softer, more vulnerable parts underneath. She didn't show him love or need or fear, and he doubted she showed them to anyone else, either. He knew that her friends had no doubts about her love for them, but he thought that was because she had demonstrated it, quietly, in so many ways for so many years that they accepted it the way they accepted that it would rain in April or snow in February. It was just the way their world worked.

He thought Ava's world was more complicated than that. In her world, trust seemed to be a commodity that was not easily come by, though once given, it appeared to be unshakable. Otherwise she would not have gone to Missy and Graham when she ran from Dima. He actually found it astounding that she trusted the Alpha Lupine at all. Neither of them made a secret of their animosity for the other, yet each seemed completely comfortable—in their own strange way—turning to the other for help when it made sense to do so. Graham had made no fuss about trusting Ava to survey Yelizaveta's headquarters, even though he had volunteered to enter the building with Dima when they were ready to take the vampire back into custody; if he did so, he would be putting his life into Ava's hands, trusting that she would not have provided false or inaccurate information.

Likewise, Ava had complete confidence in the fact that Graham, though quite strong enough to rip her limb from limb should he choose, would not harm her. The solidity and unthinking reflex of that belief proved it to be one of long standing, which meant that even as a defenseless human, she had felt the same way, because she trusted that Graham's love for Missy would prevent him from harming one of his wife's closest friends. More than that, she trusted that at his core, Graham was not a wanton killer, not the type of Other who would slaughter the innocent simply because he possessed the ability to do so.

Dima wanted to earn that kind of trust from her. Whether or not it was possible was another question entirely.

She had walls, his Ava, thick, high ones, some of which had been planted with briar roses to keep out anyone adventurous enough to try to scale them. He thought he knew where a few of them were and had made note of the gaps that could allow him to worm his way inside; but just when he thought he had the landscape down, he would turn a corner and find a new maze of moats and fences, and have to start all over again.

Was anyone, he asked himself, really worth all this work?

As he pondered that question, the door to the suite opened and a figure stepped inside. He could have been blind and he would have known who it was. All she had to do was breathe in his direction and his entire body went on high alert, tense and ready for action—of one kind or another.

She said nothing for several minutes, just stood with her back to the door and her dark eyes on him. He wanted badly to know what she was thinking, considered taking just a peek, but resisted. He couldn't seem to bring himself to do anything that would truly upset her or cross the boundaries she'd so clearly laid out. Seven hundred ninety-three years old, and he'd been brought to heel by a woman barely in her thirties. There were moments when he didn't think he could bear the shame of it.

He also couldn't bear to have her watching him and not know what she was thinking. He lifted the remote control, lowered the television volume to a quiet murmur.

"I thought you were going to spend the rest of the night with your friends."

She shrugged and pushed away from the door to take a seat in an armchair that angled near the end of the sofa on which he lay. "I thought about it, but they were starting to get a little Ward and June on me. I can't handle that kind of thing."

"Ward and June?"

"Pictures of domestic bliss. When Missy started talking about new ways she'd found to let Graham know she still needed a little romance now and then, even after all their years together, I panicked and ran." Her mouth curved in a wry smile. "I thought you'd be spending your time talking to your brother. After all, you certainly have a lot of catching up to do."

Dima shook his head. "We do, but I think both of us are feeling a bit overwhelmed by it. We each have a lot of old ways of thinking to adjust, and that's going to take time. Now that we've seen each other and broken through that barrier, we know we have all the time in the world to get reacquainted."

"Very true."

There was a moment of silence. Each watched the other and waited.

"I thought you might want to go over a few things about tomorrow night."

Ava finally broke the silence, shifting as she spoke to smoothly cross her legs at the knees. Even wearing a pair of old sweatpants and a baggy Columbia University T-shirt from the collection Missy apparently kept on hand for emergencies, Ava looked like a queen, elegant and calm and regal. Only the way that one manicured fingernail beat a quick, uneven rhythm on the arm of her chair betrayed the restlessness of her mind.

When Dima didn't respond, she arched a brow and pursed her lips. "You seemed . . . uncomfortable when we laid out the strategy earlier."

That was one word for it, he supposed. "I am. I think you are taking a large risk for something we could achieve in other ways."

"But not as quickly or as easily."

"Perhaps." He shrugged. "But as you have pointed out before, I am your mentor and not your keeper. If this is what you truly wish to do, I cannot stop you."

"Sure you could."

He inclined his head but kept his gaze on hers. He wasn't quite sure what she was getting at, but he knew it wouldn't pay to be caught completely unwary. "Did you want me to? I am certain that you only need to say you have changed your mind and no one would expect you to put yourself in danger, nor would they hold your change of heart against you."

She snorted. "I would."

He sent her a questioning look. More than that, he thought, might spook her.

Her mouth tightened. "I don't go back on my word. Not when there are already so many people who have a corner on that market. I said that I would go, and I will."

"It's not your responsibility."

"It might not have started out that way, but I made it mine when I volunteered. I won't abandon it now."

His mouth slowly curved into a smile. "I could have used more men like you, back when wars were fought by individuals instead of by machines and puppet masters."

She gave him a look of almost pitying disappointment. "Those wars are still fought every day, Dima. In fact, they're the only ones that matter."

Dima looked at her, really looked at her, and saw the shadows again, the ones that lurked behind her eyes when she thought no one could see. But he could. He always knew when they were there. Maybe he was the only one who had ever looked.

"Yes, they are," he said, his voice low and quiet and intimate in the dimly lit room. "What is your war over, *lyubushka*?"

"What does that mean?" she asked him, broadly sidestepping the question. "You're always calling me things in Russian, which as far as I'm concerned is a cheap trick. If you're insulting me, I want to be able to defend myself, and if you're not, then I want to at least get a charge out of a compliment now and then."

"*Lyubushka* means 'sweetie,' " he translated easily.

"What about *kukla*?"

" 'Pretty little girl,' like a doll."

Her brows rose. "What about *nen-* . . . *nenag-* . . . Damn, you use a lot of consonants." She tried again. "*Nenaglyadnaya*?"

"What are you fighting, sweetheart?" He turned her avoidance technique around to her. "What is your war over?"

"My war is never over."

"And you will not tell me what it concerns?"

Ava pursed her lips. "It doesn't concern you."

He corrected her softly. "I believe that it does."

"Why?" she shot back.

"Because everything about you concerns me. That is what happens when a man falls in love."

If he hadn't been watching her so closely, he might not have seen it. He wasn't certain it wouldn't have been better if he'd missed it. Because of all the expressions a man wants to see on the face of his woman when he tells her he loves her for the first time, this wasn't it. Ava looked as if he had shot her in the heart and left her to bleed to death on the rich Persian carpet.

Chapter 18

He might as well have stabbed her in the chest, Ava thought, dazed. Of all the things he could have said to her, all the insults he could have thrown, all the observations he could have made, that was the one phrase in this universe that was guaranteed to take the little bits of herself—the ones that she had salvaged from her childhood and painstakingly knit back together from the shreds left by her neglectful, selfish parents—to take them and throw them on the floor and stomp on them with freshly sharpened golf cleats.

What the hell had he been thinking?

Ignoring the way her heart stuttered and clenched at the words, she fixed him with a calm look of mild surprise. It cost her the soul of her firstborn child to achieve it.

"I think you must be mistaken. Maybe the stress of the last three days is getting to you. Do you take a vitamin supplement by any chance? I hear they can work wonders."

"I take it you have some doubts about my sincerity," he commented wryly.

"No, only your sanity."

He tilted his head in question. "You find it insane that a man should have fallen in love with you?"

She laid her palms flat over the arms of the chair she sat in, hoping the fabric would absorb the sweat that had begun to form there. "I think *love* is a pretty word for an ugly game. And I think that in the space of three days, the only thing a man is capable of falling into is trouble."

"I cannot argue that you have caused some of that."

Her eyes narrowed. "Let me advise you that telling a woman she's a troublemaker is not among the top ten ways to convince her that you love her."

Dima shrugged. "You have just told me that you don't believe I'm capable of loving you. In fact, you implied that you don't believe that love exists. So, really, what harm can I do myself? It seems a fairly hopeless endeavor on my part no matter what I say."

Ava tried not to let the twinge of disappointment she felt at his matter-of-fact attitude show. She had expected him to argue with her, at least a little. Her parents had always argued that they loved her.

I tell you I love you every time I talk to you! they had said, as if the words meant more than the deeds.

The less she had believed them, the more they had argued. Or maybe it was the other way around.

"Permit me to ask one question, though."

She nodded at him, suspicious of that cool-as-glacier-water tone of his.

"I was under the impression that you see the proof of love around you every day. Graham and Missy, my brother and Regina, even Rafael De Santos and his Tess seem to love each other very much. Do you not believe they have those feelings for each other?"

Ava permitted herself a short laugh. It contained very little amusement. "If you can call that love."

"You don't believe they love each other? They looked thoroughly happy to me."

"Oh, I believe they're *in* love with each other, that they believe they love each other, but I have a hard time calling something love when it requires changing or concealing a person's nature to make them fit into your life better."

He blinked at her for a moment. It took him several seconds to form his mouth around the words, "Excuse me?"

"I don't think it's love when a man makes the woman he claims to love take part in some weird werewolf ritual that involves running from a crowd of would-be rapists who are all obviously stronger and faster and more able to see in the dark than she is," Ava said, feeling the old anger she had struggled with for so long come surging back as she spoke. Suddenly it was easy to remember why she and Graham couldn't stand each other.

"Nor do I think it's love when a man changes a woman into another species of creature just so he can keep her with him for as long as he lives. Taking away someone's humanity isn't love."

Dima watched her, his cool blue eyes looking strangely soft in the dim light of the sitting room. "Have you considered that maybe it was love when those women agreed to such things?"

"Telling someone that that's the way things have to be if they want to be with you isn't love." She spoke quickly and flatly, not even needing to pause for thought on that one. "It's emotional blackmail."

He nodded slowly, as if piecing together puzzle parts and trying to decide what the full image would be when he was done. "So you were there when Graham ordered Missy to participate in a mate hunt." He said it without the inflection of a question, as if he were repeating her own words back to her. "And you were there when Regina went through her transformation."

She scowled. "Of course not."

"Then how can you know what really happened?" he asked gently. "How do you know that each of those women did not make the offer to change? How do you know that each would not make the same decision again if offered the choice?"

"'Do what I want or fuck off'?" she speculated cruelly. "What choice is there in that?"

Restless, unable to sit still any longer, she pushed up out of the chair and began to pace the small room, from door to window and back again.

"The choice to follow her heart, to take a step or not, from what I can see."

"When is that ever the choice? In all my life, I've never been offered any choice that involved following heart! It doesn't exist. The only choice is to go along with what other people want in the hope that it will make them mean it when they say they love you." She gave a short bark of laughter. Or maybe it was a sob. "Then you do what they want and find out they're not capable of meaning it and they never will be."

She stopped in front of the window and clenched her hands into fists at her sides. Emotions roiled inside her like currents in a whirlpool. She closed her eyes to keep from seeing her own face reflected in the dark glass of the window. She couldn't stand the look of pain and hope and disappointment and stupidity in her own eyes. And she certainly couldn't look at Dima, not when he watched her as if he understood some of what was going on inside her. No one could be expected to do that. Her parents never had.

But Dima could already read her too well, while she couldn't even get a hint of his thoughts from those icy eyes and stony face.

But it does, lyubimaya. *It exists right here.*

"Get out of my head," she growled, her nails digging into her palms until she thought they would draw blood. It was a good thing Misha and Reggie had brought her blood earlier this evening or she might have been tempted to open her eyes and check. "You weren't invited, and I don't want you there."

What about in your heart? his voice asked, the one she heard in her head and her heart and every other part of her weak-willed body. *Am I welcome there?*

"Don't ask questions you don't want answered."

Then why don't you ask the questions of me?

He stepped up behind her, his feet silent on the thick carpet, his movements graceful as always, but she didn't have to hear him. She didn't have to open her eyes to see his reflection pressed up against hers in the dark window glass. She could feel him, almost like another part of her own body. She was acutely aware of his breath stirring her hair, his heat radiating into her chilled skin, his head bending to hers.

Ava didn't answer. She couldn't. If she opened her mouth, she would either scream or beg, and she couldn't allow herself to do either.

Or perhaps you already know. His breath brushed her ear, then his lips. She had to lock her knees to keep them from giving out on her. *I will make no secret of it,* kralya. *You never have to ask if I will invite you into my mind or my heart, for each already belongs to you.*

Ava cursed silently. How the hell had this happened? It wasn't supposed to be like this. She had come up to the sitting room knowing Dima would be here, planning to seduce him shamelessly. She knew he was upset about her role tomorrow, and frankly, she had begun to wonder if she might have bitten off more than she could chew, so she figured a little medicinal sex would be just the thing to distract them both from their worries. If it was anything like last time, it would probably distract her from things like breathing, thinking, and remembering her own name, too, but those were the sacrifices she was willing to make. And Dima was a man—vampirism, age, and phenomenal muscle development notwithstanding— so he should have had the good manners to cooperate by tripping her and beating her to the floor.

But no. He'd had to go and start talking about love. Sex Ava could handle. She could handle affection maybe. Hell, she'd even find a way to handle vampirism, eventually. Love wasn't ever supposed to be a part of it.

Who did this to you, kralya? his voice murmured inside her head. *Who made you so distrusting of love?*

Who the hell didn't? When everyone you meet immediately tells you they love you—love your work, love your face, love your body, love your smile, love your money—right before they shove a dagger in your back, you learn a natural instinct toward caution.

His arms slid around her, crossing over her abdomen and snugging her back against him. He leaned forward and rested his chin on her left shoulder. *This isn't caution you have,* lyubushka. *It is terror.*

You try being an international modeling sensation at thirteen—which is one year after your father says he doesn't want to be your mother's husband or your father anymore, and one year before your mother finally realizes he means it and begins a slow, irrevocable slide into dementia, by the way—and let me know how you do staying confident.

There was a long pause. Ava opened her eyes to find his gaze locked on their reflection in the window. Or rather, it was locked on her reflection, on her face, and he looked somehow both sad and confused.

But lyubushka, he said, and his voice in her head was full of emotion, from pity to affection to sadness to impatience, *you are not thirteen years old anymore.*

And Ava met his eyes in the glass and burst into tears.

Chapter 19

She felt like a prize idiot.

It didn't matter that Dima treated her with all the affection people usually reserved for wounded kittens and four-year-old children. Or maybe it did matter, but it just made her feel even more ridiculous. Either way, when he heard the first choking sound of weeping, he turned her in his arms and pulled her into his chest, cradling her against him and rocking her like an infant.

Ava thought she must sound like one, but her tears were uncontrollable. She felt like a bathtub whose drain plug had been pulled. All the tears she'd been storing up since the day her father had left her came pouring out on the shoulder of a vampire when he told her he loved her. All she needed was to see a clock melt and her life would have officially become as surreal as a Salvador Dalí painting.

"Hush, *lyubimaya*," Dima crooned, his hands stroking her back, and he rocked her back and forth. "It is all right. You are all right, *nenaglyadnaya*. Hush."

She just cried harder. Her hands unclenched with

a jerk and she bent her stiffened arms, pulling them away from her sides and wrapping them around Dima's waist. She clung to him, the first time she could remember clinging to anyone since she had learned to walk, and gasped for breath in between shuddering sobs.

She heard him murmuring to her, comforting sounds and nonsense words, some in English and some in Russian. What he said, she realized, made very little difference. What mattered was that he continued to hold her and even if he was trying to soothe her and encouraging her not to cry, she knew instinctively that it was because he hated to see her so upset and not because he didn't want to have to deal with her and her messy emotions.

When she showed no signs of stopping, he scooped her up and carried her a few feet before he stopped and turned sharply around, heading for the door to the bedroom she had laid claim to early in the evening. She clung to him while he shouldered the door open and carried her into the dark room. She felt a moment's panic that he meant to tuck her into bed and leave her to cry herself to sleep, but he never took his hands off of her. Instead of laying her on the mattress, he turned and sat, swinging his legs up onto the bed and propping his back against the pillows piled in front of the headboard. Then he settled her comfortably in his lap and rubbed his cheek against hers, spreading a layer of salty tears over each of them.

"Poor little *kralya*," he murmured, and stroked her soothingly. "So many tears."

He was right. Ava hadn't known it was possible to

cry so much, and she could have lived without ever learning the truth. She felt as if something deep inside her had cracked. Or maybe more like a huge scab inside her had been ripped off, and while the pain was excruciating, she knew that once her nerves stopped screaming about it, she would find new, shiny, healthy pink skin in the place where she had always been wounded.

Slowly, very slowly, she began to calm down. She wasn't sure how long it took, though judging by the wet spot on Dima's shirt—which took up almost half of his chest—she used quite a few minutes to do so. The clenching in her chest gradually eased, allowing her breathing to smooth out and her heartbeat to slow to something like normal.

When she shuddered out a long sigh, Dima took her chin gently in his fingers and tilted her face enough to let him look at it.

Ava grimaced. "Don't say anything. I don't care how gorgeous she might be—when she cries, no woman looks pretty."

The corner of his mouth quirked up. "I think you are beautiful." He leaned down and brushed a tender kiss over her lips. "When your eyes go all red and puffy."

She smacked him. "You told me you love me. Isn't that supposed to mean you don't notice things like that?"

She couldn't believe she had said it out loud. But more than that, she couldn't believe she almost believed it.

"I said I was in love, *kralya*, not that I was blind."

"But love *is* blind."

"Not since the invention of contact lenses." Grinning, he carefully lifted her and set her down on the mattress next to him. Then he slid off the bed, pausing to press a kiss to her forehead. "Stay here. I will be right back."

She didn't have to wonder where he was going for long. He moved only as far as the attached bath, where she heard him moving around along with the sound of water running. Exhausted, she snuggled down onto the bed and laid her face on a fluffy pillow. She hadn't realized how tiring emotions could be, not this kind of emotion anyway, maybe because she didn't have much experience with them. Her father had no emotions that she had ever perceived, and the ones her mother had had cost the woman her health and her sanity. These were hardly sterling examples for Ava to want to emulate.

Again, Ava heard no footsteps, but she felt Dima's approach as surely as if there had been a cable tying them together. She looked up as he sat back on the edge of the bed.

"Here. Drink." He handed her a glass of water. "All that crying will leave you dehydrated."

She took the glass automatically, raised it to her lips, and paused. "I can drink water?"

He made a face. "Of course you can drink water. All living creatures can drink water. It is not as if it is full of nutrients your body must process. All it is full of is water."

"I was just asking," she huffed, but she was smiling behind the rim of the glass. "At this point, I figure the last thing I need to cap off my evening is a lively bout of vomiting."

He waited while she drained the water and then set the glass aside. Then he reached out to her and pressed a warm, wet cloth against the skin of her face.

She moaned in surprised pleasure. "Oh, my God, that feels amazing."

He said nothing, just quietly wiped the traces of tears from her cheeks and eyes and even her forehead. She knew tears were supposed to roll downward, but hers had apparently defied gravity. Either that, or they had been smeared in interesting directions when Dima had rubbed against her. When he was done, he set the cloth aside and watched her. Ava marveled that even in the dark, his pale eyes shone distinctly blue, and she wondered if that was due to her improved night vision or the power of his eyes themselves.

"It will not be dawn for a couple of hours yet," he murmured. "But if you're tired, you should sleep. Tomorrow you will need to be strong and rested."

"I'm not sleepy."

She watched his eyes for another minute, then lifted her hand and placed it on his cheek. She felt the rough prickle of stubble against her skin and noted how he automatically leaned into her hand, shifting to nuzzle against her palm. She felt something stir inside her, something she thought the tears might have unleashed. It stretched and blinked and saw what was before her, and it purred.

Ava drew his face down to hers, or maybe it drifted. Either way, she stretched up off the pillows and brushed her lips over his. She heard the catch in his breathing and felt the same echoed in her own chest. Something undeniable happened when they touched, undeniable and electric and terrifying and exhilarating. She didn't know if it was love, but it fascinated her.

Her lips rubbed against his, soft and unhurried, savoring the shape and texture of his mouth. From a distance it looked so hard, as if chiseled from the same granite as the rest of his face, but up close it was so soft, almost as soft as her own, and it yielded to the slightest pressure of hers.

His lips parted, making it easier for her to play with each lip in turn. She pressed kisses to the top, drawing her breath in softly until his lip clung to hers as if beseeching her for more. Then she shifted to the bottom and caught the flesh between her teeth for a split second, a stinging nip, before soothing the tiny hurt with a tender stroke of her tongue. She heard him groan and felt him sink into her, and her heart began to beat a little faster.

Her hand remained on his cheek, cradling him to her, but the other slid up and around his shoulders. She pressed down, drawing him to her, and her body ached with relief when he sank down beside her. When he aligned their bodies so that they both lay on their sides, pressed together from mouth to toe, Ava felt some tension drain out of him and felt that something inside her relax as well. Its purring grew louder.

She didn't stop to think or analyze; at the moment, analysis was the last thing she wanted. The first, she knew, was to be touched by Dima, skin to skin, on every inch of her body. In pursuit of that goal, she reached for the buttons that ran down the front of his dark shirt and began to top them free.

He pulled back for just a moment to look at her. She met his gaze but didn't bother to still her hands. Dima smiled and pressed a kiss to her forehead. Then he set out to help her.

Within the space of a minute, he was naked. Ava made an encouraging noise and reached for the hem of her T-shirt and seconds later, she followed. They lay atop the downy coverlet on the bed, face-to-face, and each looked their fill of the other. No one's eyes drifted over plane or curve, smooth skin or scarred; everything they were interested in seeing could be found in a dark or light gaze.

Ava shifted and tangled her legs with his. She adored the contrast of his hard muscle and masculine hair against her own smooth skin. She opened her mouth to speak, then hesitated. The room lay still and silent around them, no sounds filtering in from the club outside the suite—testament to Graham's family's dedication to quality . . . and soundproofing—and it seemed a shame somehow to disturb the fragile peace.

She laid a hand on Dima's chest over his heart and concentrated as hard as she could. *If I talk to you like this,* she thought at him, *can you hear me?*

He smiled and raised her fingers to his lips, brushing his mouth over them. *Even if you don't shout at the top of your mind,* lyubushka.

She flushed and pulled back a little. *Sorry.*

Do not be. It is a skill, and a new one for you. You will get better with practice.

She sighed and pressed her forehead against his shoulder. *It might have been a good idea to practice some more before tomorrow, huh?*

He dropped a kiss onto her shining hair. *It will be fine. You will not be alone, and whatever you cannot speak to me, I will pick up from your mind. All you have to do is behave naturally and keep your eyes and ears open. I will take care of the rest.*

I'll try, she promised. *It's not going to be easy, you know, having you hang out inside my head without me booting you out just by reflex.*

I'm tenacious. It will be fine.

Ava lay quietly for a few more minutes. She wanted to make love with Dima, but something about just lying here with him in the dark, skin to skin, felt so profoundly right that she was in no hurry to move things along. There were plenty of things the two of them needed to talk about, but to bring them up now would have felt like an intrusion into a sacred space.

His touch could never be classified as an intrusion. It skimmed across her cheek, down her arm, tracing the curve of the underside of one breast before his thumb stretched out to rub across her nipple, bringing the rosy little nub to a peak.

"You're pink," he observed, shifting so that he could press a kiss on the crest. "You fed decently tonight."

She wrinkled her nose. "You know, blood drinking is not generally considered a good topic for pillow talk."

He shot her an amused look. "You haven't been a vampire for long. How much did you drink?"

"I think Regina said about three bags. It made me feel better, like I had more energy," she admitted with a sigh, "but I still can't say I like the taste. Especially of the bagged stuff. It tastes bland. Like rice cakes with nothing on them."

"Exactly. You'll become a connoisseur yet."

"I somehow doubt that. I had to close my eyes while the bags were in my mouth; otherwise I thought I was going to hurl."

Dima laughed softly. "All right, so it might take a few months."

"Try millennia."

"But it strengthened you, and that is what is important. You will learn, perhaps not to like the act itself, but to appreciate what it can do for you."

"Make me able to leap tall buildings in a single bound?"

"Perhaps moderately sized private homes."

Dima pressed a kiss to her other nipple, as if he didn't want to play favorites. Then he began to dot a string of nibbling caresses across her sternum, pausing briefly to probe into the cup of her navel.

"At the moment, I think I'm content with continuing to breathe and refraining from attacking my friends. I'm pretty low maintenance that way."

He laughed against her skin. "You cannot fool

one who has survived for longer than most royal dynasties, *diva*. You are a princess, but I do not mind treating you as such."

Ava made a face and lifted her head to look down at him. "You're almost eight hundred, right?" She watched him nod. "You said something about Turks before, to Misha, but you've never told me how you were changed."

She felt his breath whisper against her skin as he spoke. "It is far from a glamorous tale, not the stuff films are made of. I was raised a warrior in a time of warfare. My father and his people constantly had to fight to defend our lands and properties, against both Turkish invaders and the Chernigovs. Each could be called a formidable opponent, but after Misha's supposed death, they forged an alliance against us."

Silently she lifted a hand to his head, stroked her fingers through the light silk of his hair.

"We fought many battles," he continued. "Endless battles. Our people were brave, but they whittled away at our numbers like a knife on wood. Eventually, enough of my men had fallen that one of the Chernigovs was able to strike me down. Unfortunately, that was not enough for our enemy. Yelizaveta's brother was just as ruthless as she. He knew of my mother's piety and thought it would cause her more pain to see me cursed in the eyes of her God than to lose me in honorable battle. It caused me more pain as well."

Ava's fingers tightened in his hair. "It sounds as if you didn't have a much easier time than I did."

"It was not something I wanted," Dima said, his

lips brushing the curve of her waist. "But it was different for me. In the world I lived in, physical strength equaled power. Having the abilities of a vampire gave me an advantage I quickly came to appreciate."

"I guess so."

He raised his head and locked that pale, knowing gaze onto her face. "You will need to learn to harness your strength, as well, *diva*," he said. "Not only for your own sake, but so you do not misjudge and injure another unintentionally."

She sighed. "I have to do a lot of things these days to keep from unintentionally hurting people, don't I?"

"Would you change back if you could? Go back to being human?"

"That's a trick question if I ever heard one. If I hadn't become a vampire, I'd be dead now, wouldn't I? I'm very happy about not being dead."

"But you would rather be human?"

"It would be easier." When he would have spoken again, she silenced him by pressing a kiss to his mouth. "I don't want to play what if. The only thing I want to concentrate on is what is, right here and right now."

She could see that he wanted to say more, but in the end, for all of his strength, his age, and his powers, Dima Rurikovich was just a man, and men could be easily distracted. She accomplished this task by lifting her top leg and draping it over his hip, opening her body to his so that when she arched and pressed her hips forward, she formed an inviting cradle that pressed intimately against his erection.

That was all it took.

With a groan, his arms tightened around her and he shifted his own hips, bringing them into alignment with hers. As he pressed forward, parting the lips of her sex with the broad head of his cock, he leaned forward until his forehead touched hers and all either one of them could see were the unfocused eyes of the other.

I know what you're doing, he said, his voice gruff and thick even in her mind. *You can't keep being distracted forever,* lyubushka. *Eventually, you will need to decide.*

She rolled her hips forward, her entire body clenching at the feeling of him sinking deeper inside her. Her eyelids drifted shut, too heavy for her to hold up, and she struggled to fill her lungs with heated, passion-scented air.

Decide whether to live or die? I've already made that decision. I'm here, aren't I?

His hands shifted, gripping her hips and urging her closer—as if they could get any closer—until she had to pull her top leg even higher, her knees now resting on his rib cage and her instep braced against his hip. He flexed his hips and sank a fraction deeper, nudging her womb with the head of his shaft. Ava gasped out a cry, overwhelmed, and trembled uncontrollably in his arms. She couldn't believe she was this aroused, balanced on the knife-edge of climax without one thrust. All Dima had done was sink slowly inside her, merge their bodies as if reuniting two halves of a whole, and then rest there, and she felt as ready to shatter as if he'd been riding her for hours, teasing and taunting and daring her to come.

You will have to decide what you want.

She heard his words, felt him suck in a deep breath, and her eyelids fluttered open to find him watching her, his eyes blazing with pale blue fire.

Will you go back to the life you knew before and make a few adjustments for your new needs?

He held himself still inside her and the need for movement suddenly and sharply overwhelmed her. She tried to thrust her hips against him, but he held completely still and his fingers flexed on her hips, pinning them in place.

Dima, she thought frantically.

Or will you embrace your new life and the new possibilities it offers? He leaned forward and captured her lips with his even as his voice sounded inside her head. There was something frighteningly, crazily intimate about that, about feeling him inside her head and inside her body and tasting him on her lips all at the same time. She could not describe the sensation, but it made her ache for something she couldn't name.

Will you seize what is offered to you, lyubushka, *or will you turn it away because it is too much, too hard, requires too much work?*

She had no idea what he meant. At that point, she barely had an idea of her own name. She had been reduced to a giant bundle of nerve endings, every single one of which burned and throbbed and strained hungrily toward release.

Dima. Somewhere in the back of her head, a detached and sane part of herself heard the pleading in her tone, the helpless need, and wondered if what she was asking—what *he* was asking—would cost her more than she was willing to pay. But in the moment, need easily triumphed over logic, and Ava resorted to the only weapon left to her.

Slowly, deliberately, she tightened her body around him and watched the flame in his eyes leap higher. She did it again, and heard a rough sound rumble in his chest. A third time, and she felt the rumble, like an earthquake, vibrate through him and into her.

"Kralya," he ground out, and she knew he praised her beauty. But the stubborn man still didn't move.

She tightened again, and shivered as the clenching of her own body around him threatened to send her over the edge without him.

Dima, she thought, and his name was a caress.

He groaned, his eyes snapped shut, and she could feel the dam burst inside him. Roughly, one hand closed around her leg, pulling it even higher and tighter against him, while the other reached between her legs from behind, finding the point where their bodies joined and pressing against the tightly stretched skin of her opening. The sensation made her entire body seize like a giant fist, and when the tension eased, she felt herself dissolving into a million tiny little pieces, a climax at once violent and yet painfully tender.

She felt his body jump inside her, felt the same kind of tension seize him, and then he was coming apart in her arms. He shook violently, like branches in a storm, and his breath strained between his lips in uneven bellows as he spent himself endlessly inside her.

Ava lay dazed and broken beside him, thinking with the few brain cells left to her that her life had just changed more profoundly in this man's arms than it had in the alley a few nights before. If she hadn't been so bonelessly, mindlessly exhausted, she would have panicked.

Instead, she fell deeply, dreamlessly, silently into sleep, her arms still wrapped around the man who held her as if he never intended to let her go. She knew that something in that thought should concern her, should add to her panic, but she couldn't think what it was. She couldn't think. So, instead, she snuggled closer, and slept.

Chapter 20

Dima had been walking around in a truly foul mood since the crack of dusk, and since he'd spent all of that time glued to Ava like a bad toupee, it was beginning to tick her off as well. A lot.

Part of her irritation with him stemmed from the simple reality that no one liked to be around someone who had a glower permanently tattooed on his face and who could barely keep a civil tongue in his head; but a considerable part of it lay in the fact that when a woman let a man see the most vulnerable parts of her soul and then had profound, emotional, consciousness-changing sex with him, she did not expect to wake up to find him pissed off and grumpy. It could seriously give her a complex.

Ava wanted to ask him what the hell his problem was, but since the ensuing discussion would likely involve strong language, graphic violence, and adult content, she thought it might be wise to save it until they weren't on a schedule for trapping an evil vampiress and half the people they knew weren't clustered around them trying to pass themselves off as useful. So instead, she ignored him with verve.

"Do you have everything you need?" Regina asked her for the ninety-seventh time in the last ten minutes.

"Yes, Mother." Ava rolled her eyes and patted the side of her reclaimed and repurposed handbag. "I triple-checked everything myself—invitation, cell phone, pepper spray, stun gun. And Missy did a fabulous job sewing up the lining so that you can't even tell there's a bug in there."

"Well, I should hope so. I doubt there's a vampire on earth who would take kindly to finding out they've been secretly recorded by a fledgling they invited into their home."

Ava gave her friend a look. "Honey, there isn't *a person* on earth who would take that kindly. It would make me a little cranky myself."

"But since it's for your own safety, you're going to make sure you keep it with you, aren't you?" Misha demanded in that tone he shared with his brother, the one that asked a question while simultaneously feeding you the only acceptable answer.

"Yes, sir. Thank you, sir. Anything else, sir?"

He ignored her sarcasm and looked at his wife. "You know, I think these changes have had a positive effect on your friend, *dushka*. I find her new attitude delightfully refreshing."

"Blow me, suck boy."

"Graham and I will be monitoring the wire," Missy said, stepping in before they escalated into violence. It was really what she did best. "If we hear anything that makes us think you're in danger, we're going to signal to the others to get inside and get you out. That won't be pretty, so you're going to keep your promise and do what any of them says will keep you safe, right?"

"I swear to the Virgin Mary and all the martyrs, you two missed your calling as kindergarten teachers."

Missy blinked at her. "I was a kindergarten teacher."

Ava rolled her eyes. "We've been over the plan nine billion times. I go in, present myself to Elvira—"

"Yelizaveta," Misha corrected.

"—Queen of the Night," she continued without pause, "and kiss some royal butt. Then I pump her for information, ask to be taken in like an orphaned kitten, and scope out her digs. Before dawn, I make my way out the back of the house where the entire Secret Service will be waiting to whisk me into protective custody lest I do something really dangerous like break a nail."

"Before *one*," Dima growled, layers of suppressed violence in his voice. "Before *one*, *pava*, or I swear by all that's holy, I will come inside for you and when I take you out, you will not let your ass touch furniture for a month."

She threw him a glare. "Charmer. I bet that attitude just kills the ladies, doesn't it?"

"Ava—," Misha began.

"Stuff it, Dracula. You and your brother can both kiss my ass instead of threatening to beat it. I'll do what you want and do it well. Contrary to what seems to be becoming popular belief, I am neither stupid, helpless, nor suicidal. I can handle this."

"We're just worried," Missy said, reaching out to squeeze her hand.

"I'm sure some of you are, but you can stop. Because I'm a big girl, and I have no intention of trying to prove how stupid I am by playing the hero or anything. I can think of better ways to kill myself than this."

"Fine," Dima growled, and pivoted toward the door. "Let's go then."

"Let us get this over with," Misha agreed.

"From your lips to God's ears," Ava muttered, and joined the procession out of Vircolac's back door.

Ava really did feel like she had the presidential Secret Service detail on her case. She rode to Wadsworth House in the back of a Town Car with Dima and Misha, pinned between them on the backseat like a sardine in a can. Neither one of them spoke to her, both of them wore grim expressions, and she fully believed that if anyone around her threatened her life, one of them would jump on top of her and pin her to the ground while the other one used excessive force to deal with the threat.

Ahead of them by a couple of blocks, so as not to cause suspicion, a plain white delivery van with no windows and the name of a local deli painted on the side was preparing to park somewhere close to the mansion so that they could pick up every word that registered with the high-tech and highly dangerous wire buried in Ava's purse. Behind the Town Car, a large black SUV with local plates and tinted windows cruised patiently, looking for all the world like it carried a bunch of regular travelers instead of a team of the Silverback Clan's most experienced and efficient werewolf soldiers.

The only way Ava could have been more protected would be if they strapped a bulletproof vest to her chest and had a marine helicopter monitoring her from overhead. Somehow, she wouldn't have been surprised to hear they had considered the idea. She was only surprised that they had abandoned it.

She could feel the tension radiating off of Dima in waves, and she wanted to think it was because he was worried for her and would have preferred that she not be putting herself in danger by entering Yelizaveta Chernigov's lair all alone, but she wasn't sure. Was he brooding because of last night? Had it not affected him as strongly as it had her? She had a hard time believing it was possible that he hadn't felt something intense. He had certainly behaved as if he had. But then again, she'd fallen asleep immediately afterward, so what did she know? Maybe he'd only just discovered that she talked in her sleep and decided it drove him crazy.

The car began to slow, and Ava felt the first twinge of nerves rush through her. She had every confidence in the measures that had been taken to protect her, not to mention in her own confidence. These felt more like the nerves she felt just before her turn on the catwalk or before the cameras began to snap—not fear for her safety, but a form of stage fright that she had learned early on only fueled her performances.

"Come and change places with me," Misha said, taking her arms and half-lifting her off the seat to shift her nearer to the door. In the background, Ava thought she heard Dima growl, but she couldn't be sure. Maybe she was just imagining it. "And remember the first rule?"

She rolled her eyes. "Yes, Mr. Worrypants. I remember."

"What is it?"

"Don't take any stupid chances."

"And rule number two?"

She grimaced. "If it would make Missy worry, it's a violation of rule number one."

"Good girl."

"Get bent."

She said it without heat and reached for the handle of the door. Before she could pull it, Dima snaked a hand out past his brother and grabbed her by the back of the neck. He leaned forward and pulled her to him until their noses practically bumped somewhere in the air over Misha's lap.

"If you get hurt in there," Dima growled, his gaze hard as ice and intensely blue, "I will kill you, understand?"

"That you're out of your mind? Completely." She blew out an exasperated breath. "Relax. You'll be with me the whole time, right?"

He muttered something under his breath, in Russian, then gave one last tug until their mouths collided in a brief, hard, bruising kiss. Then he turned her loose and sat back in his seat.

"Just keep it in mind," he grunted, and pointedly looked away from her.

Ava tried glaring at him but found it remarkably unsatisfying, given his refusal to turn his head and notice. Muttering something to herself, she opened the car door and slid out onto the cool pavement. Misha, though, both heard and understood her comment. He laughed out loud.

As Ava shut the door behind her, she heard Dima ask his brother what she had said.

"Oh," Misha chuckled. "I really don't think I could do it justice. You'll have to ask her yourself, later."

The sound of Dima's frustrated cursing followed her all the way up the block to the front door of Wadsworth House and had her whistling a happy tune as she pressed the button for the doorbell. Maybe tonight wouldn't be so bad after all.

Chapter 21

Ava wasn't sure what she had been expecting, but to have her doorbell answered by an elderly-looking man in a crisp butler's livery, complete with bow tie and frock coat, hadn't been it. She raised an eyebrow in surprise, before collecting herself and greeting him with a cool "Good evening."

"I've come to see Ms. Chernigov. I believe she should be expecting me."

The butler didn't so much as twitch an eyelash, which looked to be the only hairs on his entire face. He was completely bald with the natural look of someone who had not shaved his head to make a fashion statement. He was also cleanly shaven and had no eyebrows she could detect. The lack gave him a blank, empty expression that she found disturbing.

When minutes had passed with no response from him, including one in which he would step away from the doorway and let her in, she lifted her chin arrogantly and tried again.

"My name is Ava Markham, and I'm here to see your employer at her invitation. If you have doubts, please feel free to check with her. But for now, I would like to not be kept standing on the doorstep like an orphaned beggar."

The butler did finally step back, but he still looked about as cheerful as death's door knocker. "Wait here," he intoned in a surprisingly deep voice for a man who stood several inches shorter than Ava.

She had no trouble listening to the instruction. There was plenty to look at in the front hall of the mansion, from the intricately carved mahogany banister on the curving, marble stairway to the priceless collection of museum-quality art hanging on the walls. Ava had seen it before when she'd been inside the building for various charity functions over the years, but knowledge of the house had been limited to this hallway, the huge ballroom to the left, and the corridor behind where the ladies' restroom was located.

Besides, she realized as she gazed up at a beautifully executed portrait of an eighteenth-century husband-and-wife couple, things looked different when you were here with five hundred other people from when you were standing alone listening to your breathing echo off the intricate plaster ceiling.

Testing. One, two, three. Testing, she thought under the cover of her art appreciation flashback.

She felt a distinctly Dima-ish presence flood her thoughts and was surprised at how much better it made her feel.

I am with you, kralya, *but it is best to think of me as little as possible. None of us have had dealings with Yelizaveta in many years, and it is impossible*

*to predict what talents she might have learned. Rest
assured, I will not leave you while you are there.*

Ava smiled to herself and turned her attention to
a small landscape depicting an English country
estate in the summer. The bucolic tranquility presented there contrasted nicely with her tightly wound
nerves.

Relax, she heard just before a sharply cleared
throat called her attention back to the reappeared
butler.

"Princess Chernigov will see you," he said, absolutely no inflection in his voice, something Ava
hadn't even known was possible.

"Princess" Chernigov? Ava thought as she followed him down the hall.

*In Russia, Prince and Princess are common ti-
tles. Like Lord and Lady in England.*

She has a title.

*Her family, at one point, could claim a right to
them, I suppose, but it has been a long time since
the last noble in her family was hacked to death by
his own mistreated serfs.*

Charming family.

The butler stopped halfway down the hall before
a wide set of ornately carved double doors. Ava saw
him grip the knobs and blinked. The vampire lady
was going to meet her for a nice chat in the formal
ballroom? Interesting choice . . .

The butler pushed open the door, nodded her
through, then pulled the heavy weights closed behind
her. When Ava looked up, she found herself facing a

movie set and wondered if this Chernigov woman had hired the same decorating firm that had worked on the Council of Others' meeting chambers.

The room looked nothing like Ava remembered. Only the polished wooden floorboards appeared remotely familiar. Heavy black drapes now hung across the floor-to-ceiling windows that ran all along the two outer walls of the enormous room. Presumably they had been installed to block out the light, and the fabric looked to be expensive velvet, but the effect of it covering most of two walls was to make the place look like a funeral parlor or a sadly unfortunate disco.

No lights had been turned on in the room, but the antique chandeliers, once converted to electricity, had been lowered and candles mounted in their cups. Talk about a double whammy of a fire hazard. The tables Ava was used to seeing around the perimeter of the room were absent. The only furniture she saw were a few delicate-looking armchairs at the far end of the room. They had been arranged around the base of a small platform about two feet off the ground, and on that platform stood a chair that . . .

Ava blinked, squinted, and blinked again. No, she hadn't been mistaken. The chair on the platform could only be described as a throne, and a gaudy one at that. It looked to have been upholstered in rich burgundy velvet; the exposed wood framing the back and making up the arms and legs had been heavily, massively gilded so that the piece seemed to glitter in the candlelight.

It took a severe act of willpower for Ava not to laugh at the pretentions of it. Which was wise, because a laugh would likely have counted as a bad move.

In the chair, lounging like Cleopatra on her Nile barge, lay a woman—a girl, really—who Ava realized appeared to be no more than nineteen or twenty years old. She had fair hair in a rich shade of strawberry blonde—half-red, half-gold—and an even fairer complexion dusted with a tiny sprinkling of freckles across her snub nose. Her eyes were wide and, from what Ava could see in the dim light, dark and titled exotically at the corners. She had dressed in something out of a sci-fi fantasy movie, with long skirts, flowing sleeves, and a braided rope of leather and gold fabric wrapped and crisscrossed several times around her narrow torso.

This is Yelizaveta the Terrible? Ava thought, and wanted to laugh. *She looks like a cheerleader trying out for the school play.*

Do not let looks deceive you, Dima warned. *Remember, you look like a cold, calculating bitch at first glance.*

So? That's not an inaccurate impression of me.

When she looked at Yelizaveta Chernigov, all Ava could think of was a famous Waterhouse painting of Tennyson's Lady of Shalott. Ava fought not to smile. If this girl proved to be as hopelessly dim as that immortal character, this would be even easier than they had hoped.

Ava approached the throne and dais and noticed

that several of the chairs at its base were occupied by people with the inherent stillness and predatory gaze of vampires. Flanking the throne on either side, Ava also spotted two figures who appeared to be body-guards.

So far, everything was pretty much as they'd. Except that Ava had expected Yelizaveta to look a bit different.

You were thinking horns and a tail?

No. Well, maybe little horns. I guess I just thought she'd look . . . bigger. More grown-up.

She is as old as I am, lyubushka. *Do not let yourself be taken in.*

When she came within eight feet of the end of the throne platform, Ava halted and looked up at the other vampire through innocent eyes.

"Are you Yelizaveta Chernigov?" Ava asked, her voice carefully neutral.

She hadn't yet decided how to play this. Dima and his brother had warned her to be deferential, the way a new fledgling would be expected to behave, but she wasn't sold on the idea. After all, if Yelizaveta knew who Ava was, she could easily have gathered information on her, and wouldn't it be more suspicious to suddenly act like she'd gone from ass-kicker to ass-kisser in just a couple of days?

The woman on the throne waved her hand and a male vampire in the chair closest to the throne's right-hand side spoke.

"You are in the presence of Princess Chernigov," he said, his voice sounding as tight as his face looked. For a vampire, he appeared to be made entirely of lemon juice with pale skin stretched across the top. He was that sour. "You must make your bow."

Bow?

She stared at the lackey for a moment and raised an eyebrow. "I'm afraid I was never a Dallas debutante," she laughed, taking care to strike the right balance in the sound between amusement and self-confidence. "The, ah, princess will have to settle for a polite nod and a 'How do you do?' "

Yelizaveta leaned forward in her throne and glared at Ava. "I never settle for anything, Ms. Markham," she hissed, and Ava saw not just antagonism but quite a bit of crazy in Yelizaveta's eyes. "That's why I have an empire at my disposal."

Okay, guess we're not going to pretend to be best friends.

"Um, you do?" Ava tried to look confused more than contemptuous. Really, she did. "Wow, that's great. I'm just surprised to hear it. None of the people I asked about you seemed to know anything. In fact, none of them had ever heard of you. Isn't that odd?"

"Odd indeed." The little man at the base of the dais stood and took several steps toward Ava. As he stepped closer, she saw that not only were his sour lips pursed, they were a sickly-looking gray color, and his hands, which he held clasped together in front of him, were somehow deformed. The fingers were overly long, the knuckles too prominent, and his nails had been filed into what resembled sharp talons instead of fingernails.

After she saw that, she found it hard to look at his face.

"I'm afraid there are many things for you to learn about your new situation, Ms. Markham," the lackey continued. His eyes glinted, but in the dim light, even with her improved night vision, the pupil blended so well with the dark, dark color of the iris that his entire eye looked black and flat, like a shark's. "First, there are your manners, of course, but equally important is the fact that speaking to the wrong people about the wrong things can be very hazardous to your health."

Ava looked at him and concentrated on keeping her breathing deep and regular. "Huh, that sounded almost like a threat to me."

"And if it almost was?"

"Then I'd have to wonder why you would go to the trouble of inviting me here just to threaten me. You couldn't have tied a note to a brick and thrown it through my front window? It would have saved each of us a lot of trouble."

"But would it have been as effective?"

She paused as if to consider the question. "Probably," she answered after a minute. "I'm not ever very good at obeying orders."

Yelizaveta swept to her feet and twitched her skirts gracefully out of the way. "Perhaps it's time you learned, then. And since I value Charles' company too much to inflict the teaching on him, allow me to instruct you."

With a smile as false as her heart, she stepped down off the platform and closed the distance between them until she stood no more than two feet away. The only reason she stopped there, Ava believed, was that if she went any farther, she'd have to crane her neck to look up at a woman she probably considered her inferior.

"First, though," Yelizaveta said, her voice smooth and light and young for someone who had celebrated eight hundred birthdays, "it might do you well to understand your position here."

"My position? Wow, and I wasn't even sure I was going to get the job."

Yelizaveta ignored her wisecrack. "My name, as you have obviously learned, is Yelizaveta Chernigov. I am just over eight hundred years old, and I have spent over seven hundred and eighty of those as a vampire. I have powers you could not hope, in your naïve, little, recently human mind, to comprehend. This is why I am the ruler of the House of Chernigov, and you are merely one of my many followers."

"Followers?" Ava smiled and shook her head. "I've always found that if I get lost, a map and a good internal sense of direction are all I need to get me going in the right direction again. But thanks."

Yelizaveta laughed, a light, tinkling bell of sound that provided a sickening contrast to the gesture she used to bring Ava to her knees.

The sensation came on suddenly, feeling as if a hand was tightening around her throat to shake her. Shock immobilized her for an instant before she reached up and instinctively began to claw at her neck. Her mind flashed back to the night in the alley, and she felt fear creeping over her again.

Relax, Dima said, his voice clear and comforting

inside her head. *Remember, you cannot die this way. If she truly meant to kill you, she would go for your head or your heart. Relax.*

I thought you said she wasn't supposed to be able to do weird mind control stuff.

Apparently, I was wrong.

Well, that's *comforting!*

Still, Ava listened to his instructions and relaxed. When she stopped fighting, the tension around her throat eased, allowing her to breathe again. She glared at the vampiress.

"I suppose that's one way to win friends and influence people," Ava coughed.

The woman laughed again. "I have no desire to win friends, *suka.* The only thing I am interested in winning is the war. The fact that you can be useful to me in doing so is the only reason you have remained alive this long."

What did she just call me? Ava demanded.

A bitch.

Oh, it is on!

She let her hands drop back to her sides and lifted her chin, meeting the megalomaniacal Yelizaveta glare for glare. Granted, Ava had to stare down her nose to meet the other woman's gaze, but it wasn't her fault the vampiress had been born a midget.

"Is that right?" Ava asked, her tone implying she didn't care for an answer. "Interesting. But frankly, it makes a girl wonder what sort of state your army is in, if a week-old vampire with absolutely no special talents is the key to winning your war."

That horrible laugh sounded again, making Ava

want to slam her hands over her ears until it stopped. It was worse than nails on a chalkboard in her ears.

"So, so stupid," Yelizaveta giggled while her eyes remained as cool and emotionless as colored glass. "You mean precisely nothing to me, *suka,* and in the grand scheme of things you are capable of serving only one purpose. Your significance has nothing to do with how you are or what you can do. It is simply who you know."

"Who I know?"

The woman nodded eagerly, making Ava think she really must be a total lunatic. "Who you know! The head councilor and his wife, the Alpha of the local Lupines and his wife, everyone and his wife. But most important of all, my two oldest . . . friends. The brothers Rurikovich. They're special. I think I might save them for last."

Ava felt her blood chill in her veins. "What does that mean?"

"It means that you must exert not a speck of effort to prove yourself useful, *deshovka.*"

Cheap whore, Dima translated in Ava's head. *I think she might be having some problems with what the psychologists call "projection."*

"Oh, and what do I have to do, Yelizaveta?"

"Nothing." Another giggle. "That's what makes the plan so beautiful. You simply have to *be.*"

"Be what?"

The vampire smiled like a shark, all teeth, and performed a few dancing steps of delight. She spun to a stop and pinned Ava with her blank, doll's eyes.

"Be bait!"

Chapter 22

Dima wondered if they could expect reinforcements later in the week, because he was certain his allies had heard his shout of denial in Moscow.

"That *bitch*!" he roared, slamming his fist down on the dashboard of the van with enough force to dent the thick layers of metal and vinyl. "She got us to do exactly what she wanted and she never even had to lift a fucking finger. I'm going to pluck out her eyeballs and feed them to the crows, I swear to God."

Misha reached forward from his position just behind the front passenger seat and squeezed his brother's shoulder. "Hush," he urged. "You might still be able to hear what is going on inside, but while you shout, none of the rest of us can."

Dima hardly cared how well the bug was transmitting to Graham's high-tech monitor system, which allowed the other members of what he now feared would be a rescue team to hear the events unfold inside the mansion. He had never felt entirely comfortable with this plan of Ava's, and now he knew why. Only what he really wanted to do was be able to grab her and shake her and say, *I told you so,* but he couldn't. He had let her walk into a spider's web, and now he had to find a way to get her out again.

"Ssshhh!" Graham hissed, gesturing for quiet. He pressed a pair of earphones against his head, listening for tiny details that could prove significant while the sophisticated surveillance equipment broadcast the voices to the rest of the audience gathered in the van.

"You're telling me you invited me here just to try and lure Dmitri Vidâme and Vladimir Rurikovich to come with me?" Ava's voice sounded loud and clear inside the steel box, and slightly nervous.

Only Dima could sense the fear that flashed inside her at the thought of being the cause of his or his brother's death. Dima's jaw clenched helplessly.

"That seems like a risky card to play," she continued. "I mean, sure I know both of them, but I don't know why you would think they'd come here after me. I mean, it's no secret that Dmitri and I have never gotten along, and I've known Vladimir for all of a week. Don't they have a sister you could take prisoner? I doubt they'll go through all that much trouble to come after me."

He knew she was bluffing, but Dima found himself disturbed by how convincing she sounded.

"Oh, they'll do almost anything to stop me." Yelizaveta's voice wasn't as loud as Ava's, but thanks to the expensive spy equipment, it came through just as clearly. "There's a rumor going around that I mean to raise an army and kill what remains of the European Council of Vampires and rule over Russia and the rest of the territories in Europe myself. Sillies! As if I'd want to go back to cold, ugly Moscow when I can live in New York forever!" She giggled insanely, and Dima swore.

"Stay in New York?" Misha asked, frowning.

An instant later, Ava echoed the question.

"Of course. It's ever so much more exciting here. There's so much more to do! And the shops are wonderful. I've never seen so much luxury in one place in all my life! There's no way I'm going back to dismal old Moscow, let alone that hideous little prison in Kolomenskoye. I'd rather be dead." She paused to laugh. "No, actually, I'd rather kill Misha and Dima, and I will! They'd try to stop me. They'd try to send me back; therefore, the only way I can have what I want is to kill them both."

Dima felt Ava's heart skip a beat and then race forward for a second; then a wall suddenly slammed down between them. He wanted to comfort her, but he couldn't seem to reach her internal thoughts. He could monitor the scene through her perspective, but it was as if she had instantly cut off all emotional connection between them. Frankly, she shouldn't have had the ability to do that so early, but maybe the shock had allowed her to tap into it. It didn't really matter. What mattered was that while he could keep track of her words and Yelizaveta's responses, he couldn't tell how Ava felt about them.

He couldn't tell what she planned to do next, and frankly, that scared him more than anything else.

"I'm telling you that I'm a lousy lure," Ava informed the other woman calmly. "If you wanted to force Dmitri to come here, you should have used his wife. Even his best friend would be a better piece of bait. The warmest feelings he had for me can best be described as irritation and impatience. And as for Rurikovich . . ." She paused, and Dima could feel her shrug, rather convincingly. "Who knows what he might feel? The man's as easy to read as Egyptian hieroglyphics during a sandstorm. But after a week's acquaintance, I doubt he feels anything approaching an emotion strong enough to make him come after me. I'm afraid you've dealt yourself a very bad hand, Yelizaveta. Next time, you might want to know your targets a little better."

That mad giggle sounded again over the wire. "Oh, I know them as well as you can possibly know a man," the vampire taunted. "Both of them."

Inside the van, the brothers exchanged shocked looks, followed by identical sheepish shrugs.

"I was still human. And I was drunk," Misha muttered. "So drunk I'm surprised I was still capable. And I may have been thirty to her fifteen, but I swear to Christ, the little slut had more experience than I did."

Dima nodded. "Then it's no wonder I was so easy for her. I was only sixteen myself, and she was only the second woman I ever had. The first had known almost as little about the matter as I had."

"Both of them?" Ava demanded in their ears, and in Dima's head he felt a flash of her very real irritation. "I'm sorry, but that's just kinky."

Dima knew her irritation was more with him than with Yelizaveta, and he couldn't blame her. He wished he'd never slept with the little psychopath himself, but boys did many stupid things when they were only sixteen and their hormones were raging. Not to mention what happened when they got bored six hundred and some odd years before the invention of television.

"Admittedly, it was several centuries ago," Yelizaveta continued, "but I've found over the years that men very seldom change in any fundamental sort of way. You see, the biggest weakness that each of those fools have is their ridiculous sense of honor. They've always been too noble for their own good. So you see, once they learn that I have an acquaintance of theirs—a *female* acquaintance, no less—in my power, they'll be tripping over themselves trying to be the first one to save you."

"I'm telling you, you're wrong. They don't care enough about me to try to save me."

"They don't have to care about you at all."

The vampire's tone was growing bored, and Dima was growing impatient with the delay. He gestured to Misha that they should prepare to move, but his brother shook his head.

"Not yet," Misha murmured. "We don't know enough about the situation inside. Unless Ava can tell you how many men she can see with Yelizaveta."

Dima cursed himself for not asking as soon as she entered the room. He'd caught her impression of people sitting in chairs near the throne, but she hadn't counted them, and he hadn't insisted she do so immediately. He had thought they would have a little more time. And now, since she had cut him off, he no longer had the option of getting the information from her.

"I don't know," he admitted, "but it can't be that many. She didn't have much of a reaction when she walked in there. If Yelizaveta had an army on hand, Ava would have noticed."

"That's not a good enough answer." Misha met his brother's gaze evenly, which drove Dima crazy, because he knew the other man was right. "Not too many could mean no more than fifty, and those aren't odds I want to take on, not even with the Silverbacks to guard my back."

"Or it could mean less than a dozen. We could take those easily."

"But we don't know for sure, do we?"

Reluctantly, Dima jerked his head no.

Misha raised a brow. "And I'm assuming that for whatever reason, Ava is not providing you with that information?" He barely waited for the acknowledgment. "What did you do to piss her off?"

"I have no idea," he answered honestly. "From what I can recall, I did nothing."

"Well, take my advice and apologize anyway when you see her again. It makes everything involved in this mating business go much more smoothly."

Dima shot his brother a sideways glance. "Mating? Who said anything about mating? I certainly never said I had taken a mate."

Misha patted him on the shoulder. "It's all right, *bratok*. It comes to us all eventually. Trust me when I tell you that it's just less painful when you give in."

Not, Dima reflected grimly, *if the woman you had chosen for your mate was being held prisoner by a violent, sociopathic vampire with delusions of grandeur and a dislike of ever being told no.*

"They don't have to care about you at all," Yelizaveta repeated. "They just have to care. Misha cares about his wife, that is obvious to the whole world, and his wife, the sniveling little thing, cares about you. He might damn you to hell, but if losing you would cause his wife a moment's pain, he would save your life at the expense of his own."

Dima could read the truth of that in his brother's expression. It didn't matter what the cost was; he would always do what he could to keep his wife from pain or grief.

"And if Misha comes for you, it is inevitable that Dima will come for him," Yelizaveta chortled. "Poor little Dima was ever following after his older brother, wanting to grow up just like Misha. Well, I will make them happy. I will kill them in one blow, so they might spend all the rest of eternity being dead together. Aren't I thoughtful?"

"As a concrete floor," Ava replied. "Even if Misha were insane enough to try to rescue me for Regina's sake, why would you think that Dima would come chasing after him? They haven't seen each other in hundreds of years. That seems to indicate to me that they might not be all that fond of each other."

"Oh, that's just them being stubborn, and it's already forgotten. I knew that once I threw them together they would let the past slip away. They were

too close when they were young not to build on that
bond again as soon as they were forced to actually
see each other."

"What do you mean, 'forced to see each other'?"

"Once I threw them together again. You were the
perfect tool for that, *shalava* [slut]. Your connection
to Misha brought you to my attention, and once I
saw you, I knew Dima would slobber all over you
like a dog. He always fancied a dark girl so he could
press all that pale muscle of his against her. And, of
course, once you were in danger, that nobility of his
would do the rest. He would never leave you to suffer if he could prevent it so easily."

Dima's mind reeled. Yelizaveta was implying that
the attack on Ava hadn't been an accident. But how
could that be true? How could Yelizaveta have planned
something so seemingly random?

"I should thank you for making it so easy. You
really should try not to walk the same route between
your home and Misha's every time you go there,
suka. Why, if someone wanted, they could just lay
in wait for you and grab you as soon as you walked
by. It would be so entirely easy."

The vampiress giggled again.

The occupants of the van heard a moment of silence.

"Then I wasn't changed accidentally," Ava finally
said, her voice curiously flat and disinterested.

Dima frowned. It wasn't like her not to show any
emotion at learning such a significant detail. Something was wrong. He could feel it.

"Oh, stars no, *suka*! I planned that, just like I

planned everything else. If you hadn't bitten Jimmie, he'd been instructed to feed you a few drops of blood, just to get things going. While I knew Dima couldn't resist saving you, *I* couldn't resist the idea that you'd suffer while he did it."

Chapter 23

Dima was out the door of the van and halfway across the street when something large and pissed tackled him from behind and wrestled him to the pavement. He cursed mightily and drove an elbow backward, getting a grunt and a muffled oath for his trouble. When he drew back his arm for a proper punch, someone caught it in mid-air and held tight.

Looking up, he saw Misha holding his clenched fist between his two hands; turning his head, he found Graham's Lupine eyes staring down at him. Neither looked very happy, and neither appeared to have any intention of letting go.

"You can't do this, Dima," Misha snapped. "You know you can't, and I know how much you want to. Believe me, I do. But if you charge in there now with no strategy and no idea of what you'll be getting into, you'll only make things worse."

"That is where you're wrong." He spat the words out through clenched teeth, barely able to speak through his anger. "Right now, there is no worse. She has Ava. She has *my woman* inside that house.

I'm going to get her out if I have to raze the entire building to rubble."

"Which would only make things worse," Graham grunted. "You heard just as well as I did that your Russian bitch-friend set this all up as a trap for the two of you. If you were planning to let her catch you, you could have at least given us enough warning so we could go home and catch a little couch time with our wives."

Dima bared his teeth at the werewolf. "You want me to just leave her there?"

"Of course not. But we have to use our brains on this one. The only way to get Ava back safely is to have a strategy." He watched Dima's face as he spoke, and gradually he began to let go of the hand he had caught in mid-punch. "One of us needs to keep a cool head and start with a plan."

Graham snorted and levered himself off of Dima's legs where he'd had him pinned. He was rubbing a hand over his rib cage and wincing. "Yeah, well, you first, sucker. For some reason, I'm in more of a beat-it-till-it-squeals mood." He shot a glance in Dima's direction.

The vampire looked at them consideringly. He appeared lost in thought for a few moments; then the contemplative expression was edged away by one of devious pleasure.

"I think," he said, his mouth curving into a smile, "that we should give Ms. Chernigov what she wants."

Graham stared. "You want to let that psycho-tramp stay in the city and continue to make our lives miserable until we die of old age and she goes on to make our children's lives miserable?"

"Of course not, but what if the council were to make the offer? What if they came here in person and offered her asylum?"

"I think she'd jump at the chance. But I also think she'd be bored in six months and looking to start another war."

Misha nodded. "Exactly."

Dima scowled. "So we let her start her war?"

"No, we let her fight it. And once she's exhausted, we swoop in and carry her back to prison."

"Forgive me if I say that sounds a little simplistic, but, well, it does."

"Only because you are not considering the possibilities." Misha shook his head, still smiling. "The first step to making such an offer would be to get the head of the council here to negotiate, wouldn't it?"

Graham rolled his eyes. "Oh, sure. Let's just add another target for her to take aim at. While we're at it, we'll just invite the mayor of New York City along for the ride, shall we? Then she can wipe out everyone who matters around here in one fell swoop."

"Now you're thinking like Yelizaveta," Misha scolded.

"I'm what?"

"You're thinking about the benefits *you* get by arranging things a certain way, but you're neglecting to consider the other possibilities in such a scenario."

Dima levered himself into a sitting position. He

had finally begun to see the strategy his brother was suggesting. "Possibilities such as the targets that she gathers into one convenient place might not oblige her by dying so easily."

The Silverback Alpha looked from one brother to the other and shook his head. "The two of you are out of your minds. *That's* your plan? Get Rafe here and let her think she can kill all of you in one glorious shot, and then surprise her by fighting back?"

"You make it sound so . . . primitive."

"Because it is!"

Misha leveled him a glance. "You have a better idea? One that can be arranged and executed within the hour? Because I don't like the chances of us having much more time than that to work with."

Graham opened his mouth, shut it, opened it again, then frowned. A minute later, his expression cleared and began to curve into a smile, one a lot like the one Misha had recently worn.

"Well, first," Graham said, reaching out a hand and helping to swing Dima back to his feet, "I suggest we give my assistant a call and see if her husband has any plans for this evening."

There were moments in a person's life that they remembered forever—a first kiss, the passing of a loved one, the birth of a child. Ava didn't even remember what happened next ten minutes later. All she knew was that the rage at Yelizaveta Chernigov that had been building since the moment she announced her intention to harm Dima exploded when the bitch revealed that she had intentionally robbed

Ava of her life by ordering a henchman to convert her into a vampire. And that Yelizaveta had known it would cause Dima pain to watch Ava suffer, yet had done it anyway, pushed her over the edge.

Unfortunately, that was the last thing she remembered until she regained consciousness in a small room, made of stone, and smelling of damp rock and distant soil. A basement, she guessed, which narrowed it down not at all. When she tried to press her memory for more details, all she encountered was a blank wall and a huge, throbbing headache.

She groaned and reached up to cradle her head, thinking that might be the only way to keep little chunks of it from falling off and bouncing on the floor. When her arms encountered some kind of resistance after moving only a few inches, her eyes flew open and she swore, with great feeling, in Catalan.

"Thirty-four years I've gone without once getting tied up, either professionally or recreationally, and now, after a week as a vampire, I manage it twice."

It hurt to turn her head, but then, it also hurt to breathe and, she suspected, just to exist, so she gritted her teeth and craned her neck until she could see the knotted ropes that bound her wrists above her head to the head of a small iron cot. The move sent a wave of nausea rolling through her and she said a prayer of thanks that she'd actually woken up, because if she didn't have a concussion, she would eat her own shoes.

The very thought sent her stomach into another round of protests, so she took a moment to relax and let it settle back into stillness while she thought.

She couldn't really tell how much time had passed, except to acknowledge that since she was awake, it was most likely still nighttime. Or maybe nighttime again. But she didn't feel stiff enough to make her think she'd been tied like this for hours, so she was willing to bet on choice number one.

She wore the same clothes she had carefully donned a few hours ago, a slim pair of dark, pinstriped trousers that flared in the leg and a severely tailored vest of the same fabric, lined in black silk. On her feet were the same Gina boots she had worn the night of her attack. She had been willing to potentially sacrifice herself for the cause, as it were, but not another pair of shoes. A woman had to draw the line somewhere.

Thankfully, she realized, pulling her knees toward her chest until she could rest the balls of her feet on the cot's thin mattress, whoever had bound her this time had not been as thorough as Dima. They had neglected to tie her feet.

While she tried to decide how that might be helpful, she tugged experimentally on her hands. The knots held, and there wasn't all that much wiggle room to work with. Frowning, she considered her options.

To her surprise, she actually had very little fear for her own safety, at least for the moment. Since she knew Yelizaveta planned to try to use her to lure Dima and Misha to the mansion, she knew no one would be by to kill her before the brothers showed up. What she didn't know was when they might appear or what would happen once they did. Better to find out for herself, she decided, than wait around here to have someone bring her the news right before they chopped her head off. That kind of ending did not fit into her plans.

In order to shake up the evening, though, she'd have to find a way to get herself free from her current situation. Too bad Dima wasn't in the next room again, waiting to untie her as soon as she woke up.

The thought made her tense. He had been listening to her conversation with Yelizaveta. She had tried to block him out when the psycho had started to threaten him because she'd been afraid that with him in her head, she wouldn't be able to hide their connection from the vampiress, and she hadn't wanted to add any fuel to an already-blazing fire of craziness. She thought she might have managed it partially, but she had still been able to sense his presence in her mind, and she knew he could have been listening to the eavesdropping device along with the others, anyway. In any case, he would have an idea what had happened, and he might be a little bit worried about her safety and well-being right now.

Damn it, she was going to have to do some explaining when she finally got ahold of him.

Sighing, she closed her eyes to help her concentrate and began trying to locate his mind with hers.

For the first ten minutes or more, she had absolutely no luck. She just couldn't manage to get around the painful throbbing in her skull. It made the kind of concentration she needed to complete the difficult task impossible to come by. Every time she thought she might have found a tenuous thread of communication, her head would throb and she would lose it, forcing her to start all over again. Finally, she began to anticipate the sharp pains and to count on their ebb and flow like a metronome. That helped, and her second set of attempts was more successful.

She located the thread of their earlier communication easily enough. Dima had been careful to make it obvious so that if they were interrupted, as they had been, she would be able to find him again. The problem was that when she picked the thread up, she could follow it only a second before she seemed to hit some kind of barrier between their minds.

Visualization can be really helpful, she remembered him saying when he'd given her a crash course in basic telepathic communication the other night. *If you have trouble with a task, picture it in concrete terms. If something feels heavy, picture a weight that you need to lift; if it feels messy, picture straightening up papers or sweeping debris out of the way. Whatever works. There is no right or wrong way to do it.*

She hoped like hell he was right, because she felt like an idiot when she pictured a drywalled, taped, and painted wall in her head with a piece of blue string the color of a glacier trapped between the bottom of the wall and the floor underneath. Then she painstakingly imagined a door in the wall just where the string was, reached out, and carefully pulled it open.

In her mind's eye, a blast of wind tore through the

opening with the force of a hurricane and sent her staggering back at least three or four feet.

Where the bloody hell have you BEEN, *woman?!?!?* Dima's voice roared in her head at a volume so high, she thought her eardrums might actually be physically affected by it. *I thought you might be* DEAD! *Do you have any idea how that made me feel?*

Mind you, I'm just guessing here, she thought, trying to regain her balance, *but perhaps a tad concerned?*

This was met by a silence that gave Ava a small concern of her own.

When Dima spoke again, he managed a normal volume, but his words vibrated with the tension caused by such a tight hold on his self-control.

We can discuss that later, he ground out. *First, you must tell me if you are hurt.*

Not as far as I can tell. Someone must have hit me in the head, because that aches like nobody's business, but I'm not bleeding, and I don't detect any broken bones.

She thought she sensed a sigh of relief.

All right. Good. Where are you now?

She lifted her head slowly, in deference to the knowledge that it could explode or fall off at any moment, and looked around her. The narrow chamber looked like nothing so much as a nun's cell. It had bare stone walls, a bare stone ceiling, and three pieces of furniture: the cot on which she lay, a small wooden table—more like a stool really—standing against the opposite wall about halfway to the door, which bore a candleholder and three candles, only one of which was lit. It had burned almost all the way down, and she realized that if she wanted to retain the meager light, she would need to get herself untied soon, so she could put out the candles. The only other furniture was behind her head, pressed against the wall behind the head of the cot; it was a seven-foot-tall wooden wine rack that stretched all the way from the floor to the ceiling, with semicircular notches all along the front for the wine bottles to rest in. It was empty and covered with dust.

The only information the room offered was to confirm what her sense of smell had already told her—she was in a small room in the basement of an older building. With luck, it was the same building she had walked into just after dusk that evening.

I'm not positive, she told him, *because I was unconscious when they moved me, but it looks like I'm in the basement of the house. It's a tiny little room, completely stone, that looks like it used to be used as a wine cellar.*

Is anyone there with you?

No. I was alone when I woke up a little while ago, and no one has come in since.

Can you open the door and take a look around outside?

Um, I'll have to work on that, she said after a moment's hesitation.

Why? What's wrong?

She sighed. *They tied me up. Until I get free of the rope, I'm not going to be going anywhere.*

He cursed. She was really going to have to learn to speak Russian one of these days.

All right, then, I want you to stay put, he instructed. *We're going to be coming for you, but things could get . . . messy. If we know where you are, we won't have to worry about you being in the way. So stay there until Misha or I come for you, all right?*

No! Dima, you can't! That's exactly what Yelizaveta wants. She's trying to trap you into coming to my rescue so she can kill you. You can't come for me! I can get myself out of this.

Hush, lyubimaya. *I know. I heard Yelizaveta tell you her plans, but I promise you, nothing will come of them. You cannot trap a wary adversary, da?*

Maybe not, but you can still outnumber him and chop his head off! Dima! I want you to listen to me! Stay. Away. From. Here. *I got myself into this situation, and I can get myself out. I don't need you to come charging in here like the cavalry to rescue me. I'm a big girl, and I can take care of myself. I always have.*

Lyubimaya, he said tenderly, and she swore she could feel his fingers touching her face, *don't you see that this is the reason I must come for you? I must do this for you, because no one else ever has.*

Then the door she had created in her mind slammed shut, and when she raced back to haul it open again, she found it had been carefully bricked up from the other side.

"Dima!" she screamed, and set to work frantically on freeing herself from her bonds.

Chapter 24

Noah Baker may have been human, as Dima learned, but he had a trick or two up his olive drab sleeves that had made him quite useful even among his Lupine pack-by-marriage. He had been waiting when the truck carrying Dima, Misha, and Graham had pulled up outside the home he shared with his wife in Gramercy Park, and he had greeted the newcomer with quiet strength. He had also wasted about five seconds doing that before he got down to the business of loading bags and boxes of mysterious "equipment" into the back of the truck.

"I was in the army before the pack lured me away," he told Dima, grinning. "I was Special Forces, but Graham made me an offer I couldn't refuse."

Behind them, Graham snorted. "*Sam* made you the offer you couldn't refuse. I just gave you a job."

Noah wriggled his eyebrows. "Like I said, they're a hard bunch to resist."

Dima nodded and stowed another bag. "What did you do in the military?" he asked as the human loaded the last of his gear.

The man's face bloomed in a grin wide enough to cross the Black Sea. "Demolitions."

Then he slammed the truck's back doors shut and jogged around to climb inside the passenger compartment. Dima followed, feeling a stirring of exciting hope in his chest. A useful man to have around, indeed.

Graham drove, blithely ignoring the safety and welfare of himself, his passengers, and nearby pedestrians, as any good New York driver would. "Were you able to get everything you needed?" he asked, glancing at Noah in the rearview mirror.

The human nodded. "Pretty much. I'd have liked some narrower fuse cable, but what I have will do the trick. It just won't look as pretty."

"We're after function," Misha assured him. "Not form."

Noah grinned. "Ah, but the form is half the fun."

From the front seat, Misha glanced back to where Dima sat behind the driver. "You're okay with this?" he asked.

Dima barked out a sound something like a laugh. "Not even remotely, but I can't think of anything better, so what the hell? I'll give anything a try."

Graham rolled his eyes and swerved around an Asian delivery person on a bicycle. "Now that's the positive attitude we like to see."

Misha glared at him. "And how would you feel if it were Melissa in that building?"

"Come on, D, don't try and piss me off." Graham frowned, his hands tightening on the steering wheel. "There's no comparison. Missy is . . . hell, Missy is practically an angel. There's no living creature on this earth who's ever met her who hasn't liked her, and every damn man she meets falls half in love with her at first sight, the bastards." The pride and love in his voice were obvious. "Ava is an entirely different story. She's a stone-cold—"

"She is my mate," Dima bit out, leaning forward and catching the Lupine's gaze in the rearview mirror. "I suggest you take care in how you describe her."

Graham's eyes widened and his jaw bounced off his collarbone. "You're shitting me!"

Misha slapped the side of Graham's head. "*Mudak!* Dumb shit. Do you think we'd be doing this for just any woman?"

"I thought you were doing it for Reggie! Everyone knows how she feels about Ava. I mean, no one understands, but everyone knows. The two of them can't be in the same room anymore without trying to strangle each other, but you can bet that if you ask anyone, they'll say the reason no one has killed Ava yet is because they know they'd have to take on Reggie to do it, and that means they'd have to take on you, too."

Dima reached forward and smacked the same spot his brother had. "Do not speak so of my woman," he snarled. "And certainly do not ever mention her death again if you do not wish to witness your own."

Graham scowled. "Hey, I didn't mean I was going to kill her. I'm in the same boat as Misha. She might get on my last living nerve, but Missy loves her like a sister. No way in hell am I going to do anything to upset Missy. Not when it comes to her friends. With these girls, friendship is like a blood oath. They take it *seriously.*"

"As do we," Misha agreed.

Dima grunted. "Fine. But I will hear no more insults directed at my mate, is that clear?"

"Absolutely." Graham held up two fingers in the Cub Scout salute. "Just let me ask you one thing. Are you sure you know what you're getting into?"

Dima thought of Ava, of her entrenched arrogance, her volatile temper, and her stubborn insistence on running the show—all the shows, everyone's show—all by herself. Then he thought of her dark eyes cloudy with desire, of her incredible strength, of her neglected past, and he nodded.

"One hundred percent certain. There is not a doubt in my mind, and there is no other woman for me."

Graham nodded and stepped on the gas. "Okay, then. T minus thirty-seven minutes and counting. Rafe will meet us at the mansion, and we can get this show on the road!"

Graham was grinning until out of nowhere Noah leaned forward and slapped him hard on the side of the head.

"What the shit was that for?" he growled, barely dodging a double-parked car while he glared at the other man in the mirror.

Noah grinned back. "Just for luck. I was feeling left out."

Rafe met the men on the sidewalk three blocks from Wadsworth House near the van where the rest of the

Silverback team had camped. "Any trouble?" he asked as the other four approached.

Graham shook his head and gave a coded knock to the van's back door. "Nah. We're good."

The door opened a crack and Missy stuck her head out.

Graham pressed a quick kiss to her lips. "Anything?"

She shook her head. "No. We're pretty sure they must have destroyed the purse. Either that or they searched it, found the bug, and destroyed it, but we didn't hear anything that would indicate they'd located it, or that they suspected anyone was listening."

"Good."

"What about Ava?" Dima demanded. "Has she made any contact?"

He wasn't sure which answer he'd been hoping for, but his gut clenched when Missy shook her head.

"No, she's still quiet. But that's a good thing, right? It means she's staying put like you told her to."

His jaw clenched. "With Ava, it's impossible to tell."

"Amen," Graham muttered under his breath. Missy smacked him. He jerked his head around to glare at her and lifted a hand to rub the stinging spot. "All right, I've had about enough of that!"

The group ignored him.

"All right," Misha said, taking a look around and nodding. "Let's gear up."

For the four men whom Yelizaveta had tried to lure into a trap, that meant very little. They knew that the chances of their being allowed into her presence while clearly armed were slim to none, so they didn't bother to carry any weapons. Not where they could be seen, at least. Dima never went anywhere without a long, slim blade strapped to his boot, and unless his brother had changed drastically over the years, he doubted Misha would be without a knife of some sort, either. Rafael De Santos was himself a weapon, a jaguar coiled in a man's skin, with teeth and claws that could rip a body in half with one swipe, and you would never know it from glancing at his lean, elegant form, unbearably chic in a tailored Italian suit. Between the Felix and Dima's older brother—also wearing an expensively tailored jacket, though this one had been dressed down with sharply pleated black trousers—Dima felt like a poor relation, dressed as he always was in black BDU-style trousers, battered black boots, and a close-fitting black pullover shirt in a wrinkle-free, moisture-wicking, temperature-regulating fabric. At least Graham—another weapon in human clothing—was wearing jeans, even if they and the button-down shirt he wore with them did sport designer labels.

Noah and the Silverbacks took slightly more outfitting. Thanks to Noah's military connections, each one carried a 5.56 mm M16 assault rifle fitted with night scope, laser sight, and flashlight, and had a small M9A1 pistol strapped to his side. They also each wore a high-tech communications headset to allow them to communicate with the other members of the team. In one of the pockets of his trousers, Dima had secreted a small handheld communicator, like a walkie-talkie on steroids, that operated on the same frequency as the headsets. Just in case. Noah alone carried a backpack over his shoulders, filled with goodies Dima didn't know the names of and probably shouldn't be able to testify about anyway.

No one wanted to blow up Wadsworth House, of course—that would leave a pretty conspicuous hole in the neighborhood that might be hard to explain—but Noah had the skill to set off any number of different explosions, from ones that blew out an area no bigger than a door lock to ones that could blow the entire island into pieces that would rain down over southern Connecticut and northern New Jersey for days. They all hoped the only explosions they needed tonight would be in the first category.

When all the team members had suited up, Graham gathered them around and went over the plan. The Silverback team, led by Noah, would enter the house secretly through an old trap door that Rafe had discovered on a set of historic plans of the building. It had been sealed off since the mid-1800s, but the toys in Noah's pack would make short work of that problem. He even had a few that didn't make noise, although those weren't his favorites by any means. Once inside, they would sweep through the basement, picking off any troops Yelizaveta had with her and securing Ava's safety. Two of the men would break off and escort her to safety while the others continued to clear the building from the bottom up, eventually joining Dima, Misha, Rafe, and Graham upstairs to secure the capture of the primary target, Yelizaveta Chernigov. It would not be the neat and tidy capture Dima had planned on, but it would work and it would put this mission behind him so that he could concentrate on more important things. Like his future with one intensely infuriating woman.

"Is everyone clear?" the Alpha asked, getting a series of decisive nods in return.

"All righty then." Noah grinned, gesturing with his rifle for the Lupines to follow him. "Let's get this party started, ladies!"

Dima watched the expertly trained men blend into the shadows and took a deep, calming breath. Every single one of the Lupines Graham had picked for this team had extensive military or police training, and by the time they were halfway down the block, Dima had a hard time picking them out from their surroundings. They were all very good at what they did, and if he could trust Ava's safety to anyone, he could trust it to them.

But that didn't mean he liked trusting it to anyone but himself.

He felt a hand on his shoulder and turned to see his brother watching him with dark, sympathetic eyes, but those eyes didn't encourage him to be afraid; they imparted a strength and solidarity that had Dima's spine straightening and his lips firming in resolve. He nodded at the other men.

"You heard the human," he said, turning to face the path to the mansion. "It's time to take care of a small piece of business, gentlemen. If you'll all follow me?"

As one, four tall, powerful men of The Others strode forward, shoulder to shoulder, ready to take on the world for the only two things in it that mattered: justice and love.

Chapter 25

The damn stubborn knots just wouldn't come loose. Ava worked on them until her fingertips went numb, but she just couldn't get enough leverage in her position to take any of the strands in a tight enough grip. Without a good grip, loosening the ties was impossible. She needed another plan, and quickly. A glance at the candle on the table nearby told her that her time with any kind of light source was running out.

At least she had two things to be happy about: First, the pounding in her head had settled down to a dull throb, so that she didn't stir up a wave of nausea every time she moved her skull so much as an inch in any direction; and second, she had remembered an old documentary she had watched on the National Geographic Channel that had discussed the method by which embalmers in ancient Egypt had used an instrument made of heavy wire—much like a modern coat hanger, the narrator had pointed out—and bent into a hook at one end to remove the brains of those being mummified by pulling them down and out of the nose. She had decided that would make a lovely way to kill Dima for cutting her off the way he had. She couldn't wait to get home and pick up her dry cleaning so she would have the appropriate materials to get to work.

Craning her head, she made another examination of the ropes binding her and caught a glimpse of the wine rack behind her. Her brow furrowed. It was hard to judge distance from this angle—upside down and flat on her back—but she was guessing the cot was no more than about two feet away from the rack. She wouldn't have much room to maneuver.

Provided, of course, that what she was planning was possible outside of Olympic gymnastics and Cirque du Soleil.

Taking a deep breath and offering a silent apology to the tailoring gods, Ava wrapped her hands around the rope that bound them and pulled it tight. Using the pressure this generated as leverage, she contracted her abdominal muscles tightly, hoped her trainer was worth his money, and began to pull her lower body up off of the mattress. Tucking her knees up close to her forehead, she reflected that she hadn't exactly been thinking of situations like this when she started taking yoga five years ago, but when she felt the toes of her boots brush against the wood of the wine rack, she didn't suppose her intent mattered. All that mattered was that all the blasted flexibility she'd hammered into her body was about to come in handy.

Strangely, it was her back and not her abs that protested the strange position of her body. It grumbled out a warning when she shifted a couple of inches toward the foot of the cot, flexed her feet, and did a backward somersault off the head and onto the stone floor of the chamber.

The small amount of play in the rope allowed her to shift her shoulders, wriggle her wrists, and end up with only that last joint bent at an awkward angle. As far as Ava was concerned, that spelled complete success. Bending her head, she set her teeth to the rope that bound her and began to pick the knots apart with her teeth. Her dentist might kill her the next time he saw her, but then again, once he got a look at her new fangs, maybe he'd offer her a sugar-free lollipop instead.

When the butler opened the door to Wadsworth House, a flicker of surprise showed beneath his blank mask. It was there for only an instant, but Dima caught it, and it gave him a small sense of satisfaction. The man could probably get thrown out of the butlers' union for that, and Dima would only laugh and point.

"We're here to see your mistress," Misha informed him brusquely. "You may take us to her."

The fact that the butler did not ask their names or tell them to wait while he announced them told Dima that Yelizaveta had been expecting them. That was fine, because she wouldn't be expecting the outcome.

They were led a few paces down the hall to a set of double doors with leaves and berries carved around the edges of the heavy panels. The butler didn't knock or hesitate, merely pushed the doors open and ushered the gentlemen through. He did not follow but closed the door behind them with a distinct snap. The second snap, Dima concluded, had been the sound of a key turning in the lock. Yelizaveta, it seemed, planned for them to stay awhile.

Even though he'd gotten Ava's impressions of horrified amusement when she had first stepped into this room, they hadn't prepared him for the sheer scope of the ego that the décor betrayed. It also hadn't informed him that he would recognize the floor plan as an improvised copy of Yelizaveta's father's great hall outside of Smolensk. She had arranged the furniture around a dais at one end, just as her father had, and had placed the largest chair she could find atop the elevated spot like a throne.

Kazimir of Chernigov, Dima recalled, had possessed enough ambition to rule all Russia but less intelligence than it required to rule his own family. Although the official story had him dying at the hands of an assassin sent by a foreign king afraid of Kazimir's power, Dima suspected that the truth lay a little closer to home. Like in the hands of his only son and Yelizaveta's older brother, Stepan. A dagger, Dima assumed, in the back. The Chernigovs, after all, loved tradition.

Another echo of Kazimir's hall was the two dozen guards who encircled their leader's dais, swords and axes and maces at the ready. Clearly, they intended to do this old school. The image sent a pang of nostalgia arrowing through Dima's chest. Sometimes, he missed the gory old days.

"Ah, finally you have come to visit, old friends," Yelizaveta greeted them in Russian with an open sweep of her arms and a smile as treacherous as the sea. "I was afraid that you intended to ignore me forever. 'Did their mothers teach them no manners?' I asked myself. And then I remembered: Their mothers had been useless whores!"

Her laughter tinkled through the room. Dima felt Misha beside him, felt the tension in his body, and somehow his outrage was tempered by the knowledge that his brother shared it.

"You're not going to goad us into rash action with insults, Liza," Misha answered in English, his deep voice carrying easily across the ballroom. "And you are the one displaying bad manners. Two of your guests do not speak our language. You should address us in ways the entire company can understand."

Her mouth formed a little moue of annoyance. "You are such a taskmaster, Misha darling," she said. In English, this time. "But I will humor you. After all, you do not have much longer to live."

"I'm afraid you are mistaken about that."

"I don't see how. I wanted you to come here so I could kill you. You came here, and now I will kill you." She shrugged. "It is really very simple."

Rafael stepped forward, drawing Yelizaveta's eyes. They promptly widened. The Felix tended to have that effect on women. His wife, Tess, often complained that he got whistled at on the street more often than she did. Something about his dark hair, dusky complexion, and bright, feline green eyes drew women like hummingbirds to sugar water. Or maybe it was his inherent grace, and the old-world charm he wielded like a weapon. Either way, it appeared not even a half-sane vampire was immune.

"Well, hello," Yelizaveta purred, brushing her guards out of the way so that she could step down off the dais and stalk toward him. "Now this is a real shame, that we haven't met before, Mr. De Santos." She approached within a few feet of the men and stopped to bat her eyelashes at the Felix. "It is Mr. De Santos, isn't it? I've heard so much about you, and I have to say the rumors didn't even do you justice."

Rafe gave a courtly little half bow, and Dima wondered how he managed it without choking. "Miss Chernigov—," he began.

She stopped him, her smile going tight for a second. "Princess," she corrected. "Yelizaveta. Please. Let's not be so formal and stuffy."

"Princess," he acknowledged. "It is quite an event to finally meet you. Your reputation precedes you."

"Oh, I hope you haven't been listening to these two naughty boys. I'm sure they would like to tell you all sorts of horrible things about me, but I'm certain that the truth would leave you stunned."

"Is that so?" Graham asked, his expression bland but for one archly raised eyebrow. "Please, you'll have to share it with us. The truth, that is."

Yelizaveta barely spared the Alpha a glance. Instead she stepped closer to Rafe and held her hands out in entreaty. "You look like a man who understands freedom, who values it. These monsters"—she pointed at Dima and his brother—"want to see me imprisoned. Locked in a cage for the rest of eternity! A civilized person wouldn't treat an animal so poorly, let alone a woman."

Dima growled. "Your 'cage' has twenty-seven rooms, all the modern amenities available to mankind, and a staff of thirteen, plus guards, *highness*," he mocked. "I'm sure there are many in this world who would trade their lives for yours in an instant."

Her eyes narrowed at him. "I don't care what they would do, *ublyudok*. I care that the European Council has no right to pass judgment over me, let alone to imprison me forever with no hope of release."

"You wouldn't be in prison if you hadn't killed a prince, Liza," he pointed out. He didn't mind being called a bastard. He'd been called worse. By the woman he loved, in fact. "You killed more than one. And humans. And probably others we don't know about. I'd say that the punishment perfectly fits the crimes."

"You know nothing," she hissed, dropping her hand and her act of sweetness and light. She stepped back away from the men and called her guards to her with a flick of a finger. "But it hardly matters. Because soon enough, you'll be nothing. Just an unpleasant memory to be erased with vodka and merriment."

She raised her hand, preparing to send the guards into attack, but Rafe's voice stopped her.

"Not so quickly," he said, easing forward so smoothly, you could barely tell he was moving. "I have a feeling there are things we could offer you that might make it worth your while to keep us alive, Princess. At least some of us."

Dima could see interest flicker in the vampire's eye and silently urged the Felix on. He had caught the woman's interest. All he needed to do was keep it for a few more minutes, just to buy them some time. The twenty-four guards in the room were too much for the four of them to handle on their own. If the guards had been human it would have been different, but these were vampires, and not just vampires but trained warriors. Yelizaveta never went anywhere without some, so Dima knew they would be skilled fighters. At the moment, the odds were in favor of the bad guys, but once Noah and his squad made it up to the first floor, things would even out. Noah only had nine men with him, and two of those would be getting Ava out, but the twelve of them could easily handle the twenty-four vampires. Two against one were odds Dima liked; six against one were not.

"If you were to kill all of us now," Rafe continued, inching forward, not steadily but whenever he saw her interest pique, "you would get rid of the Russians, but you would lose the opportunity for so much more."

She raised her chin and tilted her head, clearly listening. "How much more? What else can you promise me, Feline?"

The man smiled the jaguar's smile. "I am head of the Council of Others, Princess. I can promise you many things."

"List them," Yelizaveta ordered, crossing her arms over her chest and tapping a slipper-clad foot rhythmically against the polished wood floor. "If any of them interest me, I might allow you to live."

Rafe purred. "Oh, I think you'll find what I have to say very, very interesting."

Chapter 26

The first thing Ava did when the ropes slid free was dash over to the little table and light a second candle from the flame of the first. She made it just in time. Even as she lifted the second candle away, the first one guttered itself in hot wax and went dark.

The second thing she did was lean over and vomit onto the stone floor; and that was when she discovered one of the most important parts of being a vampire—when you stopped eating solid food, vomit became meaningless. There was really nothing in her stomach to come up.

Clutching the candle in one hand and her aching head in the other, Ava crept toward the chamber door and pressed her ear against the thick wood. She didn't hear anything.

At least not until the door was yanked away from her head and she tumbled out into the dark corridor with a squeak of surprise. When she saw the man who had opened the door, her fear morphed immediately into confusion.

"Noah?" She did a double take, then another one

for good measure. "What the hell are you doing here?"

He pressed a finger to his lips in the universal signal for quiet and nudged her back into the room she'd just left. When he'd shut the door behind him, she saw him lift a hand to the sleek black earphone he wore and press a button twice. Three seconds later, she heard a double clicking sound, and Noah turned his attention back to her.

"We're here to get you out," he said, his voice low and nearly soundless, less carrying than a whisper. "Marc and Geo are going to be here in a minute. When they get to you, do exactly what they say. They're going to lead you out the way we came in and take you back to the club. You'll be safe there until the rest of this is over."

"Get me out? Wait at the club till this is over?" Ava had no idea if she could keep her voice that low, so she didn't even try. She spoke normally, if a bit angrily. "What the hell are you talking about? I'm not going anywhere except back upstairs to give that bitch a piece of my mind!"

When she tried to brush past him, he grabbed her shoulder and shook his head. "You can't go up there. It's too dangerous. My orders were to get you out the back way, and that's what I intend to do."

She scowled at him. "I don't care if you and your intentions plan to repave the road to hell in yellow brick. You're not going to shuffle me out the back door so that Dima can come in the front without worrying I'll get in his way. If she shows up here, he'll be walking into a trap. Unless, of course, the

Mega-Bitch of Moscow is already dead when he arrives."

Noah shook his head again, and Ava took a really good look at his face. Then she said a word in Catalan that her mother had once denied knowing, let alone teaching her.

"He's already here, isn't he?" she demanded. "He's up there right now, the bastard, and he was going to have you send me home to bed like a good little girl." She threw up her hands and stalked toward the door. "I swear to God, when I'm done pulling his brains out through his nose, I'm going to see if I can pull his entire head out of his ass using the same methods. I might need a bigger tool, though. You know, since the damned thing's been wedged up there so long now. It might be really stuck."

Again, Noah caught her before she made it back out into the hall. She glanced down at the hand on her arm and then up into his eyes. "You know I could break those fingers now, don't you?"

"Absolutely. And you know that I'm aware of at least ten different ways I could kill or incapacitate you with my bare hands in under ten seconds, right?"

"Absolutely." She waited a minute, then lifted her brow. "So what are we going to do?"

She saw him thinking, literally almost watched the gears turning for a few beats, then heard him sigh.

"Compromise," he offered. "I'll take you upstairs—I won't make you leave with Marc and Geo *if* you agree to follow my orders the same as the rest of the men on my team. Do we have a deal?"

Ava didn't hesitate. "Deal."

She made a mental note to buy Samantha a thank-you gift when all this was over. She knew very well to whom she owed this man's reasonableness.

Noah sighed and traded her the candle for the flashlight he removed from the barrel of his rifle. He looked as if he already knew he was going to regret this.

"Here. Stay close and cover the beam when I tell you, okay?"

"Okay."

"Now, a few quick things." He took a minute to show her some basic hand signals for directions, slow, stop, halt, and hide. She committed them to memory and tried to hide her impatience. Finally, he reached around her to open the door and eased outside.

"Remember," he murmured, "stay close." Then he led the way back into the darkness.

Yelizaveta had listened when Rafe promised her asylum from extradition back to Russia and when he offered her the unconditional support of the Feline breeds in the city, but her eyes lit up when he began talking about giving her the council.

"You understand that elections are not held until next year," he said, his voice full of promise. "But I have begun to think about retiring from my position, and I don't believe I am being presumptuous when I say that my choice for my successor will hold a great deal of weight with the voters. Especially with the Inner Council."

Dima could practically see the vampire drooling. She didn't just want revenge, he realized, or to build herself an army to conquer her old homeland. She wanted everything. She wanted to rule the world, and like her father before her, she believed she would manage the task. In that moment, Dima finally grasped the extent of Yelizaveta's insanity—of the insanity that had tainted her entire family like a blood-borne infection—and he knew that she could never be returned to prison, because she would always be planning her next escape. No prison could ever be made escape-proof; so as long as a woman like Yelizaveta lived, there would always be a risk of her escape, and while there was a risk of her escape, there would always be a risk to him and to his family. Somehow that mattered more to him now that he intended to claim Ava as part of that family.

He would not allow her to be hurt.

He slid one hand inside the pocket of his trousers, the pocket that held the small communicator he'd slipped in there earlier. While Rafe tried to convince the madwoman that he could be bought for the right price, Dima pressed the button on the device three times in rapid succession. A few seconds later he felt three rapid twitches against his palm and he felt a grim sense of satisfaction. The cavalry was on its way.

Casually, he shifted his weight, as if growing impatient, catching Graham's eye with the movement. Frankly, it wasn't difficult to feign the boredom. What was tough was believing that Yelizaveta was stupid enough to believe that they would stand by and let Rafe strike a bargain that involved their deaths without protesting. But now it was finally time to act offended.

The plan had been that Graham would make the first move. He would confront Rafe, argue that he wanted no part of this betrayal, and start a fight. The brawl would stir up some chaos and distract the guards from the stealthy arrival of Noah and his backup forces. They would surround the guards, Rafe and Graham would join in the fun, and they would all live happily ever after.

That *had* been the plan. But then, no one had bothered to describe the plan to Ava.

Ava had obeyed every single order, request, and signal from Noah Baker for the last fifteen minutes. As far as she was concerned, she'd built up enough good-deed karma to last her until next Christmas. At least.

She had stayed as quiet as a mouse all the way through the basement and up the back stairs into the kitchen. She'd taken off her boots and carried them so that her heels wouldn't make noise on the bare floors. She had even hidden in three different corners and alcoves so that she would be safely out of the way while Noah's men disposed of some of Yeliza-veta's patrolling guards.

So Ava figured that by the time they reached the doors from the narrow back hall to the ballroom, the men she was with should have realized that all bets were now off. Was it really that big a surprise when, as soon as Noah eased the first door open, she slipped past him and hurried into the room?

Ava felt Noah reach for her arm and miss, and

even though he didn't breathe a whisper, she could feel his curses bouncing off her back as she edged toward the back of the dais. Back here, she realized, was where Yelizaveta's minions had stored all the other bits of furniture and decoration Ava had been used to seeing in the ballroom. They had actually hung the heavy black drapes about eight feet in front of the windows on this side of the room and taped heavy black plastic, the kind used to line ponds and water gardens, over the glass.

Using the clutter as cover, Ava moved silently toward the center of the room and the space where she knew the dais to be. When she reached the barrier of the curtains, she raised her gaze to the fabric and searched out the nearest seam between panels. Finding one, she twitched the cloth aside just a hair's breadth and peered through.

She didn't quite have a clear view of anything. What she could see was the back of Yelizaveta's throne, a small crowd of bodyguards armed with medieval weaponry, and glimpses of several male faces, one lethally charming, the others just lethal. Somewhere in the mix, she knew, was the madwoman, but it took a moment to find her red-gold head. She appeared to be standing somewhere in front of Rafe instead of sitting on her throne. Ava could see that Yelizaveta had stepped a couple of feet away from her guards, but not far enough for anyone to get a clear line of attack, she imagined.

The one thing Ava didn't see was the lemon-sucking flunkey who had spoken for Yelizaveta earlier that evening.

God, had it really been just this evening? she wondered, shaking her head. It felt like lifetimes ago.

Letting the curtain reclose completely, Ava turned to warn Noah that a significant member of Yelizaveta's cheerleading squad seemed to be missing, only to discover that Noah was missing, too. In fact, all of the men were, except for the one who stood right behind her, with his eyes glued to her head and his hands on his rifle. She didn't have any trouble realizing what had happened—Noah had taken advantage of her distraction to set his troops into motion, leaving one man behind to ensure that she didn't throw herself into the breach and get herself into trouble. Noah had counted on her knowing that the key element of a surprise attack—that being surprise—would be negated if she kicked up a loud fuss about his heavy-handed tactics before the first shot was fired.

Damn his manipulative little hide.

Sparing her watchdog a withering glare, Ava took a very deep breath—then another—in an attempt to regain control of her temper. When she thought she could relax her lips without giving in to the urge to scream, she turned back to the curtains and peered out again. It didn't really look like anything had happened. No one had moved so much as a hair on their heads, but she could feel the tension in the room ratcheting up several notches and she knew it had to be more than just her. She felt as if she could write her name with her finger in the air and still be able to read it after enjoying a nice cup of tea.

Straining to hear what they were saying, she could make out the words if she listened hard enough. Her hearing had improved since her turning, but the speakers were Other as well and kept their voices low to avoid sharing the details of the discussion with everyone present, and the drapes absorbed and muffled much of the sound.

"—do you think?" she heard Rafe ask, presumably of Yelizaveta.

"I don't really think that matters," she heard Graham snarl, and realized, to her surprise that he was talking to Rafe, arguing with Rafe. "I think that before you go trading away promises of loyalty, you ought to consult with the parties involved, old *friend*."

Rafe turned to face the Lupine, which put his back to her, so she couldn't hear his reply. What she could hear, though, was Graham's vicious snarl and the insult he threw at the Felix's head. Rafe responded by throwing a punch, and the two of them turned on each other like rabid animals.

Ava couldn't believe her eyes, not that Rafe and Graham—who had been friends for years numbering into the decades—would have such a vicious argument, and not that they would indulge in such risky, stupid behavior in front of an enemy. Something was not right about this.

Then Ava saw a blur of movement along the other curtained wall and she realized what part of the picture had been missing. Graham and Rafe had been serving as the decoy while Noah's men put themselves into strategic positions around the room to prepare for the coming confrontation.

They were lucky, she thought, that she had realized the truth so quickly, or they might have had a very different situation on their hands. She would make very sure to point that out to them just as soon as she got the chance, too.

She held her breath and watched as nine large shapes distributed themselves around the perimeter of the room. She had to marvel at their abilities, because even though she knew they were there, she had to really look to pick out where each one was hiding.

Then Noah gave a signal and the first shot rang out, echoing through the massive space. Near the front of the dais, a tall, fair-haired vampire blinked, then collapsed to the floor, a blooming patch of red now decorating the outside of his chest above where his heart had recently been.

The game was on.

Yelizaveta gave a furious scream and ordered her guards to kill everyone. She sprang at the man closest to her, who happened to be Rafe, and managed to get a claw or two into him before he twisted and shivered and landed in front of her on four compact and furry feet. At least, compact for a jaguar the size of a small pony. Clearly furious, she tried to slice at him again, but he was too fast and much too agile for her to lay a hand on.

Around them, the rest of the room had erupted into chaos, Yelizaveta's guards leaping at the enemy. The Silverbacks had to drop their guns after the first shot, since in the melee they couldn't be sure who they might hit. Several of them shifted, taking on the forms of extremely well-made timber wolves in varying shades of gold, red, brown, and black. In the mix of fur, Ava also noticed a tawny wolf whose fur was colored silvery white like a mantle across his back and shoulders.

The others had joined the fighting, and Ava could see vampires beginning to fall all around them, most of them turning to dust, but one or two just falling to the floor and beginning a rapid version of natural human decay. What she did not see was Dima. Looking around, she found him and his brother consulting briefly with Noah, and then saw them move with pride of purpose toward Yelizaveta. In his hands, Misha carried a set of handcuffs and a long length of silver rope, while Dima bore a new-looking roll of gray duct tape.

Ava winced, then thought about it and shrugged. The bitch had it coming to her.

Ava was paying so much attention to Dima, trying to keep watch over him, as if something terrible would happen the moment she took her eyes away, that she almost didn't notice the something terrible approaching.

Then another sliver of movement caught her eye, and she turned her head again. Charles, the lemon-sucking, manicure-needing, hideous skin tone–sporting vampire flunkey of this evening, slipped out from behind the drapes at the other wall with a small, sharp, obviously well-balanced dagger in his hand. She saw him raise the arm that held it over his head, saw the glint of hate and madness in his eyes, then saw him focus all that malevolent force on Dima. She screamed and let her instincts rule her. Raising her own hand, she let fly one of her poor, battered, beautiful boots, straight at the vampire's head.

Ava had been aiming for his throwing arm and had hit his head, but since he took the three-inch heel right between his eyes, she wasn't about to quibble. Either way, he screamed, the knife flew harmlessly off course, and she got to see Dima spin safely around, lock eyes on Charles, and fly at him with a muffled roar. The ends justifying the means right there, even while she watched.

The soldier behind her, however, was less of a go-with-the-flow sort. When she moved, he panicked, probably thinking she meant to run into the middle of the room and join the fighting, and he shoved her to the floor and covered her with his body.

She screamed and tried to buck him off, but he simply dug in his heels and hung on.

For God's sake, what had they told these guys about her? she wondered, realizing for the first time how closely a vampire and a werewolf could be matched in strength. They were treating her as a sort of combination between Mata Hari, Harry Houdini, and the Incredible Hulk. Flattering, certainly, but hardly accurate.

When she failed to throw off her human—or maybe make that Lupine—shield, she settled on a particularly foul curse and lifted her head.

"At least let me move the curtain," she snapped when he would have stopped her from reaching out and twitching the fabric aside. "I need to see what's happening out there!"

The soldier grunted and shook his head. "I'm sorry, ma'am, but I have orders."

Ava told him exactly where she planned to shove

his orders and reached out again. She was just barely able to touch the fabric with the tips of her fingers, but when she thought she had it, it was whisked out of her hand and brushed aside, leaving a wide gap through which she could clearly see the rest of the ballroom. Or she would have been able to see it if her field of vision hadn't been completely obscured by a pair of long legs and big feet clad in unrelieved black.

Despite the Lupine still physically pinning her to the floor, Ava smiled up at the vampire and smiled. "Did you get her?"

Dima half-turned, allowing Ava to see the room beginning to quiet down behind him. Misha had bound an irate Yelizaveta to a chair with rope and was now taking great delight in sealing her lips with a strip of the duct tape. Charles lay, also bound but blessedly unconscious, on the floor where Dima had tackled him.

Ava breathed a long sigh of relief and let herself relax. "Cool. It looks like we won."

Dima shook his head. "Not quite yet. There's still one last piece of winning I need to do."

She looked up at him and frowned. "What do you mean? Did I miss something? What else could you possibly need to win? The Nobel Prize?"

"Your heart."

Chapter 27

It was never fun getting the police involved in this kind of thing, Dima reflected grimly, but times had changed and he and people like him had to learn to change along with them. So Rafe summoned the police, who made everyone wait around to give a statement before they were allowed to leave. Since Dima had been involved in the capture of a known fugitive and had been the victim of an attempted murder, while Ava had been kidnapped and held against her will for several hours, they were among the last of the crowd to be allowed to leave the mansion.

Adrenaline still pumped through Dima's body, partially from the fight and partially from the discussion he knew he was about to have with Ava. Frankly, he couldn't decide which one was likely to be more challenging. If he had been alone, he would have walked back to the Vircolac club, but he could see Ava fading and could feel the first stirrings of dawn beginning below the horizon. He needed to get her tucked into a bed where the sun couldn't touch her as soon as possible. There would be time enough for their discussion tomorrow.

He had to remind himself of that several times over the next hour, during the time it took to pour her into a cab—where she proceeded to crawl into his lap and snuggle during the trip to the club—and then into bed, where she pressed her naked form against his as if it were the most natural thing in the world, and drifted immediately into sleep.

Dima lay beside her, exhausted but far from sleepy, and stared up at the ceiling. His rational mind had a hard time accepting that he'd known this woman for only as many days as he could count on one hand, but then again, his rational mind had very little to do with his feelings for her. It wasn't rational to fall in love so quickly, even if Misha said it had happened to him the first time he laid eyes on Regina. It wasn't rational to love a woman who could drive him completely out of his mind with rage or lust with equal ease. It certainly wasn't rational to feel as if the presence of one particular woman dictated whether or not any day or night before him was likely to be a good one.

None of it was rational, and Dima couldn't have cared less. How could he, when he fell asleep with his woman in his arms and a smile on his face?

He woke with the niggling feeling that he had overslept and that this fact was significant for some specific reason. When he finally lifted his eyelids and saw Ava's dark brown eyes looking down at him, he remembered exactly why.

"Good evening," she greeted him, the corner of her mouth twitching into a smile. "I thought you were going to sleep forever, and I was just working myself up to be mad at you for it, because I'm really starving."

He stared up at her and lifted a hand to brush several stray strands of dark silk from her face. "Marry me."

She blinked; her smile disappeared. "What?"

Somehow, the confusion on her face made him feel all the more certain. He felt himself smile.

"Marry me," he repeated, and tugged at a lock of her hair. "You really don't have any choice. I'm the only man in the world, or any of the more populated dimensions I can think of, who would ever be willing to take you on. So make it official and marry me."

Her eyes narrowed as she stared down at him. "I can't say that's the most romantic proposal I've ever heard," she commented sourly. "The only man willing to take me on, my ass."

He grinned and rubbed his hand over that portion of her anatomy. "Oh, I'm sure there are thousands, tens of thousands, who would be willing to take on your ass. It's your mouth I think they'd have trouble with."

"It doesn't seem to bother you."

"I love your mouth." He pressed a kiss to her lips to prove it, and found himself sinking unintentionally deeper, savoring the sweet, sleepy flavor of her, still warm from sleep and soft from dreams. It was several minutes before he could pull himself away. "Wow, I *really* love your mouth. But it does have a tendency to . . . how can I put this? . . . slice a man's balls off when he least expects it."

"Now be fair. I have no problem slicing off a woman's balls when necessary," she said, dropping her haughty mask into place. The teaming of it with the disheveled hair and breasts barely covered by a wrinkled sheet made him want to tumble her backward and love her senseless. But first things first.

"That's right. So really it's for the sake of all humanity—no, all living beings in general—that you have to marry me. A sacrifice to the greater good. You can just lie back and think of England. I promise to do all the work."

She stared down at him, her mouth softening and curving. She looked like she couldn't quite believe what he was saying, but that she wanted to with all her heart. "You do realize that you're saying you've just proposed to me because I'm such a horrible person that no one else will ever want me, and even if they do, I'll be so mean to them that in order to preserve the future happiness of everyone everywhere, you'll make the ultimate sacrifice and marry me."

He nodded. "In a nutshell."

"Wow. You're quite the romantic."

She shook her head, and he could read in her expression that she was baffled by this new, more lighthearted side of him. Frankly, he was a little surprised himself, but then again, he couldn't remember the last time his heart had felt so light. He wasn't sure if it was from the completion of his mission, the capture of his family's old enemy, or the realization that he had found the woman he would love for the rest of eternity, but he was betting on the last one.

"Come on," he urged, pulling her down for another kiss, this one longer, deeper, but just as sweet. "Marry me. You have to marry me."

She drew back and pursed her lips as if debating the possibilities. "If I do, will you promise to teach me to speak Russian?"

He blinked in surprise. "Of course, if you would like. *S udovol'stviem.*"

"Which means?"

" 'With pleasure.' "

This time, she leaned down to kiss him, and her lips lingered, making his heart and his sex tighten. When she drew back, he opened his eyes and saw his own love reflected there, and he began to smile.

Ava sighed. "Oh, all right." She accepted his proposal just as graciously as he had given it, and it made him want to laugh. "I suppose I'll have to marry you. After all, if no one else will want me, there can hardly be any hope for you."

"What do you mean?"

"Sweetheart." She smiled at him, wicked, and ran her hand over his bare chest, her fingers light and teasing. "You must have realized by now that after me, every other woman on earth is going to seem completely bland and colorless. I can't possibly let you suffer like that."

Dima laughed, a deep, bed-shaking belly laugh that nearly sent her tumbling down onto his chest. She braced her arms and locked her elbows to keep herself from falling forward.

"I didn't think it was quite that funny," she told him coolly.

"I know." He grinned. "That is because you are

the most arrogant, vain, high-opinioned woman in the entire world." When she began to look truly offended, Dima reached up and pressed his thumb to her lips to keep her from speaking. "But the most frightening thing about that, *nenaglyadnaya,* is that you have every right to be so, because you are the most amazing woman I have ever met in seven hundred and ninety-four years on this earth."

Ava softened, visibly, and melted down over him. "That, my dear, was a very good save." She snuggled closer and let herself begin to relax. "You know, you never did tell me what that means."

"What what means?"

"Nenaglyadnaya."

"Ah."

He cradled her against his chest and smiled into the darkness of the quiet room, feeling for the first time in a very long while that everything was right with his world, because of the prickly, arrogant, stubborn, breathtaking woman who had entered it.

"It has two meanings," he told her softly, stroking his hand over her hair and savoring the feeling of a perfect future stretching out before him.

"What's the first one?"

"Literally translated, it means 'the woman at whom I could never grow tired of looking.'"

She was silent for a minute, and he could feel the wonder and hope radiating from her, two emotions he knew she had not let herself feel in a long time. Not when it came to things like love.

"That's beautiful," she finally said, pressing a kiss to his chest. "What's the second meaning?"

"Well, that one is the simple truth." He waited until she tilted her head up and met his gaze, brown eyes melting into blue. "That is what I will call you in my heart for every day of my life," he promised.

"What is it?" she demanded, love and laughter shining in her eyes.

"Beloved."

Don't miss the novels of The Others, a scorching-hot series
from *New York Times* bestselling author

CHRISTINE WARREN

YOU'RE
SO VEIN
ISBN: 978-0-312-94792-7
ISBN-10: 0-312-94792-5

THE DEMON
YOU KNOW
ISBN: 978-0-312-34777-2
ISBN-10: 0-312-34777-4

ONE BITE WITH
A STRANGER
ISBN: 978-0-312-94793-4
ISBN-10: 0-312-94793-3

SHE'S NO FAERIE
PRINCESS
ISBN: 978-0-312-34776-5
ISBN-10: 0-312-34776-6

WALK ON THE
WILD SIDE
ISBN: 978-0-312-94791-0
ISBN-10: 0-312-94791-7

WOLF AT
THE DOOR
ISBN: 978-0-312-94553-4
ISBN-10: 0-312-94553-1

HOWL AT
THE MOON
ISBN: 978-0-312-94790-3
ISBN-10: 0-312-94790-9

AVAILABLE FROM ST. MARTIN'S PAPERBACKS

...and look for Warren's story, "Devil's Bargain," in a
sensational new anthology
HUNTRESS
ISBN: 978-0-312-94382-0
ISBN-10: 0-312-94382-2

Coming in July 2009 from St. Martin's Paperbacks